THE WAY OF WATER
WATER WITCH
BOOK TWO

TONI CABELL

CHAPTER I

"This is *your* coronation—not mine! I'm queen by marriage only. We'll be asking for trouble if you insist on bestowing a crown on me tomorrow." Solace folded her arms and watched Rhees pace around the king's drawing room. With its gilded furniture, heavy, maroon drapes, and portraits of every previous monarch arrayed on its walls, the chamber was designed to intimidate rather than welcome.

Solace hated the room and itched to redecorate, but there was no money in the treasury for anything so frivolous. In fact, there was very little money at all. The palace's previous occupant, King Neuss, had bled the kingdom—and its overworked inhabitants—nearly dry.

Rhees ran a hand through his dark, unruly hair, which curled over the collar of his shirt. Tall and muscular, Rhees looked more like a rancher than a royal, in his simple chambray shirt, gray slacks, and riding boots. After completing one more circuit around the room, he turned back toward Solace and Chancellor Ghrier, seated on a cluster of burgundy sofas at the opposite end of the room.

"But you sparked the rebellion," Rhees waved his hand

at Solace, "divining for water right under old Neuss's nose. And you stopped him on the battlefield too. You've earned this crown."

Chancellor Ghrier smacked the plush carpet with his walking stick. The golden silk rug muffled the sound effect, so Ghrier lowered his white eyebrows and waved his cane in the air instead. "Your wife is quite right. By law and custom, she is technically the queen consort. There is no precedent for a double coronation, nor would I recommend it."

"Even if there's no precedent, I can't see the harm. Why not do it anyway?"

Ghrier smoothed down his snowy beard before answering. "Politics, as Solace has rightly pointed out. While most of Toresz wholeheartedly welcomes you as the new king, we know there are pockets of resistance from everyone whose palms were greased by Neuss and his thugs. You must follow the letter of the law so there can be no grounds for finger pointing later. As for Solace, the people appreciate all she has done for them. However, she is neither a royal, nor your equal in terms of bloodlines." Ghrier gave Solace a quick bow from the shoulders. "I am sorry to be so blunt."

Solace smiled. "No apology needed. You're simply stating the truth."

Rhees reached Solace in several long strides and tugged her from the sofa. "As far as I'm concerned, you are the people's queen—and queen of my heart." He drew her into his arms, his brown-black eyes filled with longing, with the same aching need she felt inside her chest.

They'd not seen each other for nearly a month, their new duties sending them in different directions. Solace had returned to the palace earlier that morning, exhausted from a three-week trip divining for new water sources. Rhees was gone when she'd arrived, inspecting security for his coronation the following day. Solace hoped they could find time to escape together from the confines of the palace and their new, all-too-public lives after the ceremony.

The door to the drawing room opened, and Rhees brushed his lips against hers before releasing her. "We'll find time for ourselves once all this ceremonial hoopla is past," he whispered, "I promise."

"I'll hold you to that promise."

Someone cleared his throat, and Solace turned toward the door. The footman bowed and ushered in a rumpled-looking traveler. A thick layer of dust coated the visitor's boots, and his rough tweed jacket was out of place inside the fussy drawing room.

"Arik! Well met, what a welcome surprise. Did you arrive with my father?" Solace swiftly crossed the room, smiling at her oldest friend, the man who'd loved her before Rhees, and judging by the yearning in his warm, brown eyes, loved her still. Solace smothered a sigh. She'd wished, hoped, that Arik had moved on by now.

Arik was a well-built man with thick, black hair and beard, and a deep, tan complexion a shade darker than hers. Where Rhees was often brusque, bordering on surly, Arik was courteous, an optimist at heart. Arik gave her a quick, tentative hug before stepping back. "Soren sent me in his stead, and before you start to worry, your father is fine. His sciatica is acting up, and he and my dad need to finish the spring planting."

Arik turned toward Rhees, who'd joined them, and bowed. "Congratulations on your pending coronation, Your Highness...and on your nuptials. You've married the best woman in two kingdoms."

Rhees stood beside Solace and draped an arm around

her waist. The two men stared at each other, Arik coolly assessing her new husband, Rhees glowering in return. *Arik knows the truth. Dad would have told him why I'd gone missing for half a year. He must hate Rhees almost as much as my father does. I don't blame either of them. I'd hated Rhees for nearly as long, until I realized I loved him with an equal ferocity.*

Rhees squared his jaw, grunted thanks, and drew her closer. Despite the fact he was the handsome new king of Toresz, Solace knew Rhees was still insecure when it came to her feelings for him.

Solace broke the awkwardness, introducing Arik to Ghrier, who reminded them they were overdue at the Great Library for the dress rehearsal. The massive, drafty, old library had been the original palace and was still used for coronations and other royal ceremonies. Ghrier offered to show Arik the way to the library, and they left by horseback.

Rhees went to the cloakroom and returned wearing his leather duster and wide-brimmed hat. He helped Solace into her gray cape, which needed to be laundered following her long trip. They departed through the rear of the palace, where their driver waited with a sleek, black carriage drawn by four white horses. Solace noticed the staff had repainted the vehicle to hide Neuss's crest, replacing it with Rhees's blue-and-gold royal seal.

Rhees sat across from her with a loud sigh, their knees grazing as they settled into the velvet benches. Solace leaned back against the upholstered squabs of the carriage and closed her eyes. She was exhausted, and the last thing she needed was the extra drama of Arik and Rhees in the same proximity, even for just a few days.

She berated herself for not returning to the palace earlier so she could rest before the coronation. But there was simply so much need inside Toresz, so many families without access to fresh water or enough decent food or adequate shelter. She'd pushed herself to divine for a few more water sources, and then a few more. Solace hadn't seen her healer yet, but she expected a long lecture about her stubborn refusal to take it easy.

Rhees fidgeted on the seat opposite her, grumbling under his breath. Solace decided she needed to address the Arik situation head-on and opened her eyes. "I know you're fuming over the fact my father sent Arik, so just come out and say it."

Rhees slapped his thighs with his open palms. "Of course I'm mad. It's so blasted awkward, having your ex-beau staying with us. We have more than enough drama without Arik pining for you right under my nose."

"I don't know what I can do about it now. Let's try not to let this ruin your special day." Solace reached over and took one of his rough hands in hers. She ran a gloved finger over his calluses, earned through years of sword fighting and the kind of hard, manual labor most kings and princes never dreamt of doing.

Rhees reached out his free hand to cup Solace's cheek. "Arik was right about one thing—I did marry the best woman in two kingdoms—nay, all the kingdoms." He leaned toward Solace, their lips inches apart, when the carriage gave a sudden jolt. Rhees heaved another sigh. "Soon, my love, very soon. Just a few more days, and the visitors will be gone and we'll be alone."

"As alone as two people can be inside a palace full of servants and advisors." Solace chuckled. Their driver stopped the carriage, and Solace peeked out the curtain at the soaring, sand-colored Great Library. Fluted columns lined the front entrance, with two stone lions guarding either side of the poppy-red double doors. A wide, stone staircase, worn in the center from years of use, ascended from the street to the doors.

A good-sized crowd milled about on the sidewalks, probably hoping to get a glimpse of the new king and queen. Solace noticed a large carriage parked halfway down the cobbled street, with a green-and-black insignia on the door she didn't recognize. Of course, Urhl was packed with visitors in town for the coronation. Neighboring kingdoms —Yelosha to the west, Censarra and Gwynvalla to the north, and the numerous small, satellite states to the south —were each sending a royal delegation.

Rhees brushed aside the footman and insisted on helping Solace out of the carriage. They passed through the library's double doors and entered the four-story atrium. Balustrades ran around each of the floors overhead, with shelves of books running at right angles all around the hall, a booklover's paradise.

Solace's eyes widened as she peered around the main floor, which no longer looked like a library. Wooden pews formed neat rows on either side of the atrium, creating a wide aisle down the center of the room. A large dais had been erected at the end of the aisle, with Rhees's heavy, hand-carved wooden throne occupying the front of the platform. Blue and gold banners dangled from the second-level balcony. Solace caught a faint whiff of the incense that would be used in the ceremony.

Royal guards milled about, some hanging banners, others waiting for orders. The men and women wore blue tabards, with Rhees's royal seal embroidered in gold thread on their fronts and backs. Gold coifs covered their heads, and swords hung in scabbards from the leather belts at their waists.

Rhees's aunt Fenwith had been at the library most of

the day, fretting over last-minute details. Even though her nephew was now king, Fenwith still wore plain cotton dresses and aprons when she was working, which was nearly all the time. She drew Solace into a tight embrace. "I've been so worried. You were gone too long, and I can see the dark circles under your eyes. I *knew* I should have ridden with you. No one else forces you to rest like I do. If it hadn't been for this coronation business, which Ghrier insists we have to do by the book, I *would* have gone with you. But first—"

Solace arched an eyebrow at Rhees, who smiled at Fenwith. "You're quite right. Let's get this over with so we can all relax, and Lace can get some much-needed rest. Looks like Ghrier just arrived. I'll go see if he's ready to begin."

Fenwith watched as Rhees walked toward the double doors. She squinted at Arik, standing next to the chancellor. "Who's that nice-looking young man? Do you suppose he's one of Ghrier's new legal clerks?"

Solace shook her head. "That's Arik, my friend from Yelosha. My father is so busy at the farm right now he sent Arik in his place."

Fenwith gave her a shrewd look. "He's the lad who wanted to marry you, as I recall. I reckon your father sent the dashing young Arik along in case you changed your mind about Rhees."

Solace bit her bottom lip. Fenwith was probably right about her father's motives. Although Soren did have sciatica, and he did have the planting to finish, he could have asked Arik to complete it for him. "That's not going to happen," said Solace, "but at least Arik will return home satisfied I'm happy here. Perhaps he can convince my dad as well."

"Perhaps," sniffed Fenwith before she dragged Solace over to make the introductions.

Ghrier banged his walking stick on the flagstone flooring and waited until the buzz of conversation around the atrium settled down before bowing to Rhees. "I believe we are now ready, sir. Shall we begin?" Rhees gave him a firm nod, and the chancellor continued. "Alright then. Let's assemble by the double doors. We'll begin by walking down the center aisle. Once we proceed from the back to the front, please go to your assigned locations."

Ghrier explained the order of precedence and where everyone would be sitting, starting with Solace in the front row, facing the dais on the left. Across the aisle would be Rhees's aunt Fenwith and uncle Chelyss, who was elsewhere at the moment, running errands for his wife. The three rows behind them were reserved for the large number of royal visitors in Urhl for the coronation. Rhees, Ghrier, and Brother Evryst, who was running late, would ascend the dais and turn to face the crowd. Lastly, a dozen royal guards would stand behind the king, providing additional security for the event.

Ghrier led them through the processional and ceremony, making a few minor adjustments as they rehearsed. Halfway through the second run-through, one of the squires guarding the entrance dashed inside. A man and woman followed at a stately pace behind him, both attired in regal robes of green-and-black houndstooth.

Rhees walked down the aisle toward the newcomers, Ghrier trailing him. Solace rose from her pew to watch, her brow furrowed in confusion. *What are these royal visitors doing here, interrupting our rehearsal? Are they simply confused about the date, or is this something else entirely?*

The squire bowed and then shouted, his voice quivering, "His Majesty, Rhees, King of Toresz, may I present His Majesty, Valyss, King of Censarra and his sister, your ah... your hmm..."

The Censarran princess stepped in front of the bumbling lad. A pretty though pouty-looking woman, she had glossy, dark brown hair plaited like a crown on top of her head, light beige complexion, and hazel eyes. She wore a beaded, low-cut green gown beneath her robe, and a tiara on top of her braid. Her brother pushed aside the young squire and drew abreast of the princess. King Valyss appeared to be about thirty, with similar coloring to his younger sister, although he was slightly taller and considerably stouter.

Valyss addressed Rhees, his voice booming in the still air of the atrium. "King Rhees Demore *Orillya*, congratulations on your ascension to the throne of Toresz!" Valyss placed extra emphasis on Rhees's surname, which had been a closely guarded secret until the revolt. Concealing his lineage had ensured Rhees's safety. If Neuss had discovered Rhees was the true heir to the crown, he would have never reached adulthood.

Valyss continued, "I wish you a long reign, with lasting peace and prosperity. Our two kingdoms share a common border, which makes us neighbors and allies. Even more important, we share the bond of kinship. And now, without further preamble, it is my great pleasure to present Her Royal Highness, MaudeLyn, Crown Princess of Censarra, my dear sister—and your betrothed!"

CHAPTER 2

"My *what*?" thundered Rhees, glancing around at the empty pews inside the library's atrium. "I've never laid eyes on this woman in my life!" The royal guards stepped off the dais and inched closer, their mouths hanging open. Fenwith left her seat and moved behind Rhees, probably for moral support. Solace, shocked to her core, remained standing in the front pew.

Rhees must have recalled his manners, because he gave the princess a quick bow and turned to her brother, standing in the wide, center aisle next to his sister. "Er, with apologies, sir, but I have no idea what you're talking about. I fear there is a grave misunderstanding. Furthermore, I am already married." Rhees spun on his heels, glancing wildly about the room until his eyes landed on Solace.

She hurried over to join Rhees, her heart thundering in her chest. *What kind of game are these two playing?* Most royal marriages were carefully negotiated business arrangements. Love never seemed to enter the equation, which Solace thought made for a very long, sad life together. *But no such betrothal contract could have been made with Rhees, since no one knew of his claim to the throne.*

Rhees squeezed her hand, as if to confirm her presence. "May I present Her Majesty, Solace, Queen of Toresz."

Crown Princess MaudeLyn, who was eight or nine years older and half a head taller than Solace, peered down her nose at her. Solace resisted the urge to smooth the folds of her simple, square-necked, wine-colored day gown, which was exceedingly comfortable but far from royal. Other than the new robe and gown Solace had commissioned for Rhees's coronation, she'd had neither the time nor the desire to drain the treasury further by ordering an entirely new wardrobe.

The Censarran king and crown princess did not bow to Solace, as they had for Rhees. They bestowed barely perceptible head nods, and Solace felt Rhees stiffen beside her at the insult. Valyss said, "With all due respect, the crown princess's claim is an old one, and given your consort's youthfulness, I daresay takes precedent."

Rhees sputtered, "Please explain yourself, sir."

"Your brother Heris, Crown Prince of Toresz, was eighteen at the time of his unfortunate demise, was he not?"

"Aye," grunted Rhees. "What does Heris have to do with this?"

"Everything!" replied Valyss and MaudeLyn simultaneously. The king continued, "Our fathers had jointly signed the betrothal agreement between Heris and MaudeLyn the previous year. My sister's dowry was deposited in your treasury, and your father graciously expanded our mining rights along a disputed section of the border. All was well, or so we thought, as MaudeLyn and our family traveled into Toresz for the wedding ceremony.

"We made it halfway to Urhl, when we were turned

away, for our own safety, by a small group of soldiers fleeing the capital. And that's when we learned the awful truth: King Meade and his family had been murdered. We turned back with heavy hearts, and MaudeLyn, who was sixteen at the time, went into mourning. She later married Munsey, Crown Prince of Gwynvalla, who has since passed away without producing any heirs. MaudeLyn was content to remain in Gwynvalla, until we heard the most remarkable news—until we heard about you!

"We were delighted to learn King Meade had a second son, a legitimate heir who'd escaped Neuss's assassins. As Heris's younger brother, not only are you ascending to the throne, but you may now fulfill the betrothal agreement as required by law."

At the mention of a betrothal agreement, Rhees had stopped fidgeting. By the time Valyss finished speaking, Rhees had grown completely still, and his palm was sweaty as he gripped Solace's hand. Solace knew nothing about the arcane laws governing royal families, but her stomach clenched just the same. *Could Rhees be under some legal obligation to the pouty crown princess? But we're married!*

MaudeLyn had been watching Rhees's reaction throughout her brother's explanation. She gave him a small head nod. "I know this comes as a shock, but it does not change the truth of the matter. As Heris's only surviving brother, you are legally obligated to fulfill the betrothal agreement in his place, to place me under your protection, and to produce heirs who will honor both your brother and you."

Ghrier dismissed the royal guards clustered in the aisle behind them, and waited until they'd departed from the atrium before he limped forward, thumping the floor with his walking stick. Rhees introduced Ghrier, adding, "Could you produce a copy of the betrothal papers so my chancellor may examine them?"

"Of course." Valyss reached into a brown leather pouch at his side. He pulled out a scroll, carefully wrapped in a layer of linen, which he handed to Rhees, who in turn gave it to Ghrier. The chancellor hobbled over to one of the pews and instructed the tongue-tied young squire to hold a pillar candle overhead so he could read. Ghrier withdrew a pair of half-moon spectacles from inside his jacket and began to review the document.

Everyone else remained standing around awkwardly in the atrium's center aisle. Solace considered inviting the king and crown princess to sit down in one of the pews but quickly dismissed the idea. After all, they'd traveled to Toresz not to attend Rhees's coronation ceremony, but to disrupt it. They intended to insert themselves into Rhees's life and shove her to the margins.

Ghrier peered carefully at the document, turning it over several times. Finally removing his spectacles, he replaced them in his pocket and hauled himself to his feet. He dismissed the squire, instructing him to guard the double doors so there would be no intrusions, and then he shuffled over to Rhees and Solace. Ghrier sighed, which told Solace all she didn't want to hear. She struggled to take a deep breath, her heart twisting in her chest.

"The agreement is valid—signed, witnessed, and sealed by all parties." "However," he said, holding up his index finger, "royal betrothal law also stipulates that if a man *is already married*, he is under no obligation to marry his brother's widow. That is clearly the case here." Ghrier handed the scroll to Rhees, who quickly scanned its contents before returning it to Valyss.

"Chancellor Ghrier is correct. My marriage to Queen

Solace nullifies the requirement that I marry the crown princess," said Rhees.

Valyss drew his brows together. "We wish to examine your betrothal papers and marriage contract to satisfy ourselves all is in order." Solace's palms were as clammy as Rhees's. *Do they have any inkling what truly happened between Rhees and me?* She dismissed the notion; only a trusted few knew the all the facts, and they wouldn't be traveling far and wide telling tales.

Rhees grunted, "The betrothal papers are in Yelosha with Solace's father"—not so; there had never been any such agreement—"however, we can produce the marital contract, if that would suffice?" Now that last part was true. Brother Tomyss, the abbot of Tor Monastery at the time, had performed the marriage ceremony in front of witnesses.

Valyss glanced at his sister, who inclined her head. "Very well. In the meantime, would you be so kind as to prepare our chambers for us? We look forward to seeing the palace once again and breaking bread with our Toreszan family this evening."

The room fell silent, and Solace was so stunned she temporarily lost the power of speech. *These two royal disruptors want to stay in the palace with Rhees and me, while we sort this out? How abominably rude! Then again...MaudeLyn had been betrothed to Heris, which makes her Rhees's sister-in-law...and mine as well. Argh.*

Chancellor Ghrier must have realized the necessity of providing accommodations for members of the royal family. He cleared his throat and motioned to Fenwith, who bowed as Ghrier introduced her as the king's aunt and chief mistress of the court. Fenwith assured Valyss and MaudeLyn they would be most welcome to stay at the palace with their brother-in-law and his wife. MaudeLyn puckered her lips at the mention of Rhees's wife but said nothing more.

After Valyss and MaudeLyn left—the crown princess wished to do some sightseeing in Urhl—Rhees threw his hands in the air. "This is preposterous! I'm of a mind to toss these imposters out on their ears and be done with it."

Arik, who'd been standing in the center aisle behind Fenwith, stepped forward. He narrowed his eyes at Rhees, and Solace heard the barely controlled anger in his voice. "Since your chancellor has confirmed the betrothal agreement is legal, the king and crown princess are far from imposters. Let's hope, for Solace's sake, *your* marriage contract is in order. We both know there was never any agreement between you and her father. If it were up to Soren—and up to me, I might add—you'd be behind bars, sir, instead of wearing a crown!"

Rhees's hands curled into fists at his side. A vein popped on his forehead as he faced Arik. "How dare you come here in Soren's place and then proceed to insult me to my face!"

"At least I'm not stealing from you behind your back," hissed Arik, his pupils dilating. "Or kidnapping anyone." He took several steps toward Rhees.

Solace's heart raced; she'd never seen Arik so outraged. *Is Dad just as angry at Rhees? If so, will they ever reconcile? Or will I always be worrying about my father and my husband coming to blows?*

Solace threw her hands in the air and stepped between the two men. "Stop this one-upmanship right now!" She glared first at Rhees, then at Arik, who muttered an apology and stepped back. "This has been a very stressful afternoon. I suggest we return to the palace and have tea before we're required to entertain Valyss and MaudeLyn this evening."

"An excellent idea," said Ghrier. He turned to Rhees and added, "Meanwhile, I'll send a courier to alert Brother Evryst. He'll need to bring the marital certificate along with him. I'm glad you maintained a signed copy at the monastery, since that old fox, Neuss, destroyed all the royal records."

Ghrier and Arik left for the palace together, while Fenwith sat across from Rhees and Solace in the carriage. Solace slipped her gloved hands into the pockets of her gray cape and chewed her bottom lip, wondering how they were going to deal with MaudeLyn and Valyss during the coronation ceremony. At the very least, they needed to sit together. The king's wife, sister-in-law, and brother-in-law needed to show unity.

Rhees folded his arms and sat in stony silence. Solace knew he was furious with Arik for coming to Urhl in place of Soren and for speaking so frankly. Solace exhaled, and Fenwith patted her hand. "This will all be sorted out soon enough, have no fear."

"Let's hope you're right." Solace heard the strain in her voice.

Rhees scowled. "What does Solace have to fear?"

A look passed between the two women, and Fenwith leaned forward. "How can you be so dense?"

Rhees thrusted out his jaw. "What are you saying? Speak plainly, please."

Fenwith shook her head. "Fine. If it's plain speaking you're needing, then listen up. If there is anything wrong with your marriage certificate—which we all know was hastily drawn up and witnessed—then what becomes of our dear Solace?"

Rhees drew back against the carriage's velvet cushions, a look of horror on his face. "There's no cause for concern over the paperwork. But if even if there were, I'd never abandon Solace." He turned toward Solace, sitting beside him on the bench, and brushed a lock of hair back from her forehead. "You must know that, my love."

Solace placed her hands on either side of Rhees's handsome, anxious face. "Of course I know how you feel, but..." The carriage pulled to a rocking stop, the footman opened the door, and the rest of Solace's words were swallowed up in the commotion of their arrival. As Rhees turned to give her a hand down, she silently finished her thought, *but if our marital contract doesn't pass legal scrutiny...I also know what you must do. And where would that leave me?*

CHAPTER 3

"SOLACE!" RHEES CALLED OUT. SHE'D STUMBLED, LOST IN HER own private world as they ascended the palace's stone steps, but Rhees was beside her in an instant. He gripped her arm and didn't let go until they reached the landing. Rhees yanked open the heavy wooden door at the rear of the castle, the entrance closest to the stable yard, and asked a startled maid to fetch them tea.

He guided Solace into a small, simply furnished room they'd adopted as their private parlor. There wasn't a hint of gilt or glamor anywhere. Solace sank onto one of the faded blue-and-white sofas in front of the fireplace. She absent-mindedly adjusted the books spread out on the round, white coffee table, her hands shaking slightly.

Although it was late spring, and the days were beginning to warm, Solace found herself shivering. Their new home always seemed chilly. Rhees must have noticed and handed her a woolen throw before leaving in search of Ghrier. Meanwhile, Fenwith bent down, her knees creaking, and started the fire herself rather than seeking a servant.

Solace slipped her hands beneath the blanket and frowned, unsure how she would navigate dinner that evening. She'd have to ensure the table linens, settings, food service, and seating arrangements were in perfect order for the Censarran king and crown princess.

However, she was more concerned about her husband and her oldest friend from Yelosha. Although Arik was usually mild-mannered, he had a spine of steel, and the two men would be exchanging fisticuffs soon if she couldn't smooth things over. But how was she supposed to do that when Arik had only spoken the truth?

She shook her head. She'd deal with any fallout between Arik and Rhees if and when it happened. That particular worry paled in comparison to Crown Princess MaudeLyn, who wished to be much more than Rhees's sister-in-law. Solace sipped her hot tea and glanced at Fenwith. "I think you're as worried about this old betrothal agreement as I am."

"Aye." Fenwith placed her gold-rimmed, blue teacup on the table. "I don't like it at all. At a minimum, we're obligated to recognize the kinship. But if..." Her voice trailed off.

"But if there's anything amiss with our marriage certificate," said Solace grimly, "Rhees is legally obligated to MaudeLyn."

"But Rhees loves you!" Fenwith drew her silver eyebrows together. "And you've shared the same bed, which is not something that can be nullified."

Solace let out a shaky breath. "You're too kind to say it, but let's be frank. If the paperwork is found wanting, I'd be ruined—and I'm not yet eighteen! No one else would look at me the same way again or welcome me into their homes. Well, except my dad. He'd be furious, but he wouldn't turn me away."

"And I'll not turn you away, either." Arik had entered the room without Solace noticing. She pulled back against the sofa, startled. "Forgive me," he said, "I didn't mean to eavesdrop. I stopped by to ask Mistress Fenwith where to unload my bags."

Fenwith rose from the sofa. "I'm so sorry. With all the commotion, I never showed you to your chamber. Please follow me."

Arik thanked her, but his brown eyes were troubled as he scanned Solace's face. "I spoke the truth earlier. I truly hope the marital contract is in order. I know it would break your heart to leave this place and the people you've grown to love, and to leave *him*. But I promise you this—I will look after you if the worst comes to pass. I will take you home to Yelosha."

"You'll do nothing of the kind! How dare you even suggest such a thing, in my own home no less! I demand you leave at once, you cur!" Rhees hovered just inside the doorway, looming and angry.

Arik turned toward Rhees, his back stiffening. "What did you call me?" he spat out.

Solace hopped up from the sofa and for the second time that day, sprang between the two men. "Stop this nonsense immediately." Ghrier hastily limped into the parlor and shut the door behind him.

Solace turned to Rhees. "You entered halfway through a conversation and took Arik's words out of context."

Rhees glowered at Arik over her head. "I know what I heard. He still wants you."

Arik blew out a puff of air. "You obstinate fool! I want to aid Solace, if the worst happens and you're unable to fulfill your vows to her." Arik shook his head and addressed Fenwith. "Never mind about my chamber, ma'am, I'll see myself to the nearest inn." He brushed past Rhees and Ghrier, the door closing behind him with a firm click. Solace was tempted to call him back, but she knew things would escalate further if she did.

Rhees ran a hand through his dark, wavy hair. "I'm sorry, Lace, but it's just as well Arik stays elsewhere this evening, at least until after the ceremony. We have enough to worry about."

Solace compressed her lips, shaking her head. "You were incredibly rude to my oldest friend. Arik would never do anything to dishonor either one of us, and you owe him an apology the next time you see him."

"Fine," grumped Rhees. "I'll apologize for your sake, not his." He glanced at Fenwith, stoking the fire, and Ghrier, who'd sat down on one of the sofas. He was balancing a teacup on his lap while helping himself to an almond biscuit from the platter on the coffee table. "Why are all of you expecting the worst? We merely need to produce our marital record for Valyss's inspection. I'm already married to the only woman I've ever loved. Now please, can we have a simple cup of tea in peace?"

Fenwith handed Rhees his tea and gave him a friendly nudge toward the sofas. "Of course; here, have a seat. I'm sure you and Ghrier still have details to iron out for tomorrow. Solace and I need to provide instructions to the staff regarding accommodations for Valyss and MaudeLyn."

Rhees lowered his brow but didn't argue with his formidable aunt. He sat down across from Ghrier with a grunt as Solace followed Fenwith from the room.

"You're amazing," whispered Solace.

Fenwith looped her arm through Solace's and chuckled. "You're doing just fine yourself. Rhees is so stubborn he needs a strong woman—he needs you—to help him stay focused." She headed toward the carpeted stairs leading to the family's private wing.

"Where are we going? I thought we were giving instructions to the staff."

"*I'll* be meeting with the staff in a moment. Meanwhile, *you're* going to get some rest. Your new lady's maid won't be starting for another few weeks, so I'll send one of the upper maids when it's time to prepare for dinner with the snooty princess and her stout brother. Stars almighty, what a pair of in-laws!"

Solace grinned and allowed herself to be coddled by Fenwith, who guided her to the family's wing on the second floor. They entered Solace's oversized chamber, located across the hall from Rhees's even-larger suite. A mish-mash of pink, green, blue, and yellow ruffles, lace, and florals scuttled across the walls, carpets, draperies, four-poster bed, sofa, and winged-back chairs. Solace would have to redo this room, if only to avoid getting a migraine every time she entered.

Solace pulled back one of the floriated drapes to peer at the Tor Mountain range. Beyond the peaks, out of sight of the palace, the Toreszan hill country unfurled all the way to the Yeloshan border and the brown hills of home.

What's Dad doing right now? Still working in the fields, most likely. And then later, after supper, he'll take Barley out for one more walk and smoke his pipe before turning in for the evening. He'll be up before dawn tomorrow, doing exactly the same thing, in a never-ending pattern of rising, working, resting, and rising again—and content with his life.

Solace sat in the pink, tufted chair next to her bed, undid the dozen buttons on each boot, and slipped them off her feet. She gratefully wriggled her toes in the plush carpet, a swirl of gold, blue, pink, and green flowers. Everything about the palace was so different from the simple, three-room cottage she'd called home for the past seventeen years.

Fenwith pulled back the covers, and Solace tumbled into bed, still wearing her day gown. "Thank you, Fen," she murmured with a yawn. "'Tis true, I'm worn to a frazzle." She'd started the day feeling tired, which was normal after a water-divining trip, but the events of the past few hours had drained her remaining reserves of energy.

"I'll send Brother Evryst up when he arrives," said Fenwith.

Solace groaned. "He's going to give me another lecture." Evryst was not just head monk of the Tor Order, he was also a master healer who'd saved Solace's life when she'd been stabbed by one of Neuss's goons. The monk was impossibly bossy when it came to her health regimen and would no doubt find a reason to scold her.

Despite all that had happened, she fell asleep immediately, startling into full wakefulness when a baldheaded man with a long, black beard and dark, penetrating eyes bent over her. He held a narrow, silver tube in his right hand. "I'm still alive, Evryst," she commented wryly.

"Hmm," he grumbled. "I'll be the judge of that." Brother Evryst was nearly always politely deferential, except when he was in healer mode, which brought out his grump.

"Take a deep breath...and another..." Evryst frowned as he put the silver tube away in his black bag. "You've been straining your heart again, my queen. I've half a mind to put you on bed rest, effective immediately."

Solace gasped. "But Rhees's coronation is tomorrow! We have guests from every kingdom and province here in Urhl—and then there's King Valyss and Crown Princess MaudeLyn, who—"

"Who have no business showing up a decade after Prince Heris was murdered and demanding to be recognized as kin! Even worse, they're questioning the legitimacy of your marriage. I hate the thought of turning over the certificate for their inspection." Evryst sounded as angry as she felt.

He rubbed his bald head sheepishly. "I guess I'm not behaving much like a monk. But I'm furious at the pair of them for inserting themselves into what should be a joyous occasion for all of us, and especially for you and Rhees."

"Aye, so am I." Solace blew out a puff of air. "But once they examine the marital contract and are satisfied, I'm sure they'll be ready to leave for their own home. Speaking of which, where is the contract?"

"I turned it over to Ghrier, who wishes to review it in private tonight. He will provide it to Valyss tomorrow after the ceremony."

Solace nodded. "Well, I suppose I'd better start getting ready for this evening's dinner with our out-of-town, unexpected kinfolk."

Evryst stood up. "I meant what I said about your heart. I will order you to bed if you continue to ignore my advice."

"I promise to take things more slowly, after the coronation, after Valyss and MaudeLyn leave, and after my life returns to a semblance of normalcy."

"See that you follow through," said Evryst. "Although I wouldn't wait for normalcy—your life has been anything but."

CHAPTER 4

It's just as well Arik has taken himself to an inn for the evening, thought Solace. *Even he couldn't lighten the mood around this table.* They were in the formal banquet hall, a huge room generally reserved for state dinners, with dark-paneled walls, blue-and-gold painted ceiling, rich tapestries depicting various battle scenes, and a long, massive table set with white linens, gold dinnerware, and brightly-burning candelabras

Rhees and Solace, anchoring the table's head and foot, sat in intricately-carved wooden chairs. Evryst, Fenwith, and Chelyss sat on Solace's left side, and Ghrier, MaudeLyn, and Valyss sat on her right. The remaining thirty-odd chairs that normally ringed the table had been shoved against the walls, unoccupied.

Solace had been feeling elegant, even regal, in a peach-colored, satin evening gown that had once belonged to Ellanora, Rhees's mother. One of the palace maids had arranged Solace's glossy, black hair in a mass of ringlets that tumbled, like a waterfall, down her back. Then Solace spotted MaudeLyn, whose dark brown tresses had been swept up in a bun and dotted with tiny jewels, leaving her neck and shoulders bare. The crown princess's dress, a beaded, glittering, copper affair, caught the candlelight every time she reached for her fork. Solace decided the woman's entire ensemble was designed for one purpose—to grab attention.

Chelyss glanced around the table with a barely perceptible sigh and scratched his gray beard. Solace knew he was far more comfortable shouting instructions at young squires, his peaked cap squashed onto his thinning hair, than attending a state dinner wearing his finest blue tabard. Chelyss was helping Rhees re-establish a school for the future knights of Toresz, which Neuss had shut down, after first murdering all the knights inside the palace.

Solace was thankful Fenwith had encouraged her to take a nap; otherwise, she would have struggled to stay awake as Valyss droned on about new farming techniques in Censarra. She hid a yawn behind her linen napkin when Valyss described an irrigation system he'd designed for one of his estates, which distributed water from a nearby lake onto their fields.

Rhees asked Valyss about crop rotation, which led to a discussion of climate and topography in the two kingdoms. Censarra was renowned for its ten thousand lakes, low green hills separated by gently sloping valleys, and rich farmland. By contrast, Toresz was dusty, brown, and mountainous, where fresh water was scant and pantries ran bare by the end of winter. Yelosha was no different. Solace recalled one particularly harsh winter, when she and her dad had split their last potato four ways for dinner so Arik and his father would have something in their stomachs that night.

MaudeLyn, who'd barely contributed to the conversation throughout the meal, placed her fork and knife across her empty plate and swiveled her bejeweled head toward Rhees. "It must be difficult to keep the rabble in check with so much scarcity—and so little water. It's marvelously convenient to have a water witch at hand, don't you think?"

Rhees sputtered, "Solace is not a witch! She is extraordinary...and singularly gifted when it comes to divining for water sources. Please refrain from any further name-calling, madam."

MaudeLyn didn't answer. She merely shrugged her slender shoulders and sipped from her wine goblet.

Solace lowered her brow in disgust. MaudeLyn was the worst sort of royal, entirely self-absorbed and out of touch with the people she ruled. "Toreszans aren't rabble," said Solace. "They're hard-working men and women who've been oppressed for the past decade. Ensuring they have enough water to provide a cup to their little ones is my privilege. If you think that's a witchy ability, so be it."

The crown princess sniffed and glowered down her long nose at Solace. "There's no need to be defensive. I think it was brilliant of King Rhees to secure the services of a water diviner during the rebellion. Although he might have gotten carried away afterward."

Valyss shot his sister a warning glance, but the princess ignored it. "The king didn't have to go so far as to bed you and then call you—a Yeloshan commoner—his consort. The more accurate term is concubine." Valyss's mouth had formed a silent *O* during his sister's little speech.

Solace dropped her napkin on the table and rose from her chair, her insides quaking. She bit back a rude retort and paused to take a steadying breath before addressing the room. "Please forgive me, but I must retire early. I've been divining for these past three weeks, and Toreszans now have twenty-two additional water sources they didn't have a month ago. However, my energy is flagging, and this conversation isn't helping."

Rhees pushed back his heavy wooden chair and stood up, his brown-black eyes flashing darkly at MaudeLyn before he trained them on Solace. His face softened as he gazed at her. "I'll escort you to your chamber, my dear." Solace ached to be in Rhees's arms, but not now, not when such a cloud of uncertainty hung over everything, including their marriage.

"There is no need to disturb yourself, sir," Fenwith spoke stiffly as she moved to Solace's side. "Please remain with your guests. I'll ensure Queen Solace is well looked after." Solace noticed Fenwith chose to refer to her as queen rather than queen consort, as if to make a point with MaudeLyn and Valyss. Rhees's wily aunt did nothing by accident.

Rhees canted his head at Solace, who nodded. "Very well," he mumbled as he dropped back down into his chair. "Carry on."

Valyss cleared his throat and asked Rhees when he might see the marriage certificate. Solace didn't hear Rhees's reply, as Fenwith hurried her out of the room and closed the door behind them.

"Speaking of witches!" breathed Fenwith, fuming.

Solace frowned, replaying the princess's words inside her head. The carpets muffled their footsteps as they walked down the long hallways and ascended the stairs to the family's wing. They reached Solace's chamber, where a maid sat on the pink, tufted chair, dozing. Solace dismissed the sleepy woman. She couldn't tolerate anyone in her chamber at the moment, other than Fenwith.

"MaudeLyn is awful," agreed Solace, "but I wonder

whether she's only saying what other royals are thinking. Perhaps in their eyes I am little more than Rhees's concubine, the convenient little water witch whom he'll soon grow tired of."

Fenwith was unbuttoning the back of Solace's gown but paused. "Nonsense. MaudeLyn is an unhappy, miserable woman. She can't tolerate seeing any other woman—especially someone she considers beneath her notice—in a loving relationship with a handsome, virile man, let alone a king. I understand Crown Prince Munsey, her deceased husband, was nearly fifty when they married. Apparently, the only thing he made love to was his bottle of bourbon. Nay, it's abundantly clear to me that MaudeLyn wants what you have. She wants Rhees to look at her the way he looks at you, which is never going to happen."

Solace carefully stepped out of the evening gown and wondered whether Ellanora had ever felt as she did: entirely out of place, an imposter who should turn right around and head back to the hills. Solace slipped a buttery soft, yellow nightgown over her head—another of Ellanora's hand-me-downs—and sat in front of her dressing table, brushing out her long, wavy hair. "I'll not rest easy until Valyss and MaudeLyn have reviewed the marriage certificate and are heading home."

"By this time tomorrow you'll have your wish. The issue shall be settled, and we'll be rid of the nasty crown princess and her uncalled-for dramatics."

"Let's hope all is truly settled. I want no more surprises."

Fenwith wished Solace goodnight and paused at the door, resting her hand on the crystal knob. "Aye," she said softly, "let us hope that's the case."

Solace placed her hairbrush on the table and looked

longingly at her bed, which the maid had turned down. She knew Rhees would come to her as soon as he could, his need as fierce as hers. He'd take her in his arms, kiss her until she trembled, and then turn toward the bed, intent on spending the night with her—and Solace wanted him just as much. They'd not been together for weeks, the separation too long, the evenings too lonely without Rhees at her side.

But what if Valyss were to discover something irregular about their marriage tomorrow, and even worse, Ghrier concurred? After all, nothing about their relationship—and their love for each other—could be considered *regular*. Solace loved Rhees despite their dreadful beginning, his miles-long stubborn streak, and his less-than-pleasant demeanor when crossed. She gave a soft chuckle; if the spoilt princess knew the true Rhees, she might grab her brother and hightail it out of Urhl before the coronation.

Solace shook her head. That was wishful thinking and she knew it. The crown princess wanted Solace's title, position, and husband. And if Solace's marriage contract, which had been hastily penned and executed, didn't pass muster —where did that leave her? MaudeLyn's betrothal agreement would take precedence, at least until Ghrier's brilliant mind thought of some loophole. No, she decided, Rhees needed to remain at arm's length until this was settled. They would have to spend one more night apart, until they could prove they were legally conjoined.

Solace settled onto the flowery sofa with a lemon-colored throw and one of her mother's old story books. She left all the candles lit while she waited. She must have dozed, because the soft knocking she heard in her dreams became more urgent. Solace woke with a start and hurried to the door, calling, "Who is it?" although she knew it would be Rhees.

"'Tis me, my love. Let me in."

Solace opened the door and stepped aside so Rhees could enter. She didn't want to have the conversation they needed to have while he stood in the hallway. He'd be raising his voice shortly, and while the servants would hear the shouting, they'd not be able to make out each word. She hoped their guests two floors above would not hear anything.

Rhees held his arms out, an open invitation, but Solace placed her palm flat against his muscled chest. "We must wait."

He drew his dark eyebrows downward. "Why?" he barked hoarsely. "It's been three weeks and two days."

Solace took his hand and led him to the sofa, while she moved over to the adjacent winged-back chair. Solace feared if she sat next to Rhees, she'd wind up in his lap, all her resolve melted. Her pulse raced as she gazed at her glowering but gorgeous husband, the crease on his brow deepening as she explained her reasoning.

Rhees finally exploded. "*But we are married!* No one, particularly not some husband-hunting princess, is going to cut the ties that bind us! I don't give a rat's tail if MaudeLyn and Valyss find some 'irregularity' in our paperwork. Who cares?"

"I care, and so should you. Do you really believe we could carry on as before, knowing our marriage was illegal? Our enemies would have a field day. We must, *you* must, follow the law you will be swearing to uphold in the morning."

"What are you saying?" rasped Rhees, his eyes flashing in anger, his fury now directed at her rather than Maude-

Lyn. "Be frank with me, Lace. It's been a long day, and I'm in no mood for subtlety."

"If the worst happens, and our contract doesn't withstand Valyss's scrutiny, I'm saying we would have to separate." Rhees sputtered, but Solace spoke over him. "Just for a short while, until Ghrier could work out a legal solution to the problem."

Rhees jumped up from the sofa and stalked to the door, his back rigid. He spun around and spat out, "Fine. I'm going to rouse Ghrier at once. He's the one who wants to wait until after the coronation tomorrow. I'll happily awaken that smarmy king and his snooty sister from their slumber. Let's get this over with tonight!"

Solace hurried after him. "Rhees, no. It's way too late. If I can wait twelve hours, so can you."

Rhees sighed deeply, his broad chest heaving. All his anger seemed to drain out of him, replaced by a weary sadness. "I don't want to wait," he murmured quietly, shaking his head. He extended one callused hand toward her, and she stepped closer. Rhees picked up a lock of her hair. "But I will wait...for you...and only you." He brushed his lips against her forehead and then hastened from the room.

Solace leaned against the door, her head in the crook of her arm. She let the tears trickle down her cheeks—willing herself to stay put, feet planted firmly on the carpet—as she resisted the nearly overwhelming urge to dash down the hall after her hurting, bewildered husband.

CHAPTER 5

Solace opened one eye, noted the bright beam of light streaming through the gap in her draperies, and came immediately to full attention. *It's Rhees's Coronation Day—and I'm already late.* She'd forgotten to provide the sleepy maid with wake-up instructions. Solace had hoped for extra time to get ready. Instead, she'd be rushing through her morning toilette and skipping breakfast if she wanted to arrive on time for the ceremony. Rhees would have to leave for the Grand Library without her.

As she flung off the covers and pulled the bell rope to ring for her maid, Solace's thoughts turned to the anger—and pain—in Rhees's eyes when she'd sent him away the previous evening. *Just a few more hours, and Rhees will be crowned King of Toresz. Valyss and MaudeLyn will be on their way back to Censarra, empty-handed. And Rhees and I can go on as before, only better, without any unfounded threats or intimidations from sulky in-laws.*

Little more than an hour later, Solace gave her hand to the footman as she exited the carriage alone. She adjusted her floor-length ceremonial robe, a whirl of paisley in cobalt blue and gold, the royal colors of Toresz, with touches of claret and ivory running through the swirls. Beneath the robe, she wore an ivory satin gown with a gold lace overlay and tiny blue beads at her waist, cuffs, and hem. Although Solace hadn't wanted a tiara, Rhees had insisted, and so she selected the simplest one she could find inside the royal vault: a slender, golden half-crown, with tiny blue sapphires and sparkly diamonds embedded in its delicate scrollwork. Her maid had swept her black hair into a partial bun, with half her wavy locks tumbling down her shoulders.

The footman extended his arm to escort Solace through the library's little-used side entrance, away from the crowd lining up in front. He deposited her in the small vestibule with a bow. She spotted MaudeLyn sitting with Fenwith in a tiny, cramped office across the hall. Chelyss and Valyss stood stiffly next to the cluttered, overflowing desk, the women having taken the only chairs in the room.

MaudeLyn wore a snowy white gown with a low-cut V-neckline; her robe of gauzy silver was artfully draped across her shoulders, providing an unimpeded view of her full bosom. The platinum crown on her head flashed with a dizzying number of gems as she turned to address Fenwith. MaudeLyn looked like a princess bride heading to the altar, and Solace had little doubt that was her intention.

Solace tried not to let MaudeLyn make her feel inferior, but the crown princess was beautiful, royal, and self-assured. Squaring her shoulders, Solace slipped past the librarian's office unseen and followed the sound of lowered voices—Rhees's, always half a decibel louder than the rest—along with Ghrier's gravelly hisses and Brother Evryst's milder murmurs.

She opened the door to a storage room and slipped

inside. Boxes of books and scrolls, waiting to be sorted by the busy library staff, were stacked along the gray walls behind the three men. Ghrier was clad in a white robe with a multi-colored stole draped around his neck. Evryst looked like he'd just emerged from a monastic service, in his long, hooded, navy habit neatly cinched at the waist with a red rope. But Rhees took her breath away. He wore a flowing, blue-and-gold coronation robe that accentuated his wide shoulders. A richly embroidered, golden tunic and dark blue slacks peeked out from beneath the folds of his robe, and a thick circlet of gold sat on his black, wavy hair. The circlet would be replaced with a crown during the ceremony.

Rhees glanced away from Ghrier, his scowl dissolving when his eyes alighted on Solace. "Lace...you look so beautiful," he breathed, his voice husky, "a true queen, in every sense of the word."

Solace smiled up at him but couldn't help noticing the furrowed brows of the other two men. Ghrier and Evryst seemed anxious, probably because Rhees wasn't listening to their advice. She arched an eyebrow. "Anything I should know about, gentlemen?"

Rhees waved a hand dismissively. "Merely a small disagreement about our in-laws. Ghrier and Evryst believe MaudeLyn must sit next to you, as our 'sister.' Valyss would sit in the same row as well. I don't want to publicly elevate them like that. I'd prefer for them to be seated behind you."

Solace had no knowledge of royal protocols—after all, this was the first, and probably the only, coronation she'd attend—and she looked to Ghrier and Evryst for guidance. "What is proper, under these circumstances?"

Brother Evryst bowed. "It is expected that any siblings,

or siblings through marriage, be seated with the monarch's spouse—"

"Or directly behind them," interrupted Rhees.

"Only in instances where there are a large number of siblings, and a second row is required," clarified Ghrier.

Rhees threw his hands in the air. "Alright, I concede. I hate the thought of that woman in the same row as my wife, but for appearance's sake, I'll agree."

Evryst nodded. "Very good. Of course, that brings us to the second consideration."

"Which is?" grumbled Rhees.

"The audience's attention will naturally be diverted when MaudeLyn and Valyss sit in the first row, since no one will have any idea why they are being afforded such an honor. I suggest we have them seated a good five minutes before the ceremony starts. As they proceed to their seats, the sergeant of the guard will announce them and their relationship to you, via Heris, your deceased brother. That way, MaudeLyn and Valyss will receive the recognition they crave, and the gossipy chit-chat will be mostly over by the time we actually begin."

Rhees and Ghrier scratched their beards as they considered Evryst's cagey suggestion, but Solace laughed out loud. "Brilliant! Leave it to our favorite monk to stage the entrance of our untimely in-laws."

Everyone, even Rhees, chuckled and some of the tension eased, but Solace could sense Ghrier was still uneasy, which she attributed to general nerves rather than their unwelcome new relations.

Ghrier and Evryst left to oversee final arrangements and ensure MaudeLyn and Valyss, as well as Fenwith and Chelyss, were properly announced and seated. As the new king's surrogate parents—Fenwith and Chelyss had raised

Rhees after Ellanora and King Meade were killed—they deserved their own place of honor for the ceremony.

Rhees took Solace's two hands in his and drew her closer. She started to object, not because of the unfinished business with MaudeLyn, but because she couldn't afford to mess up her well-manicured appearance. Rhees grunted, "What's wrong now? Can't I show you any affection without meeting resistance?"

"Of course you can," said Solace, "just so long as you don't touch my gown or hair or face. I need to look my very best when seated next to the voluptuous crown princess, who believes she's in competition with me."

Rhees let out a throaty growl and tugged Solace closer, until they stood a hand width apart. He used his gloved forefinger to tip up her chin and peer into her eyes, his breath warming her face. His brown-black eyes were deadly serious as he gazed into hers. "Neither MaudeLyn nor anyone else, nor anything else, except death itself, shall be able to separate us. We are meant for each other, regardless of what your father and Arik might think, or what Valyss and MaudeLyn might hope for."

Solace's heartrate soared, all her doubts about her suitability to be Queen of Toresz vanishing. She might be a foreign-born commoner with a peculiar, witchy gift for divining water, but she and Rhees belonged together. She loved this obstinate, grumpy, ruggedly handsome man with a fierceness that left her breathless—and he loved her in equal measure.

Solace removed her glove and touched Rhees's face, his dark beard soft beneath her fingers. "Aye," she whispered, "'tis true we fit together—like hand to glove, horse to bridle, hearth to home."

Rhees blinked slowly and let out a long breath, as if he'd

been waiting to hear her say the words aloud. He stepped back, raised her hand to his lips and kissed it. "Ready?"

Solace slipped her glove back into place and nodded. "Aye, it's time for you to wear the crown of your father, and his father before him, and for us to get back to living our daily lives."

Rhees guided her out of the storage room toward Ghrier, Evryst, and the monk's able assistant, Brother Alyn, waiting in the atrium's lobby for the start of the ceremony. Alyn had piercing brown eyes, a long, dark beard, and black hair he pulled into a single, thick plait. Like Evryst, he wore a long, hooded, navy habit, but instead of a simple rope tied around his waist, he'd strapped two swords onto his sturdy leather belt. Despite his fierce appearance and reputation as a warrior-monk, Solace knew Alyn was also a poet who wrote notes to himself in iambic pentameter.

Royal guards in blue tabards milled about, some to participate in the ceremony, others to guard the doors to prevent anyone else from entering the packed building, and the rest to provide general security. Solace knew Ghrier was worried about potential trouble from some fringe group claiming Neuss should still be king, likely paid off by one of his thugs still hoping to resume their criminal pastimes.

Brother Alyn began lining up the royal guards for the processional, beginning with the two banner bearers, one carrying the blue, gold, and ivory striped flag of Toresz, and her partner bearing King Rhees's royal seal. Rhees's good friend and head knight, Sir Kryss, followed directly behind the banners, the ceremonial longsword strapped to his waist. Two more knights lined up, and then Alyn nodded at Rhees, who took his place in line, followed by Solace, two more royal guards, then Ghrier, Evryst, and four more knights.

Alyn, carrying the Noble Carta, brought up the rear. The ancient tome, bound in cracked, scaly, brown hide, contained Toresz's earliest written laws, including the provision that no one, not even the king or queen, was above the law. Kings were required to uphold the laws of the land and to punish transgressors, including royal ones. This enabled Rhees to hold his crazy uncle Neuss accountable for the horrific crimes he'd committed during his reign.

Ghrier nodded at a lone knight, a brass trumpet in his right hand, standing in front of the atrium's double doors. The trumpeter pivoted, entered the atrium, and blew three long, somber-sounding notes through his horn. The din of conversation abruptly stopped as all eyes turned toward the back of the atrium. Solace took a deep breath. Her stomach tightened with nerves as she followed Rhees, who walked at a stately pace. She found herself admiring how dashing her husband looked as he proceeded down the aisle in his robe, the royal seal of Toresz—a golden lion's head peering out of a lapis blue circle—draped across his broad back.

She spotted Arik, wearing a new black suit he must have ordered for the occasion, seated four rows behind her pew. Warmed by his presence on this historic day, Solace was grateful her Yeloshan friend had made the long trip. Rhees reached the front of the room, and Solace stepped out of line into the pew on the left, where MaudeLyn and Valyss were already seated. The crown princess had managed to take up half the row, her robe billowing around her. When Solace turned to take her seat, she had to push some of MaudeLyn's finery out of the way. Her sister-in-law let out a small harrumph of annoyance, as if Solace were the unwanted guest versus the other way around. Solace ignored MaudeLyn and trained her eyes on Rhees.

The ceremony proceeded as they'd rehearsed. Brother Evryst opened with a prayer of thanksgiving, and then Chancellor Ghrier gave a short speech laying out Rhees's lineage in the long line of Toreszan monarchs, a not-so-subtle reminder he was King Meade's only living son and therefore, the sole heir to the crown.

Brother Alyn held the heavy tome in front of Rhees, who placed one hand on the book and the other over his heart. Ghrier recited the royal oath, and Rhees repeated it, his voice booming across the atrium. "I solemnly swear to uphold the Noble Carta in all circumstances, to protect Toresz from our enemies, foreign and domestic, and to faithfully execute my duty as king to the best of my ability."

Solace had been leaning forward, listening intently to each word of Rhees's oath. As he finished, a sense of peace settled over her, and she leaned back with a soft sigh. Despite all the hard work to come and the conflicts as yet unseen, Solace knew Rhees was where he belonged—leading Toresz forward and putting Neuss's dark deeds behind him.

Rhees sat on the ancient throne, and Evryst stepped behind him. The monk first removed the gold circlet from Rhees's head, and then he picked up the heavy, jewel-encrusted crown of Toresz. Evryst raised the crown high for all to see before he placed it firmly on Rhees's head. Rhees pounded his chest with his right fist, and then flicked his hand outward like a bird taking wing—the classic Toreszan salute familiar to knights and commoners alike. The royal visitors politely applauded, while the Toreszans in the crowd whistled and cheered, pounding their chests and flicking their hands in reply.

Rhees's eyes sought out Solace in the front pew. He

pounded his chest a second time, and then brought his fist up to his lips for a kiss before flicking his hand toward his wife; only lovers used this modified form of the greeting. Rhees tented his eyebrows at Solace, who felt embarrassed to be the center of so much attention, but she'd not let Rhees down. Solace repeated the gesture, and Rhees's face relaxed. He nodded, his mouth turning up at the corners.

In that single, perfect moment, as Solace beamed at her husband, her heart strumming in her chest, she had no doubt they could face whatever came their way. But then Valyss gave a throaty cough, MaudeLyn tapped her shoe impatiently, and someone started to boo and jeer behind them. A handful of other protesters joined in, all of them shouting, "Rhees is an imposter! King Neuss Now!"

Solace felt herself deflate, her hand going to her throat as she waited, as they all waited, for the men to be subdued. A scuffle broke out in the center aisle, as guards swarmed in to remove the dissenters. One of men broke free and charged down the aisle toward Rhees, a dagger in his right hand. Several of the princesses in the front rows, including MaudeLyn, screamed and swooned.

Solace turned in her seat, anxious lest the man take a swipe at Rhees, and regretting her decision to leave her pearl-handled dagger and her sling and stones behind in her chamber. She could have slipped them into her reticule, although the sling would have made her purse too bulky, and she couldn't have used it in the crowded room. Her blade, however, would have come in handy right then. Solace vowed to never go weaponless again, despite Rhees's gentle chiding that she was no longer a Yeloshan hill girl who needed to protect her sheep.

The dagger-wielding man dodged around several

guards, slashing one of them, as he raced up the aisle. He made it almost to the front, when a well-built Yeloshan man dashed out of his seat and tackled the thug to the ground. Several other guests piled on and helped Arik restrain the man, who hurled insults as the guards hauled him out of the room. Arik and the other guests dusted themselves off and returned to their seats, but Solace's brief euphoria had evaporated.

Ghrier used his walking stick to pound the floor, but a hundred different conversations buzzed around them. MaudeLyn, who'd collapsed against her brother, complained of a headache. Rhees rose from the throne and gave a hand signal to the trumpeter in the back, who blew a short, lively trill.

Rhees's rich baritone boomed across the room, which had the desired effect of quieting down the jittery crowd. After thanking the many royal guests, visitors, and citizens in attendance, he asked for a moment of silence to recall all who had perished under Neuss's regime. Solace heard many sniffles and even some gut-wrenching sobs behind her.

Rhees took a deep breath and cried out, "On this first, official day of my reign, we are reminded again of our divided kingdom. Not everyone wants to embrace a new Toresz. Some would gladly return to the old ways and deny our people enough food to eat and water to drink. While the war against Neuss has been won—that crafty old fox sits in the palace dungeon, awaiting trial for his crimes— our battle against oppression, violence, and greed is far from over!"

Rhees paused and peered from side to side, his eyes sweeping over those who'd gathered to see the new king of

Toresz. A hush fell over the atrium as everyone waited for him to continue. Rhees held up his hands, palms out, as if he were welcoming them home. "However, my friends and neighbors, this is a time for celebration. We're entering a new chapter in Toreszan history, and I promise our best days are yet to come. Therefore, let us go forth from this place rejoicing in our new beginning, grateful to all who sacrificed so much on our behalf, and mindful of what more we must accomplish!" The crowd broke into loud cheering and applause.

The trumpeter played three long notes, followed by a short trill, and everyone rose from their seats. Rhees stepped off the dais and waited for Solace to join him. They walked, hand-in-hand, down the center aisle. As they passed Arik, Rhees gave him a head nod, and Solace murmured her thanks. When they reached the lobby, two royal guards hurried Rhees and Solace to a staircase. Although Solace didn't think there would be any more security incidents, she appreciated putting some distance between Rhees and the rest of the crowd.

They took the stairs up to the next level, where book-lined shelves ran in neat rows from the balcony overlooking the atrium all the way to the other side of the massive library. Fenwith, Chelyss, MaudeLyn, and Valyss followed them onto the second floor, and Solace forced a polite smile on her face. She'd managed to forget about the crown princess for a short while. They gathered along the wrought-iron railing and waved to the crowd as they departed the atrium. When MaudeLyn started blowing kisses to the onlookers, Solace had to grit her teeth and refrain from rolling her eyes.

The sergeant of the guard opened another set of doors

that led outside into the bright sunshine. Rhees and Solace stepped onto the small terrace and waved at the Toreszans cheering in the mobbed street below them. Solace inhaled deeply, grateful the coronation was behind them. They had only to get through the review of the marriage certificate, and they could put MaudeLyn and Valyss out of mind for good.

After several minutes of waving at the good-humored crowd, the sergeant beckoned them back inside. Evryst soon joined them, followed by Ghrier and Arik, speaking amiably about the spring planting season. Solace felt Rhees stiffen beside her when he spotted Arik, but she murmured, "He is here on behalf of my father, nothing more."

"It is never nothing more," Rhees grumbled.

A thin man with a pointy, black beard, gray skullcap, and somber expression on his face slipped up the stairs. He scurried over to Valyss and MaudeLyn and bowed, his gray robe fluttering around his boots. Ghrier greeted the last arrival, and then thumping the floor with his walking stick, led them between the towering rows of books to the other side of the library.

As they passed through the philosophy and meta-physics collection, Solace itched to browse through the books rather than follow the chancellor. Suddenly, she had a strong urge to do anything other than watch Valyss and his advisor review her marriage license and wait for them to pronounce her and Rhees legally wed—or not.

Ghrier pushed open a heavy walnut door and stepped aside to allow everyone to enter the room ahead of him. Solace glanced up as she passed through the doorway. The old chancellor's bushy white eyebrows drew together, and he tried smiling bravely at her, but she couldn't miss the sad, defeated expression in his eyes.

Solace's insides froze, her stomach clenching into a mass of knots. *Ghrier knows something is wrong with our paperwork. That's why he postponed this meeting until after the coronation—to give us one perfect moment, Rhees crowned king with me by his side—before our lives are torn asunder.*

CHAPTER 6

THEY ENTERED A READING ROOM, WITH POLISHED WOOD FLOORS, long tables that had been pushed against the wall on their right, and a row of windows with taupe drapes running along the wall on their left. Directly opposite them stood a single, narrow table in front of an unlit fireplace, with ten burgundy armchairs arranged in a semi-circle around it.

"Please, make yourselves comfortable. We'll begin momentarily," said Ghrier, who suggested the two kings should sit next to each other and face the table, to ensure an optimal view. Rhees guided Solace to her seat and then sat beside her, with Fenwith, Chelyss, and Ghrier filling out one side of the half-circle. Valyss sat next to Rhees, with MaudeLyn, Evryst, Arik, and the Censarran with the pointy beard sitting on the other side.

Two servants served tea, bite-sized sandwiches, and biscuits to the guests. Solace's hands shook as she took a sip. Ghrier waited until the servants withdrew and then invited the stranger from Censarra to join him at the table. Ghrier reached inside his white robe to withdraw a roll of parchment that he spread out on the tabletop, anchoring each page with small, round pewter weights.

Ghrier rotated around to face them, leaning heavily on his stick. "We are all gathered here for the same reason, and we each have a vested interest in the outcome. As King Rhees's chancellor, I am on hand to ensure we adhere to Toreszan law." Ghrier bowed to the stranger on his left. "And Chancellor Zeffen of Censarra shall be doing the same on behalf of King Valyss and Crown Princess MaudeLyn, the plaintiffs in this matter.

"Brother Evryst of the Tor Monastery witnessed the marriage ceremony between King Rhees and Queen Consort Solace. Sir Chelyss Demore, Mistress Fenwith Demore, and Mister Arik Lariato represent the families of the defending parties in this matter. Are there any questions before we begin?"

King Valyss cleared his throat. "Neither my sister nor I wish to be thought of as plaintiffs; after all, we are related through the betrothal agreement with dear, departed Crown Prince Heris. We are interested parties who simply wish to confirm for ourselves the legality of the king's marriage to his consort. We understand the nuptials were hastily arranged and performed in the middle of the night, which does raise some questions."

Rhees reared back and looked as if he were about to say something, but he must have spotted Evryst shaking his head ever so slightly. Arik flattened his lips, his face hardening as he stared at Rhees, who glowered back defiantly. Arik crossed his arms and glanced away, but Solace sensed the tension between them ratcheting up again, leaving a bitter taste in her throat.

The two chancellors turned their backs on the room, and Zeffen leaned over the table to read the document. He slowly, methodically reviewed each page, sometimes back-tracking to re-read a paragraph. When he finally reached the end, he paused to tap his finger on the last page, and then he faced the room. "I am curious on several points. Firstly, why did the queen consort sign using two different names, er, Solace Blu, also known as Lace Blusari? Which appellation appears on her Naming Day certificate?"

Solace had forgotten she'd signed using her birth name, and the name on the false paperwork Rhees and his uncle Chelyss had secured somewhere in Toresz. Her mouth felt suddenly dry, and she cleared her throat before answering the second part of Zeffen's question. "My given name is Solace Blu, sir."

"And when did you acquire the alias Lace Blusari?" How should she answer? She wouldn't lie, nor should she have to; she'd done nothing wrong and wouldn't shrink back now from the truth, which unfortunately did not paint Rhees in a good light.

Rhees cut in smoothly. "When my uncle Chelyss secured Solace's immigration papers, the local office misspelled her name. We hadn't gotten around to correcting the error by the time we married, so Solace signed with both names."

Zeffen pursed his lips. "That is highly irregular."

Ghrier tapped the floor once with his stick. "But by no means illegal."

Zeffen conceded the point with a small shrug and addressed Rhees. "I recommend you ensure the queen consort's name is correctly spelled on all future documents."

Rhees smiled. "Aye, sir, an excellent suggestion."

The tense moment passed, and Solace felt herself relax ever so slightly, until she realized the Censarran chancellor wasn't finished. "Now onto my second, or I suppose third, question: is the queen consort's father still living?"

Zeffen looked directly at Solace and waited for her reply. Flushing under his steady gaze, she sensed everything hinged on her answer. But there was only one answer she could give. "Aye," said Solace quietly, "my father is planting his crops as we speak."

Zeffen angled his head slightly to address Rhees. "Then please explain, sir, why her father failed to sign the contract?"

Rhees thrust out his bottom lip. He glanced at Ghrier, then at Evryst, before replying, "My father-in-law was in Yelosha at the time. Solace had no other male relatives inside Toresz." He raised his shoulders in a half-shrug. "Why does it matter?"

"On this point, our kingdoms share the same, unequivocal law." Zeffen brought his hands together, the fingertips touching, and rocked on his heels. "In order to marry, a woman must obtain the permission of her father, or if he is deceased, another male relative. The only exception would be if all her male relatives were deceased. Since the queen consort, er, since the young lady's father is very much alive, you neglected to observe this critical requirement." Zeffen stopped rocking and declared forcefully, "Therefore, sir, your marriage contract is null and void."

"I knew it!" shrieked MaudeLyn triumphantly. "I told you so, Val. I knew they weren't truly married."

A sharp jolt of pain shot through Solace's chest and radiated down her right arm. She hunched her shoulders forward and took small, shallow breaths, wondering whether she was suffering from shock, or exhaustion, or a broken heart—or all possibly three—and fought to remain calm. She hoped Rhees would do the same.

But Rhees leapt from his chair and stalked over to the table. "What's the meaning of this?" he hollered at Zeffen. "Of course we're married."

Brother Evryst and King Valyss hopped up simultaneously. Evryst murmured something about needing to see the contract, although Solace knew he was as familiar with the document as Ghrier, while Valyss sided with his legal advisor, proclaiming his expertise in the matter. MaudeLyn rose from her seat, curled her upper lip at Solace, and joined her brother and Zeffen.

Fenwith reached across her chair to grip Solace's hand, and Chelyss moved into the chair vacated by Rhees. He nodded at Solace. "You look peaked. Why don't we take you back to the palace? You can rest up whilst all this legal mumbo jumbo is sorted out. We're not needed here at the moment."

"No, thank you." Solace felt lightheaded and slightly breathless but shook her head firmly. "I'll stay here with Rhees until this is resolved." *One way or another*, she thought. Although the raised voices on the other side of the room dashed any hopes for an amiable resolution.

Arik crossed the room and knelt down in front of Solace, his brow furrowed. "This may take some time to sort out," he explained, "and some things may be said that you'll find upsetting. I think you'd be better off returning to the palace with the Demores. As your father's representative, I'll remain here to protect your interests in the matter."

"My interests?" Solace twisted her hands in her lap. "I am interested in one thing here: to return to the way things were before MaudeLyn and Valyss entered our lives, but I don't believe you or anyone else can accomplish that."

"Well, not that, I'm afraid...but I will ensure your reputation does not suffer as a result. They will know the truth —about him!"

Fenwith gasped, and Solace's eyes welled up. "Oh, no, Arik, you mustn't! Promise me you'll not breathe a word."

Arik narrowed his eyes at Rhees, who was waving his arms and yelling at both Zeffen and Valyss. Arik let out a long, low breath and rose from his knees. "Fine, I'll not speak of it, but only to save you from further heartache. For now, I'll see what Chancellor Ghrier recommends, since King Rhees will make little progress with all that shouting."

Solace watched as Arik pulled Ghrier aside, the two of them exchanging urgent whispers that she found just as upsetting as all the raised voices. Rhees must have noticed Arik, because he lowered his voice, turned his back on Zeffen, and sidled closer to his own chancellor.

The whispering didn't last long, however. Rhees growled at Arik and gave him a hard shove in the chest. Arik was no pushover and jostled the king of Toresz right back. Solace knew if any royal guards had been present, Arik would have spent the rest of the day in the dungeon, despite the fact Rhees had started the scuffle.

Solace's temper flared—at her husband for antagonizing Arik, who was only trying to help—and at MaudeLyn and Valyss for using the law to upend their lives. She stormed across the room, her insides quaking, her temples starting to throb, and hissed, "Arik isn't the enemy here. He's conferring with Ghrier and trying to help."

Rhees stared at her through bloodshot eyes. "He wants to take you back to Yelosha, to your father."

"If it's between living here as your mistress and dealing with MaudeLyn on a daily basis," said Arik through gritted teeth, "or returning home where she is cherished and loved, then of course the latter course would be best for Solace."

Solace didn't need either Arik or Rhees making decisions on her behalf. "Arik, while I appreciate—"

"Lace is cherished and loved right here!" snapped Rhees. "You're not thinking of her best interests, but how you can get her away from me. Well, I won't let that happen."

Solace drew her eyebrows together. "But that's not—"

MaudeLyn's cool voice carried across the room. "Gentlemen, perhaps we could work out a compromise." The room grew suddenly silent as everyone turned toward the crown princess.

"What do you have in mind, ma'am?" asked Ghrier curtly. Solace thought the chancellor had reached the limits of his patience with MaudeLyn and Valyss.

MaudeLyn swept across the floorboards and aimed her remarks at Rhees. "I meant what I said yesterday. I think it was brilliant of you to secure the services of such a talented little water witch, and your people adore her. Why wouldn't they? They're finally able to dig for their own wells without fear of prosecution from Neuss. And you're obviously fond of her. Here's my proposition: she can move into the palace's guest wing, and you can visit her...oh, let's say...two evenings a week. But the rest of the time, you shall be my husband—in every sense of the word."

Rhees's jaw dropped, and the dull ache in Solace's temples spiked into a migraine. Rhees found his voice first. "Solace is my wife. I don't give a rat's tail about some antiquated law regulating royal progeny. She stays, and you, ma'am, may go!"

The pain in Solace's head eased slightly at Rhees's words, but deep down in the pit of her stomach, she knew MaudeLyn would never leave. The law favored her claim.

Zeffen cleared his throat. "Sir, as the new king of Toresz,

you have just sworn to uphold the law of the land, which includes even 'antiquated' laws you might not care to follow. One cannot simply pick and choose which laws to obey. We are all of us, even kings, queens, and chancellors, obligated to observe the law."

Rhees crossed his arms. "This is outlandish. I refuse to observe this law."

Valyss gave a mirthless laugh. "Oh, I think you shall, when you consider the alternative."

Solace felt a chill run through her at Valyss's not-so-subtle threat. "Please explain yourself, sir," she said.

"You need me to spell it out?" Valyss's eyes flashed darkly. "If the king of Toresz does not agree to MaudeLyn's very reasonable proposal, then we shall ensure everyone across this kingdom and beyond knows he is no better than his nasty uncle Neuss. We'll paint Rhees as another lawless king, the man who refused to honor his deceased brother's betrothal, refused to return MaudeLyn's dowry —we know, of course, your treasury is empty—and conned a young Yeloshan girl into traveling with him to Toresz. He even forged a phony marriage license to trick her into bed, and then he exploited her witchy skills to help foment a rebellion, conveniently placing him on the throne. King Rhees is every bit as crafty and ruthless as old King Neuss."

Solace cringed as Valyss's accusations pinged around inside her head. *No, none of that is true. Well, some of it is partially true, but Rhees's motivations were honorable. He was trying to save his people from the horrors of life under Neuss's brutal regime—and Rhees didn't trick me into marriage—that was Brother Tomyss's idea, to protect me from Neuss's scheming. And Rhees waited for my consent; he waited until I invited him into my tent. Rhees loves me for who I am, not because I'm a water diviner who helped him defeat Neuss...I'm sure of it... right? Of course, I'm sure!*

Rhees scrubbed his face with his palm and then looked at Solace, his eyes clouded with sorrow. She knew he regretted snatching her from her father's farm, which had been horribly wrong. While she'd eventually been able to forgive him, nothing could absolve Rhees of his own guilty conscience.

He grasped her hand and tugged Ghrier's sleeve, dragging them both to the corner of the room near the windows. "I'm at my wits end, Ghrier. I know what I want to do, which is to toss the lot of them out on their ears...but what is the right thing to do?"

Ghrier glanced up at the ceiling and blew out a puff of air. Then he locked eyes with Solace and gave her a wistful smile. "Ask your wife—for that she is—in spirit, if not in the eyes of the law. Solace knows as well as I do what is right in this case."

Solace sniffed back the tears threatening to overwhelm her. She needed her wits about her. "First tell me —is there any way to rectify this legally? What if my father, or Arik in his absence, were to sign the document now?"

Ghrier shook his head. "Nay, I've already tried that. When I broached the idea with Arik, he said your father would never agree to your marriage, so he cannot, in good conscience, sign the document now. I'm afraid the old betrothal agreement still stands."

Solace winced, both her heart and head hurting so much she felt like an open wound, raw and bleeding. She reached up and placed her hands on either side of Rhees's face, his beard soft beneath her fingers, and let out a shuddering breath. "You are the king of Toresz, my love. The right thing to do, the only thing, is to adhere to the law. You must not turn MaudeLyn away."

"But I don't want to spend a single day, or night, with that woman. It's you whom I love—and only you—and always you!"

"And I love you." Solace's lips quivered at the pain and confusion in Rhees's eyes. "Which is why we can't allow her to destroy your reputation and ruin everything we've worked so hard for." Solace shook her head. "We should have known that two people with such inauspicious beginnings could never be together."

"But we'll still be together...just not the way we'd intended."

Solace raised her eyebrows. Her brilliant but obstinate husband still didn't understand. "No, my love, we won't."

Rhees let out a cry of anguish. "What? Where will you go?"

Arik had wandered closer and stopped a few feet away. "I will escort Solace home to her father."

"Never!" shouted Rhees. "My Lace will never leave me."

Solace dropped her hands and took a step back. "Would you have me stay here, as your mistress, living under another woman's thumb?"

Rhees's face contorted. He made a guttural sound, deep in his throat. "Aye, if the only alternative," he cried, "would be to lose you forever!"

Solace's voice trembled. "You'd have me live in the shadows, scorned by every respectable family in Toresz, and served up as fodder for all the palace gossip?"

"I'd never permit you to be subjected to such ridicule. I'll publish a proclamation, explaining the peculiar circumstances of my betrothal to MaudeLyn and—"

"And our illegal marriage, and my status as your paramour," said Solace grimly, crossing her arms. "What happens if we have children? Who would raise them? Queen MaudeLyn, your legally betrothed wife?"

Rhees waved his hand impatiently. "Of course not. You would raise any child of ours."

"Under the same cloud of illegitimacy you contended with all your life?"

Rhees's eyes widened. "Never. I would publicly acknowledge any child of ours."

Solace compressed her lips. "And privately, the child would be disparaged, always known as the king's illicit offspring." She shook her head sadly. "I could never be happy under such conditions. No, my love. You must stay, and I must go."

"You would leave me?" Rhees's voice broke. "Truly?"

Solace, struggling to hold herself together, nodded wordlessly. Rhees's eyes darkened, becoming black as night, and his face hardened into a stiff mask. He growled low in his throat, "Then go, and take your blasted pride with you."

Solace took another step back, startled by Rhees's mood swing, his ire so sharp it pierced through the air and shattered her, heart and soul. Pointing at the door, Rhees snarled, "But know this: if you leave me, you leave alone. There shall be no royal escort, no one to help you in any way, save your good friend from Yelosha."

"She will not go alone." Fenwith stepped forward, her voice high-pitched but firm. "Solace is my queen, and she requires a chaperone."

"Brother Alyn and I shall accompany her as well." Evryst bowed to Rhees. "Whilst the monks of Tor serve you loyally as our new king, we must honor our good friend, Solace Blu, for all she has done for Toresz."

"Do what you must, Evryst." Rhees waved the monk away, his eyes never leaving Solace's face as he spat out, "But from this day forth, your name shall not cross my lips. Solace Blu will mean nothing to me. Do you hear me? Nothing." He spun on his heels, his coronation robe twirling around his ankles, and turned his back on her.

Solace brought a hand to her mouth. *But you mean everything to me!* She stumbled blindly from the room, tears blurring her vision as they spilled down her cheeks.

CHAPTER 7

 so hard she nearly toppled over the balcony on the other side of the floor. She heard a shout as a pair of strong, steady arms pulled her back from the railing.

"Solace!" Arik spun her around to face him. "Let's get you out of here and back to the palace, so you can pack up your things."

Solace cried, "No! I can't bear to go back there. Let's leave right now...please."

"Alright," said Fenwith soothingly. She was slightly out of breath, probably from jogging to keep up. "Chelyss and I will pack for you. But where should we meet you?"

"Not here," Solace begged, "I can't face her—or him—together."

Evryst and Chelyss had followed her out of the reading room too; only Ghrier remained behind with Rhees. The monk cleared his throat. "How about if Brother Alyn and I accompany you and Arik back to the monastery? We'll leave immediately. You can spend a restful evening there while we wait for Chelyss and Fenwith to join us. Meanwhile, Alyn and I will prepare for the trip to the Yeloshan border."

Solace nodded numbly, but Arik pointed out the obvious flaw. "Solace can't ride through the streets in all her royal finery. The crowds still believe she's their queen; they'll mob us."

"She is their queen," said Fenwith fiercely.

"Leave it to me." Chelyss's silver eyebrows knitted together. "I'll find something suitable for Solace to wear. She can wait in one of the offices upstairs, out of sight, until I return."

"And I'll send Alyn out to rent a carriage without any markings," said Evryst.

"But the guards at the gate will know Solace is passing through when they examine her papers," Fenwith reminded them.

"I'll handle the guards," Evryst replied. Solace knew the head monk of the Tor Order had a way with soldiers, knights, and guards that involved wit, humor, and a generous exchange of coins.

Evryst and Chelyss left for their errands, and Arik went to pay his bill at the inn and gather his gear and horses.

Fenwith settled Solace into a small, unadorned office on the third floor, furnished with a scarred oak desk and two old, wooden chairs, most of their finish worn off. Fenwith fished around inside her reticule and handed Solace a clean handkerchief to mop her teary face.

"I'm so sorry...and so furious," fumed Fenwith. "After all you and Rhees have been through, to see your lives torn asunder by that scheming princess and her slimy brother makes my blood boil. At least you have Arik, who clearly adores you. He will give you anything you need—even his heart if you let him. I'm afraid Rhees will be far worse off without you than you will be without him. Rhees will never love MaudeLyn, nor any other woman. His heart belongs to you."

Solace hiccupped into the handkerchief and squeezed her leaky eyes shut. Rhees may have crushed her heart underfoot, but she still loved him. She felt unmoored, like a tumbleweed tossed about by the desert wind. And while Fenwith was right about Arik's feelings for her, Solace would never lead him on; she cared too much about Arik as a friend.

Then there was what Rhees had said to her, the woman he supposedly loved. Solace mumbled, "Rhees said I'm nothing to him. Nothing! He can't say that and still love me."

"Rhees is hurting so badly he doesn't know what he's saying."

Solace rubbed her temples. "He sounded pretty convincing to me. He didn't even order an escort, and you know how dangerous the roads are, especially at night."

"Rhees was trying to scare you into staying. But he should know you well enough to realize you're as stubborn, foolhardy, and brave as he is."

Solace hiccupped again and blew her nose. "That's not true."

"You're trying to tell me he's not stubborn, foolhardy, and brave?"

"Oh, he's all those things, and I suppose we're alike in that respect. But I don't think Rhees was trying to scare me into staying. You didn't see the way he looked at me in the end...his eyes went kind of flat and cold...like two fading embers." Solace shuddered. She'd never noticed any resemblance between Rhees and the one man she truly hated, his loathsome uncle Neuss, until she stared into

Rhees's dark, blank eyes. For a moment, they were just like Neuss's.

"But that's because—" A loud knocking in the hallway interrupted Fenwith's explanation, which was just as well, since Solace didn't want to talk about Rhees anymore. She was physically wrecked, her head pounding, nose stuffy, and stomach churning, and emotionally drained, an empty husk of her former self.

Fenwith threw open the door. "We're in here, Chelyss." She stepped into the hall, pulling the door closed behind her. Solace heard the husband and wife softly murmuring, and then Fenwith exclaiming, "You did what?"

Chelyss mumbled something and Fenwith hissed, "I don't care if the boy was stark naked, you shouldn't have 'lent him' your new tabard! He'll be selling it before dinnertime, mark my words."

Fenwith flung open the door and stormed inside, a page's uniform draped over her arm. "Here you go. Chelyss found a young feller about your size. While you're changing, I'm going to hunt down the page wearing Chelyss's clothes; he can't have gotten too far. I'll be back to pick up your things shortly."

Fenwith started to leave, muttering under her breath about "foolish old men," but Solace called her back. "Um… I'm not going to be able to get out of my gown without your help unbuttoning the back."

Fenwith smacked the heel of her palm against her forehead. "Of course. Don't mind me. I'm beside myself with all that's happened." Fenwith worked quickly and quietly, both women lost in their own thoughts. As she slipped out of the room, carrying Solace's robe, gown, and tiara, she said, "I'll let Evryst know you'll be down soon."

Solace wriggled into the plain, gray tunic, which had a

freshly laundered smell, probably in honor of Rhees's coronation. The brown trousers fit surprisingly well, but looked ridiculous when paired with her new, pale ivory boots. Shrugging, Solace quickly fastened the buttons on each shank, tossed the page's navy woolen cape over her shoulders, and scurried from the room.

She descended the stairs slowly, trying to be as quiet as possible. The last thing she needed was to run into Rhees or MaudeLyn, who'd sneer at the "little witch" in the page's clothes. The floorboards creaked, and Solace heard footsteps approaching. Her pulse spiked, then settled down again when she heard Arik's voice call out softly, "Solace, is that you? We have a carriage waiting."

Solace hesitated and Arik added, "Don't worry. They're already gone…Rhees, MaudeLyn, and the rest. I saw them leave."

Solace hurried down the rest of the steps. Arik's eyes widened when he saw how she was dressed. "The royal party is gone, but some of the guards are still milling about. I know you don't want to be recognized."

"Definitely not."

Arik reached inside his well-worn tweed jacket—he'd changed back into his traveling clothes—and pulled out a short cord. Holding it up, he said, "Use this to pull your hair back, and then you can tuck it more easily into your hood."

"Good idea." Solace tried smoothing her wavy chunks of black hair into a sloppy ponytail, but she'd forgotten that half her hair was still piled into a bun. As she pulled out the pins, her hands shook so badly she dropped both tie and pins on the floor.

"Here, let me." Arik kicked aside the pins, picked up the small piece of cord, and secured her tangled locks. When he finished, Arik rested his hands on the back of her shoulders for a moment, a comforting gesture that reminded Solace of home and made her eyes sting.

Her mother used to embrace her that way sometimes, a quick hug from behind before Solace took her sheep out to graze on the hills. She missed those brown, craggy hills, and her gray sheep—how many lambs would be born this spring?—and Barley, her dog. Barley had leapt in the air and knocked her over when she'd returned to the farm with Rhees last month. She smiled at the memory, until she recalled Rhees's coldness and fury just now as she was leaving, as she tried to do the right thing, the legal thing, the only thing she could do under the circumstances and still retain her self-esteem. Solace pulled up her hood and turned around to face Arik.

"That's better," he said, nodding. "If we run into anyone, turn your head slightly, stay behind me, and you'll blend right in."

"Got it." Solace fell into step beside Arik, wanting nothing more than to be out of that library and out of Urhl. She needed to put some distance between herself and Rhees and all that had happened.

"What're ye doin' 'ere?" shouted a gravelly voice from behind them. "T'other pages 'ave already left, and yer need to be headin' back to th'palace too!"

Solace had a brief moment of panic until she recognized the ancient library guard, his long, gray beard reaching to his belt buckle. She made a snap decision and threw back her hood. He gasped, took two steps back, and bowed from the waist. "Me apologies, Yer Royal Highness. I didna expect to be seein' ye in disguise, as it were."

"Mister Waryn Grosweld, I believe?" she asked.

"Aye, Yer Majesty. Please, I beg ye, not th'stocks ag'in. Wif me achin' back an' nobby knees an' sore neck, 'tis pure torture at me age." Solace wondered how frequently the old man, who'd somehow survived under Neuss's reign, had been placed in the stocks for some misdeed. Waryn continued, "'Sides, I jes made a teensy error. No 'arm's done. I'll tell nary a soul 'bout yer get-up."

Solace had no doubt Waryn would do quite the opposite. It didn't matter what Waryn said after she left the capital. She just wanted to leave without anyone else recognizing her or slowing her down.

"You are just the man for the job I have in mind."

"I am?" Waryn's furry, gray eyebrows rose nearly to the top of his hairline.

"Aye," confirmed Solace. "I must leave immediately and do not wish to be delayed. Please go on ahead and divert attention away from me."

"Aye, ma'am. I'm 'appy to oblige, Yer Majesty." Waryn bowed and then asked, "Which doorway will ye be usin' ma'am?"

Solace tilted her head at Arik, who said, "Rear door, back alley."

Waryn lowered his eyebrows. He'd not registered Arik's presence until just then. The elderly guard glanced between the two of them, Solace dressed like a page, and Arik in humble tweeds, and he scratched beneath his heavy mop of chin hair.

Before Waryn jumped to any conclusions, or decided to seek the guidance of someone more capable, Solace interceded. "This is a matter of some urgency. Please lead the way."

Her commanding voice did the trick, and Waryn gave

them both a quick bow. He led them downstairs, skirted around the lobby and atrium, and deftly weaved in and out of the library stacks until they arrived at the back door.

A sagging, peeling, wooden farmer's cart, pulled by two skinny horses, sat in the alley. Evryst stood near the alley's egress, holding the reins to four more horses, saddled and ready. Solace assumed Arik had traveled with two of the horses, given the long trip from the hills of Yelosha to the capital of Toresz. The other two steeds would be Evryst's and Alyn's. Solace squinted at the farmer with the long, black beard perched on top of the bench seat. He seemed familiar, and when he removed his floppy hat, she exclaimed. "Brother Alyn? So you're traveling incognito too?"

"Aye." Alyn hopped down. "This was the only conveyance I could find, given the coronation. Everything else was rented out. I'm sorry I couldn't secure something more suitable."

"I suppose you will be hardly recognizable as the queen, riding in that rickety wagon and dressed like a page," said Arik.

Solace slid onto the hard bench. "I'm no longer the queen," she said shakily. "But I take your point. This should do very nicely, Alyn. Thank you."

The monk climbed up next to her and picked up the reins. He waved his hand at Evryst and Arik, who'd mounted their horses. As the they pulled away from the Great Library, Solace found the horses' clip-clopping vaguely soothing.

She focused on the rhythmic sound, on the steady drumbeat of hooves hitting cobblestones, on each bend in the road that separated her from Rhees, from their life together—barely begun and now over. As they rode through the streets, with their shops and markets and neat row homes, Solace detached herself a bit more from the capital of Toresz, and from her own bruised and battered heart she was leaving behind with its king.

CHAPTER 8

THE GUARDS AT THE GATE WERE SO BUSY WITH POST-CORONATION traffic they didn't spare Solace a second glance and waved her party right through. They rode through the gloomy, gray settlement of meager tents and ragged lean-tos that clung like a tumor to the city's outer walls. Here, the poorest Toreszans survived on the scraps and leavings of the capital's wealthier residents, by pawing through garbage heaps and sending their children into town to beg. Solace always tossed coins when she passed through but not this time. She hid her face in her hood, offering up a silent prayer for those she passed. Although her luck had run out, she was still more fortunate than they.

The cobbled streets of Urhl gave way to hard-packed soil on the road to Tor Mountain, and eventually, even that disappeared as plumes of dust rose from the wagon's wheels and horses' hooves. Solace found a cotton handkerchief in the page's cloak, which she used to cover her nose and mouth. The monks and Arik pulled up their neckerchiefs as they trotted along.

Once they were on the open road, the hard knots in her

stomach subsided into a dull cramp that worsened every time she thought of leaving Rhees behind in Urhl. She forced herself to stop thinking about him, about their past —which had been occasionally painful, but mostly sweet and passionate—and their shared plans for rebuilding Toresz together.

Tor Mountain's snow-dusted peak soared above them as Brother Alyn expertly guided the rickety cart up the steep, stony path. Solace wondered aloud whether they'd make it all the way to the ancient monastery, perched halfway up the incline. Hewn from the mountain's sand-colored rocks and stones, the abbey had been constructed in tiers, with each tier progressively smaller than the one below and topped with a red-tiled roof. Balconies ambled precariously around each of the levels.

"Not in this dray—but not to worry. We have a stabling area nearby, where we'll drop this off. We'll carry on the rest of the way by foot."

By the time Solace and the others had arrived at the entrance to the monastery, a fine layer of sand coated everything. Her feet, still encased in her stained-and-gouged ivory boots, ached as much as her head, heart, and stomach. A pair of junior monks, their cowls pulled forward to prevent them from gazing directly at Solace, guided her toward the small grotto reserved for female guests. Arik followed Alyn and Evryst to the larger pool used by the monks for bathing.

Solace had been a guest at the monastery several times and knew the routine. She accepted a piece of soap and white towel with a small bow. After the monks withdrew, she stripped off her clothes, which she left in a wadded-up ball on a stone ledge, and slipped into the cool spring. Solace washed every inch of herself and shampooed her hair twice. However, nothing could rinse away the gritty bitterness in the back of her throat that had nothing to do with sand and dust, but with her bleak, new reality.

MaudeLyn had called her a concubine and Rhees's mistress, and Solace knew that was how most people would perceive her. No matter that she'd helped to defeat Neuss, sourced water for hundreds of poor Toreszans, and believed herself married when she'd beckoned Rhees into her tent—in the eyes of the public, she was now a disgraced woman to be pitied and reviled.

Solace knew she could handle the bold stares and whispered innuendos, difficult as they would be, but she worried about her father's attitude when he found out. He'd been overjoyed to see Solace when she'd first arrived on his Yeloshan farm with Rhees. But later, Soren had shot her a look of pure disgust when she'd defended Rhees after he'd confessed to kidnapping her. Soren had slammed Rhees against the wall of their cottage, ready to pommel him. Rhees had put up no defense, which had infuriated her father even more.

When Solace had explained that her former abductor was now her husband, Soren had reluctantly dropped his fists, but only after receiving assurances from Rhees they were indeed married. Now, her father's worst assumptions would be proven true—his daughter, who'd been carried off by the rebel prince of Toresz—had dishonored her family by becoming his mistress.

Solace splashed water on her face and wondered how Rhees was faring. He'd been hurting and furious when Solace had left and no doubt was still just as miserable and angry, likely yelling at everyone who came near him. She was the only one who could soothe Rhees when he was overwrought, and she debated whether MaudeLyn would even try. Probably not; MaudeLyn had won the legal battle, and she'd take her time winning over Rhees's heart. Despite Fenwith's predictions, Solace believed that given enough time, MaudeLyn would succeed. Rhees would want heirs one day, and although she had a nasty personality, MaudeLyn was still a very attractive woman and his legally bound wife.

Solace blinked rapidly to stem the fresh tears threatening to spill over. She yearned for Rhees to wrap his arms around her right then and tell her, as he often used to, that all would be well. But nothing would be well for her—for either of them—ever again, and she had to face facts. She needed to pick up the pieces of her fractured life and move on. But where to?

Solace climbed out of the water and dried herself, grateful she could wash away the day's soil and wishing she could do the same with the day's problems. She donned a clean, linen undergarment and a navy hooded robe, both of which she found folded neatly near the edge of the grotto. After tying a white rope belt around her waist, she bent down to sort through an assortment of short, shearling-lined, brown boots until she found a pair that fit.

Towel-drying her hair, Solace considered her options. She could go home to Yelosha, where she'd be the cause of much disappointment, first her father's, because of all that had happened, and then Arik's, because she'd not marry him despite all that had happened. She could travel abroad, perhaps to one of the small southern kingdoms, where water was just as scarce as in Toresz, and water diviners were well paid for their services. However, the journey would be long, and she didn't think she could ask Fenwith or Arik or Evryst to accompany her. Besides, she had just a few silver coins in her purse, not enough to secure a ride with a traveling caravan.

Finally, she could remain in Toresz and choose a different path for herself, one that did not thrust her into public view or open her up to scorn, where she might live quietly and not be reliant on anyone else for her wellbeing. The more she considered her options, the more she liked the third one. However, she had no idea where she could go, and Arik would be opposed to her remaining in Toresz unless she had a firm plan in place.

Solace heard the swish of soft-bottomed boots in the corridor. Evryst called out, "Please take your time, Solace, and join me when you're ready."

She emerged from the cordoned-off bathing area, her hair still damp. The monk stood on the stone pathway, his hands clasped in front of him, his head bowed. "I don't believe I'll ever be ready," she whispered.

Evryst looked up and nodded in the direction of the long hallway behind him. They walked together, their muffled footfalls the only sound. "You've had a terrible shock today. I'm concerned for your health...have you any symptoms to report?"

Solace debated whether to tell him about the sharp chest pain that had radiated down her right arm earlier, but she had nothing more to lose by telling Evryst the truth. Besides, it wasn't as if he'd report it back to Rhees or that anyone other than her healer even cared at this point. Rhees certainly wouldn't be cosseting her or coaxing her to rest more and do less. She needed to decide for herself how to manage her condition.

When she described the chest pain, Evryst compressed his lips and frowned. "It's only natural your heart is more stressed than usual. I fear for you, my queen, and for your health."

Solace stopped walking and stared at the man who'd saved her life once before. "I am not your queen, Evryst."

"Ah, but you are, much more than MaudeLyn of Censarra could ever be. I spoke the truth when I told Rhees the monks of Tor would serve him loyally, and so mote it be. However, our loyalties are naturally split from this day forth, between Rhees, King of Toresz, and Solace, Queen of Toresz—the only queen we shall serve. You saved not only our nation from the grip of Neuss, but you rescued the king himself. You nursed Rhees back to health while still a captive yourself, on the road to Urhl, and you restored his ability to love again. And now, I don't know what will become of him."

"Rhees is King of Toresz!" Solace exclaimed as she resumed walking along the long, whitewashed corridor, the orange glow of flickering wall sconces adding the only spot of color. "He has countless opportunities ahead of him. What becomes of Rhees will be of his own making, unlike me, with my thin purse and borrowed clothes on my back, and my broken heart. My choices are severely curtailed."

They reached the tall, glazed windows that faced east, overlooking Urhl below. Solace wanted one last look as night fell, and torches and candles were lit across the capital. The sight was as breathtakingly beautiful as the first time she'd peered through the windows, a shy, frightened girl from the hill country, who'd just learned the truth of why she'd been stolen from her home.

"Without you, Rhees will grow as bitter and distant as Neuss—"

"He's nothing like his uncle," interrupted Solace. Then she recalled Rhees's dull, dark eyes as he'd shouted she was nothing to him. But even at his worst, he was a far better man than the last king. "Neuss was cruel and greedy. Rhees would never abuse his power or overtax the people or encourage lawlessness."

"Agreed. However, 'Queen MaudeLyn' would."

Solace leaned her forehead against the windowpane. Evryst was right. The woman cared only for herself and what she could possess by any means possible. "Your concern is that Rhees will abdicate his responsibilities to her."

"Aye," replied Evryst softly. "I know what can happen when a man is heartbroken, when he's lost what he loves most in the world."

Solace knew nothing of Evryst's past, but she believed the monk was speaking from personal experience. "That may be true, but I don't know what I can do about it." She shrugged, her words as harsh and acidic as the bile in her throat.

"Don't leave Toresz! Don't cross the hills into Yelosha and take up your old life."

Solace didn't want to admit she'd been thinking along those same lines. Instead, she asked, "But where can I go? You know how MaudeLyn will paint me, as a 'fallen woman' who entrapped the king."

"Your friends—and you have many friends here in Toresz—would never believe that lie. As to where you might go...let us both think on it. If you are open to the possibility of remaining, then I have no doubt a solution shall present itself."

Solace snorted. "Now you sound like a monk who is relying on faith alone."

"Sometimes, my queen, faith is all we have left."

CHAPTER 9

THE NEXT MORNING FENWITH SENT A MESSENGER TO THE monastery, informing Evryst and Solace she'd been delayed another day by "that wolf in queen's clothing, ordering everyone around." Fenwith was packing not just for Solace, but for herself as well, since she'd never work for Maude-Lyn; in fact, she'd already resigned her post. Fenwith planned to remain at her farm in Shulamorn after escorting Solace to the border. Chelyss would accompany them on their trip, drop off his wife, and return to Urhl to help Rhees with the fledgling school for knights.

The palace messenger also delivered two packages for Solace. The first contained two pairs of tunics and leggings that were perfect for travel by horseback; a sturdy leather cloak; tall riding boots; a nightgown; and Solace's pearl-handled knife, two slings, and pouch of stones. The second package contained her mother's books, plus the collection of Toreszan fairy tales Rhees had given her, and several books from Brother Tomyss. Solace found a hastily scrawled note inside the book of fairy tales. "This was all I could get out before that hag changed the locks on your chamber. But worry not; I've had a spare key made and will break in tonight to finish packing."

What is Rhees thinking, allowing MaudeLyn to run roughshod over everyone, even his own aunt? Is he really so brokenhearted, as Evryst suggests, that he's willing to abandon his duties so soon? And why do I care even now?

Solace nibbled a dry piece of toast, which was all the breakfast her queasy stomach could handle. She couldn't worry any longer about Rhees and MaudeLyn and the chaos at the palace. She had enough problems of her own, including figuring out whether to return home with Arik. Since Fenwith, Chelyss, and the monks would be escorting her at least as far as Shulamorn, a border town in south-western Toresz, Solace didn't have to decide immediately. Depending on their route, they would need at least a week to cross the craggy hills and dry plains of Toresz—more than enough time to formulate a plan, or so she hoped.

Solace placed Fenwith's note on the small, oval dining table in Evryst's sparsely furnished office, which included four straight-backed chairs, one of which she was sitting on, and a plain, timbered desk overflowing with books, scrolls, illuminated manuscripts, quills, and an assortment of inkwells. The most interesting feature in the austere, white room was the telescope behind Evryst's desk, which could be swiveled to survey all of Urhl from the single, large window.

Solace went to the window and focused the viewfinder on the palace. She saw guards patrolling the parapets, a pair of pages crossing the courtyard, and in the practice fields behind the castle, several squires at bow practice. None of the mayhem described by Fenwith was evident here. The scene was achingly ordinary, as if Solace's demotion from queen to non-entity had never occurred. She took a shuddering breath and turned away.

Solace tightened her rope belt and peeked into the corridor. Evryst had left to organize their supplies for the trip. As the only female guest at the monastery, she had Evryst's private wing—office, library, and guest quarters—all to herself. Solace was in no mood for conversation anyway, not even with Arik, who was taking all his meals with Brother Alyn in the main dining hall.

Solace hadn't had a day to herself, for rest and reflection, since before the rebellion. In fact, the last time she'd had any respite was in this very spot, when Brother Tomyss had been the abbot. That was before the hasty marriage ceremony Tomyss had performed to protect her from Neuss's wily misapplication of betrothal laws. As Tomyss had explained it, either she married Rhees so she could be placed "under his protection," or remain a single woman without the "shelter" offered by a husband or close male relative. If she'd refused, Neuss would have offered her his protection, essentially forcing her into a betrothal contract with the vilest man in Toresz.

And so she'd married Rhees in the middle of the night, escaping with him to the hills beyond Urhl. Together, they'd gone on to start a rebellion in the unlikeliest way of all—by using Solace's singular gift for finding water. Solace had thought of it as helping the poorest of the poor. Rhees had viewed it as the only way to undermine his uncle's ironclad control over the Toreszan people.

But why, she wondered, *did Tomyss not adhere to the laws governing marital contracts?* The elderly monk had been a scholar and must have known what he was doing. Clearly, he'd been hoping no one would notice the missing clause that would have been signed by Solace's father, giving his consent to the marriage. And no one had noticed, until now. Poor Brother Tomyss had been tossed in the palace dungeon when he'd presented the marital contract to Neuss, and later, he'd been executed.

Then, in a moment of clarity, Solace realized why: Tomyss may have skirted the arcane laws regarding women and marriage for a just cause, but he would never have forged her father's signature. He was far too honorable for that, and in the end, he'd died to protect her and Rhees, and the hope that one day Toresz would be a better place for all.

For a brief, glorious few months, that hope had come alive—for her and Rhees—and for everyone who longed for a fairer, more equitable Toresz. Or put more simply, for everyone who wanted enough water to drink and food to eat.

And now...well...and now it was up to Rhees to see it through. Solace had done her part. Not only had she given him her heart, she'd given him the means for overthrowing the old regime, by divining for water in secret, in the hills and valleys, crisscrossing the parched land until she'd been arrested and nearly died.

Solace wiped a stray tear from her cheek. *No more crying!* she told herself. She reached for one of her mother's storybooks, but changed her mind and picked up *The Kings and Queens of Toresz*, and *The Provinces of Toresz and Yelosha: An Atlas*. Hesitating, she added a third book to her pile, *A Healer's Book of Cures* and headed to the private library down the hall.

She recalled Rhees's reaction when she'd shown him the three books she'd selected from Brother Tomyss's collection, a parting gift from the wise, old monk. Solace had just arrived in Urhl, the largest city she'd ever seen.

Rhees had arched his eyebrows. *"History, healing, and maps. Three good, practical choices. I'm impressed."*

Solace had shrugged. *"Wouldn't any proper young city lady choose something similar?"*

"I think you might be able to teach proper young city ladies a thing or two about common sense."

Solace had quoted an old Yeloshan saying. *"'The hill country is a practical teacher.'"*

History, healing, and maps, she thought. *If I'm going to remain here in Toresz, I'll need a better grounding in Toreszan geography and history. As for healing...a deeper knowledge will come in handy wherever I go.*

SOLACE GLANCED AT THE SIMPLE, whitewashed cell that had become her personal sanctuary: small shelf with tin mug and candlestick, narrow cot underneath, navy robe folded neatly at the foot, handwritten thank-you note on top.

She'd found a measure of peace each time she stayed at the monastery. Since this would be her last visit, she wanted to express her gratitude to the warrior-monks of the Tor Order, most of whom she'd never met. She had nothing to offer, no goods, no money, only her thanks and a promise to divine for fresh water if the need arose.

She wove her dark, wavy hair into a single plait, tossed her leather cloak over her plain, gray tunic and leggings, and closed the door softly behind her. Her riding boots clacking against the flagstones was the only sound in the quiet passage.

After a quick breakfast consisting of a square of toast, a cup of tea, and another bout of nausea, Solace followed the small map Evryst had left for her in his office. They'd agreed to meet in the large cavern that served as the monastery's main stable, located on the side of the mountain facing west, toward Shulamorn, and Yelosha, and her future. She mentally counted off the number of turns—three lefts, four rights, descend the steps all the way to the bottom—and then pushed open the thick oak door.

A soft neigh greeted her. "Jenx!" she cried, throwing her arms around the bay stallion's neck. "I didn't think I'd ever see you again."

Chelyss rose from a nearby bench and joined her. Solace was surprised to see Rhees's uncle dressed like a knight for battle, in his blue tabard with gold insignia, dark hauberk, and two swords at his waist. But instead of a coif or helm on his head, Chelyss wore the same old, peaked cap he'd been wearing since Solace first met him. He patted the horse's flank. "I figured you'd want to make the ride to Shulamorn with Jenx, seeing as it's the last time."

Nodding, Solace swallowed, her throat painfully tight. "Thank you..." Her voice wavered, so she tried again. "Thank you for bringing Jenx and for accompanying me, and well, for everything else too." The battle-trained stallion was Rhees's horse, which he'd given her after observing the bond between them.

"Don't you dare thank me, lass," Chelyss's voice shook. He quickly swiped at his damp cheek. "I mean, my queen."

Chelyss took a deep breath and sniffed. "I was part of the kidnapping scheme too. I'm as guilty as Rhees, but I'll not compound things by ignoring the obvious. You need an escort to the Yeloshan border, and I'll be darned if I don't help you out." He turned to leave and called over his shoulder, "We're waiting at the other end of this passage. Come join us when you're ready."

Solace ran her hand through Jenx's mane. "I hope you

are well rested, my friend. We have a long journey ahead." She leaned close to whisper, "And our destination is uncertain." Jenx blew air through his nostrils and gave a soft whicker.

She backed up six paces and then ran toward the massive horse. At the last moment, when it appeared she might smack into his hard flank, Solace pushed off the ground on the balls of her feet. She leapt into the air, grabbing Jenx's saddle horn in her left hand and gripping the back of the saddle with her right. As she swung her right leg over Jenx's broad back, she lifted her right arm out of the way and landed gracefully in the saddle.

Solace leaned over, patted Jenx's sleek neck, and whispered her thanks. She guided the horse to the mouth of the cave, where she was greeted by mounted monks dressed more appropriately for war than prayer. They wore gray breeches, short, hooded, navy habits, and silver hauberks. Dark leather vambraces covering their wrists and forearms peeked out from their sleeves, and they carried an assortment of weapons, including swords, bows, arrows, and axes.

Evryst presented her escort—five large, bearded monks. She knew Brother Alyn, of course, but the others looked so similar she'd need another round of introductions later. She swore two of the men looked nearly identical. Solace tried not to appear surprised by their warrior-like appearance, which should have made her feel more secure. Instead, it ratcheted up her nerves. *They're expecting to encounter trouble.*

A pair of carrier pigeons cooed from their cages behind one of the monks. When Solace asked their names, Alyn replied, "Peerless Petrie and Daring Dahlia." She chuckled, but he said, "In all seriousness, these birds have earned their titles."

Fenwith, who wore her own version of armor—battered leather vambraces and matching breastplate beneath a brown cloak—carried a longsword at her side. Jenx ambled over to Fenwith's horse, Caya, and gave the mare a good nuzzle. "It's good to see you, Fen."

"'Tis always good to see you, my queen." Fenwith hesitated before adding, "I tried, but I couldn't retrieve anything else from your chambers. That horrid princess placed her own guards in front of the door. I'm so sorry. Everything in the palace that's not nailed down is now hers. It makes me sick. *She* makes me sick."

"You smuggled out the most important items—a change of clothes, my books, and my slings and knife. I don't need anything else." Solace forced a smile.

Arik, the only man not wearing armor, was dressed like a farmer in cotton twill work pants, rough-spun wool cloak, and brown hat with a wide brim. He guided his horse to Solace's other side and overheard her last remark. "Whatever else you need, we can take care of in Yelosha."

"Aye." Solace nodded. "True enough." She had no intention of mentioning her doubts about returning to Yelosha, at least not until she'd formulated a viable alternative.

Solace and the others carefully descended the twisty path down Tor Mountain, the sheer drop-offs on some turns giving her sweaty palms. She knew the monks patrolled the trail at night and wondered at the amount of training, or just plain luck, required for that job. A more defensible position couldn't be found anywhere in Toresz, whether for a monastic order, a unit of soldiers, or a royal family.

Despite the fact she'd been raised in the high hills of Yelosha, Solace exhaled with relief when the last horse and rider reached the bottom. They entered the arid, brown Tor Valley, which connected Tor Mountain's jagged peak with the rest of the foothills and crags encircling the bowl-like plain. A few stands of acacia and cypress trees dotted the landscape, offering limited shade against the bright Toreszan sun.

Evryst took point, leading the group in a southwesterly direction across the valley. Solace was overheated, nauseous, and cross by the time they reached the hills on the opposite side, just as the sun slipped behind the peaks. They ascended a steep knoll and set up their camp between three large boulders that offered partial protection from the wind.

Arik helped Solace set up her solo tent after dinner. She thanked him but didn't linger for a conversation she knew he was itching to have. Instead, she crawled into her tent, pulled off her boots, and climbed into her bedroll, falling asleep to the sound of soft murmurs around the campfire. Solace woke in the morning to find her eyes nearly glued shut—she'd obviously been weeping in her sleep—and to the now-familiar knot in the pit of her stomach.

After a hasty breakfast of hot coffee and porridge, which Solace struggled to keep down, everyone mounted their horses. They wound around the knoll, their horses' hooves kicking up loose stones that skittered over the edge of the path. Solace patted Jenx's neck when they finally touched down on flat land. Another pebbly, brown plain stretched out before them, with yet another ridge of mounds and hills —all part of the Tor Mountain range—extending across the western horizon.

Before long, Solace had removed her leather traveling cloak and tucked it into her saddlebag. Although it was still spring, the strong sun had already baked the ground into fine, dusty soil. Farmers would need to be tending their meager crops, pulling weeds to ensure their tomatoes, beans, and potatoes could soak up as much water as possible from the parched land, and woe to any whose well ran dry.

It was almost second nature for Solace to access her mental map of water sources running beneath the ground, and she did so as they plodded on, spotting occasional surface variations. Where the sandy soil darkened into shades of taupe and brown, she could "see" the water running closer to the surface, a ready supply for the next generation. And where the heath paled to lightest beige, the water ran so deep that only subterranean creatures could drink of it.

Arik came alongside her as they rode. "You hardly touched breakfast this morning or dinner last evening. At the risk of sounding like a mother hen—which you've accused me of being more than once—you need to eat to maintain your strength."

Solace hunched her shoulders. "I have very little appetite, and I'm afraid forcing myself to eat will have the opposite effect."

Arik glanced behind him, in the direction of Tor Mountain and Urhl. A sharp stab of sadness and regret had pierced Solace the day before, when they'd left the monastery, and the massive mountain had finally blocked her view of the capital's spires. "I know it's difficult right now, but you must put this whole ugly chapter behind you. I'm confident that in time, you'll feel better and might even question why you ever loved that lawless man in the first place."

"His name is Rhees," said Solace stiffly. "He's not

lawless, at least, not anymore. Rhees knew it was wrong to take me, and his conscience has troubled him ever since. He's never forgiven himself, and now, after all this, he never will."

"Why do you still care," exploded Arik, "after all that's happened and all the pain Rhees has caused you?"

"I don't know." It was a question Solace had been asking herself, rolling it around inside her head, until she realized she couldn't reason her way to a satisfactory answer. "The heart is unpredictable, irrational, difficult to understand. A bit like water."

Arik's brow creased. "How so?"

"The way of water is never straightforward, but it twists, and leaps, and plunges in unexpected directions. If it were easy to find fresh water, then anyone could do it. There'd be no need for a water diviner."

"Ah," sighed Arik heavily, his earlier anger drained. "Sometimes I wish your mother's gift had passed you by. Then none of this would have befallen you."

Solace squinted at the craggy hills in the distance. "I used to think that way too but not any longer. I've made many friends here and had more adventures than I could ever have imagined back home. I'm glad I could aid poor, underserved Toreszans with my divining skills. And I have no regrets about helping Rhees overthrow King Neuss."

I have no regrets about falling in love with Rhees, either. But Solace kept that last part to herself.

CHAPTER 10

THEY BOTH FELL SILENT, AND ARIK EVENTUALLY DROPPED BACK TO discuss sheep breeds with Chelyss. Solace thought again about the contrast between her staid, stable life on the Yeloshan farm where she'd grown up, and her life since she'd crossed the border into Toresz. Much of it had been frightening and dangerous, but also exciting and even romantic, or at least until the events of the past few days.

Solace was relieved to see a slender valley nestled between two of the hills up ahead. They would reach the cool shade cast by their peaks by midday. Although their next stop was somewhat of a detour on their way to Shulamorn—they were heading more south than west on this leg of the trip—Solace looked forward to arriving in that valley for another reason. She'd see her friend Peka, who was technically Rhees's friend too. But Peka would welcome Solace and the rest of the party with wide-open arms. She wondered what Peka would make of their news about MaudeLyn and the betrothal contract. Solace didn't have too long to wait.

They entered the valley, rode past several straggly trees,

and followed the well-worn path into a tidy yard. Jenx, Caya, and the other horses headed straight toward the stable behind an old stone cottage. Bray, Peka's youngest son, emerged from the barn and called out, "Well met and welcome!" to the group. Hastening over to Solace, he held Jenx's reins as she dismounted.

Bray had chin-length, dark, curly hair, and a short, sparse beard Solace suspected he rarely had to trim. His large, gray eyes, so like his mother's, normally twinkled with mischief but not that day. Bray had something on his mind. "Mum and I just got back this morning from Urhl. Watching Rhees receive his crown was pretty cool. I'm glad I could see it before, well, before everything else."

"I had no idea you'd traveled into Urhl to attend the coronation," said Solace, confused by the last part of his statement. She couldn't imagine how he'd heard about MaudeLyn so soon. "I'm sorry I didn't see you there."

Bray shrugged. "There was a mad crush of people inside for the ceremony, and we were in the back. We stayed in town an extra couple of nights and," he hesitated, "we heard the proclamation. Everyone's stunned. I'm so sorry, Solace. Mum is beside herself over it."

Solace asked, "What proclamation?"

Bray averted his eyes. "Of several 'profoundly shocking discoveries,' according to the heralds sent out from the palace. First, Prince Heris had been formally betrothed before he died. Second, your marriage to Rhees had not followed all the legalities, making it null and void. Third, as a result, Princess MaudeLyn was the new Queen of Toresz. There were riots in the streets afterward, which was when Mum decided to hasten home. Behn stayed behind with Wilhm to see if they could find out more."

Wilhm and Behn, Peka's older son, had been friends

with Rhees since they were young palace pages together, before Neuss had murdered his way onto the throne. Unfortunately, Solace didn't think Wilhm or Behn would find out anything more, or anything helpful.

Solace swallowed down the bitter lump forming in her throat, shocked that Rhees had issued an announcement so quickly. She found herself engulfed in an embrace by Peka, who exclaimed, "Such folderol and nonsense. No one wants some coldhearted foreigner for a queen—we want you!" Peka's salt-and-pepper bun had come partly undone, and she tucked a chunk of loose hair behind her ear.

"I'm foreign-born too," Solace reminded her.

Peka waved her tanned hand. "You're from the hill country, same as us. It matters not whether you hail from the Yeloshan hills or ours. But those northerners look down on all of us, with our tawny-brown complexions and old-time customs. We'll never accept MaudeLyn of Censarra. You are our queen and always will be."

"Here, here," agreed Fenwith and Chelyss. Evryst, Alyn, and the rest of the monks added to the chorus of support for Solace. Only Arik remained silent.

"Those old marital laws should be rewritten," grumbled Bray loyally. "They're stupid...and...hurtful."

"Perhaps they will be, one day," said Solace, "but we can't undo what's already done."

"Spoken like someone born and bred in the hill country, where common sense takes precedence over antiquated laws," answered Peka.

She ushered them into her home, which was small by Urhl standards but more than double the size of Solace's little bungalow in Yelosha. Peka's front room served as the parlor, with a large eat-in kitchen behind it, and several bedrooms down the hall. A low wooden table, surrounded by two faded gray-and-white gingham sofas and four red arm chairs, occupied the middle of the room. Tallow candlesticks were scattered about, on the table and the hearth over the fireplace.

A thin woman with a slight limp entered from one of the bedrooms, and Solace ran over to give her a hug. "Maysel, I didn't realize you were here."

Maysel's pretty, careworn face lit up. "Peka invited us to stay here and help around the farm while Wilhm looks for a new job. He'll not be returning to the mines." Her brown eyes glimmered with determination. "Thanks to you and Rhees—thanks to the end of that despot, Neuss—our boys will grow up in a real cottage and not some paper-thin shack with the wind whistling through the slats."

Fenwith joined them. She gave Maysel a hug and asked to see her adorable twins. Maysel explained the toddlers were napping and took Fenwith down the hall to one of the bedrooms for a peek.

Despite her shock and pain over the palace's swift, harsh announcement, Solace felt buoyed by these three women. Fenwith, Peka, and Maysel had not only befriended Solace when she was little more than a stranger in their homeland, but later, they'd fought side-by-side with her and Rhees to overthrow Neuss. An enemy's sword had nearly ended Maysel's life, slicing her thigh during the Battle of Shulamorn.

Peka bowed to Arik, and Solace recalled her manners. "This is my oldest friend, Arik Lariato. Our fathers own neighboring plots in Yelosha and farm the land together. Arik represented my father at Rhees's coronation." Arik bowed, thanking Peka for her hospitality.

After the introductions, Peka put Brother Alyn to work, carting a crock of chicken soup out to the yard, where an old plank table and some benches had been set up in the shade of the barn. The Tor brethren had already discovered a barrel of dark ale inside the barn and wasted no time filling their tin mugs. Alyn remained outside with the other monks for their midday meal.

Meanwhile, Evryst, Solace, and her companions sat down on oaken stools around the well-worn, kitchen table. Peka ladled steaming bowls of chicken soup into mismatched crockery, which she handed to her guests, along with wooden tablespoons fashioned with rounded handles. She placed chunks of warm bread and sharp cheese on a platter, and carried a second platter outside to the rest of the group. Bray lugged a pitcher of ale to the table as Maysel and Fenwith rejoined them.

Everyone ate heartily, even Solace, who was famished by then. The conversation focused on neutral topics—weather, crops, and livestock—until Bray mentioned Neuss's old gangs, who were still harassing and robbing travelers, particularly on the less-traveled roads. They'd even taken to stealing from farmers and ranchers in the hills.

"When is Neuss's trial?" asked Arik.

"Very soon," replied Evryst. "Ghrier scheduled it for the week after Rhees's coronation. Since Neuss committed crimes against the state, as well as against Rhees personally, it makes sense for the new king to sit on the tribunal."

Bray placed his mug on the table with a soft thunk. "Who are the other judges?"

"Chancellor Ghrier and Sir Kryss. Neuss will receive a fair trial. Given the overwhelming evidence against him, however, I don't expect it will take long for the panel to reach a guilty verdict."

"Death by hanging, I suppose," Arik speculated.

"Aye," grunted Chelyss. "'Tis the norm in these cases."

Solace rose from the table, unable to listen to any more talk about Neuss or Rhees. "Peka, let me help you wash up these dishes."

"No, no, you go have a seat in the parlor." Peka shook her head. "Bray will give me a hand with the dishes."

Bray helped himself to the last chunk of bread and smeared it with butter. "I don't think we have enough water right now, Mum, so I'll wash them later."

"Why don't you have enough water?" asked Solace. "I seem to recall you have a private well."

"Our well's running dry," mumbled Bray between bites.

Peka frowned at her son. "Let's not be troubling the queen about that."

"I'm no longer 'the queen,'" said Solace firmly. "And even if I were, I'd still want to know about your water problems. If you'd like to show me the old well this afternoon, then I can divine for a new water source while I'm here."

Bray wiped his mouth on his napkin and jumped up from his stool. "I can take you there right now."

Peka shook her head. "Not so fast, son. You haven't finished your chores. Besides, you and Behn had all the fun last time, scouring the countryside with Rhees and Solace for fresh water. I want to see Solace in action."

Bray's face fell but he nodded. "Alright. But my chores won't take long, and then I'll join you."

Peka looped her arm through Solace's and guided her outside. Everyone, except for Maysel and Bray, followed them into the bright sunshine. "We'll need to bring water along to drink, whatever you have to spare," said Solace.

Fenwith, Arik, and Evryst went into the barn and returned with the water skins from their horses. Arik carried his and Solace's, a water skin looped over each shoulder. They set out on foot, Peka and Solace in the lead. Brother Alyn and the other monks came along, evidently curious to see a water diviner at work.

They walked half a mile before the old well came into view. Solace paused and held up her hand. The entire group stilled, even loquacious Bray, who must have rushed through his chores in record time to catch up. Solace inhaled the earthy scent of the ploughed field, the sun warm on her face. An orange-and-black monarch butterfly flitted over a patch of clover.

"I must ask for complete silence when I'm working, since I need to listen for any signs of water beneath the surface," explained Solace. "I'll walk on ahead of you. Please remain at least twenty steps behind me."

She approached the well and shielded her eyes from the bright sun. Pivoting in a full circle, Solace scanned the soil for any color variations but eventually frowned. The same brownish-beige hue extended in every direction, providing no visual cues to help narrow down her search.

Solace closed her eyes and listened. Bray shuffled his feet and she turned toward him, a finger on her lips. He brought his hands together and mouthed an apology. She tried again and heard a soft rustle in the leaves of the acacia tree over her left shoulder, a crow cawing somewhere off to her right, the buzzing of a bee behind her head—but nothing else, no sigh of an underground spring gurgling beneath her boots.

Solace walked a hundred paces north and repeated her actions. Bending down, she scooped up a handful of pebbly soil, took a sniff, and let it sift through her fingers. She shook her head; there was no scent or texture of moisture here. She had to decide whether walk farther north and test the soil again, or choose another direction. Solace felt as if she was working blindly, her five senses not offering her any hints just yet. Pushing a damp lock of black hair off her forehead, she plodded on ahead.

Solace walked more deliberately this time, looking for even the slightest variation in the soil and straining her ears for any murmuring below ground. She had nothing to work with, no clues whatsoever. Even so, she paused periodically to touch and smell the soil, something her mother had always instructed her to do.

Solace suddenly stopped as the mental map of subterranean water sources snapped into focus. Solace *saw* the underground water flowing deep beneath Tor Mountain, running into Urhl and extending outward in all directions. However, the image became blurry with distance. She couldn't yet connect that map with the water source she knew must exist somewhere below ground.

She closed her eyes and tried again, this time licking her finger and holding it up in the air. No one, not even Bray, moved behind her. *Ah, there you are!* She smiled. *East,* her gift whispered, *head east and you will find what you seek.*

Solace pivoted to the east and walked seventy-five paces down a gentle slope. Her gift was humming inside her head now, and Solace grinned as it announced, *Look, over there! Don't you see that patch of soil? It's not as sun-blanched as the rest.* Solace scurried to the slightly darker patch no one else had noticed, dropped to all fours, and pressed her ear to the ground. *Dig right here,* shouted her witchy water gift.

Solace exhaled slowly to quiet the voice inside her head, and then she heard it: the whisper of water beneath her. Leaning back on her knees, she scooped up the soil, rubbing it between her fingers. When she brought a handful up to her nose, she inhaled the loamy scent of water buried far below ground. Finally, she tasted the soil—it was the only way to gauge how deep to dig the well. Fifty-five feet and worth the effort, for this water source would not run out for a generation at least, perhaps longer. Solace stood up, a wide grin on her face.

Before she could say anything, Bray threw his arms in the air with a loud whoop. "You did it! You found us a new well location!"

Solace put her hands on her hips. "Did you have any doubts?"

"'Course not. But I was starting to get nervous, since it took a while for you to get your senses going."

Peka rolled her eyes and said, "Don't mind him. The sun's addled his brain. So, is this the spot?" Peka pointed to where Solace was standing.

"Aye, fifty-five feet down and you'll hit fresh water," announced Solace. The small crowd of curious friends and monks applauded, congratulating Peka for her new well and Solace for finding the water source.

Most of the group dispersed, walking back to the cottage. Solace noticed some coins exchanging hands among the monks—on the down-low, out of Evryst's line of sight—and a pair of nearly identical-looking brethren pocketing the lion's share. She realized the monks had been wagering on her water divining skills and chuckled under her breath.

Arik gave Solace her water skin, and she drank thirstily, and then he handed her a handkerchief to brush the dirt off her face. They both watched as Bray hammered a wooden post into the ground to mark the location for the new well. Then Bray left to repair a fence, and Arik and Solace retraced the path back to Peka's home.

Solace walked slowly, weary from the amount of energy

she'd expended while divining. Arik offered his arm for support, and she took it, grateful for his friendship and easy familiarity. He'd seen her returning to her father's house after water divining countless times. Arik understood she was exhausted and accepted her silence in stride.

They shared a unique bond, forged from their fathers' deep and abiding friendship, their mothers' deaths a few years apart, and the hard-scrabble life of dry farming in the Yeloshan hills. When pantries ran bare at the end of each winter, Arik and Solace had half-starved together.

Life with Arik would be safe and steady, the highs and lows predicated on the weather and crop yields, not on laws and politics and kings with mercurial personalities and black-brown eyes that bored into her very soul.

Solace patted Arik's arm with a low sigh. As she inhaled the warm, sweet air, she wondered how she could ever be satisfied on the safe and steady path.

CHAPTER II

SOLACE FELT A HAND ON HER SHOULDER, SHAKING HER AWAKE. SHE pushed it away, refusing to open her eyes. She was having the loveliest dream. Rhees had taken her into his arms and was leaning down, their lips nearly touching.

"Solace!" hissed Peka. "I'm sorry to wake you, but you have a visitor."

Solace pushed herself up from the mattress, rubbing the sleep from her eyes. She exhaled softly, her dream of Rhees fading as she recalled where she was—one of the bedrooms in Peka's crowded cottage—and why.

Solace glanced out the window. "But it's still dark." No one traveled the Toreszan roads after nightfall. She came fully awake. *What's happened to Rhees?* Solace abbreviated her question, asking aloud, "What's happened?"

"I don't rightly know. Come see for yourself."

Solace fumbled around in the dark, exchanging her nightgown for a tunic and leggings, and slipped her feet into her boots. She ran her fingers through her tangled waves and dashed out the door, remembering to tiptoe as she passed the bedroom with Maysel and her boys.

A figure, shrouded in an ankle-length, gray, homespun cloak and matching veil, stood in the center of Peka's parlor. The woman—or so Solace assumed, although it was impossible to be certain—bowed low when Solace entered the room. Peka's front door opened, and Brother Evryst slipped inside, his brow puckered in confusion, and something else. Anxiety, perhaps?

"Well met, Solace, water-gifted Queen of Toresz. We have long awaited this moment."

"Well met, ma'am." Solace bowed, feeling every bit as confused and anxious as Evryst seemed. "May I ask your name? And who 'we' are?"

The woman raised one gloved hand, palm open, in Evryst's direction. "Brother Evryst? Perhaps you would do the honors."

The tongue-tied monk found his voice. "*Tabetta?* Is it really you?" When the veiled woman nodded, he cleared his throat and seemed, if anything, even more nervous. "Magus Tabetta sits at the left hand of High Magus Rebezza, head of the Order of Righteous Magians."

"No longer," the woman replied, "I now sit at Rebezza's right hand."

"Ah," said Evryst with a small bow. "My condolences on Magus Zaria. May you serve as long and well in her stead. This is the true path."

"This is the true path," acknowledged Tabetta.

Evryst and Tabetta obviously knew each other, but Solace decided to save those questions for another time. "Who are the Righteous Magians? I've never encountered anyone from your order in my travels across Toresz."

"That is not surprising, as we keep to ourselves and do not venture far from our locus."

"And where is that?"

"Andressa Cave, located beneath the mountain of the same name," said Tabetta.

Solace rubbed her forehead, trying to recall the mountain's location, and wondering why Tabetta had appeared on Peka's doorstep in the middle of the night. She glanced at Evryst, who explained, "The Righteous Magians are a society of magically gifted women, pledged to protect and serve women in need and to use their gifts for good."

"Few men know of our order, of necessity," said Tabetta. "Our founder, Most High Magus Epinema, was hanged for the crime of 'water witchery' one hundred and fifty-three years ago. By some miracle, Epinema survived and fled into the cavern system beneath the Andressa Mountain range. Her pursuers soon gave her up for dead, and she subsisted on the fish she caught and the abundance of fresh water running through those hills.

"Epinema lived a quiet, contemplative life until she learned of a girl about her age, accused of being a witch. She helped that girl to escape and together, they formed the Order of Righteous Magians. During her lifetime, Epinema recruited, protected, and nurtured nearly thirty girls and women, all of them threatened with execution because of their gifts. And we carry on Epinema's work to this day, in secret, because we know what happens otherwise."

Solace struggled to take in everything Tabetta shared—gifted women, clandestine society, death sentences. She asked, "What happens otherwise...you mean you fear persecution? Surely, we have progressed since Epinema's day?"

Tabetta raised her gloved hands, palms open to the ceiling. "Ten years ago, Neuss executed every water-gifted woman in our kingdom. He moved so swiftly and with such stealth we were unable to rescue even one. And you have been pursued, arrested, and tried not so long ago for the crime of water divination." Tabetta paused and said more softly, "Aye, we do not trust the outside world, save a very few—such as Brother Evryst, and Miss Peka, our trading partner—and other women who are similarly gifted, including you, my queen."

Solace looked down at her boots for a moment and then raised her head. "Perhaps you have not heard the king's pronouncement—"

Tabetta put up her hand, palm outward. "High Magus Rebezza 'saw' it."

"Oh, was she in the capital yesterday?"

Evryst said gently, "Rebezza is over ninety years old and doesn't travel very far physically."

Solace tilted her head. "Then how..."

"Rebezza is sight-gifted," he replied.

Tabetta must have noticed Solace's furrowed forehead, because she explained, "High Magus Rebezza is a seer. On the morning of King Rhees's coronation, Rebezza had a powerful vision. She fasted and prayed, and when the same vision recurred the next two mornings, Rebezza sent me to this farm to intercept you. She anticipated you would be here four days after the king's coronation."

Solace's knees wobbled, and her stomach roiled inside her. She gripped the back of the nearest chair to steady herself, awed at Rebezza's ability to pinpoint her location. "What did the high magus 'see?'"

"That our water-gifted queen must learn of our existence. As to the rest of her vision, High Magus Rebezza wishes to speak with you. She has shared nothing else with me."

Solace glanced at Evryst, who nodded at her, as if in answer to her unspoken question: *Can Tabetta and the Order of Righteous Magians be trusted?* She had no knowledge of the distances involved, or whether a visit to Rebezza would take her closer to the Yeloshan border or farther away. And what would she tell Arik in the meantime? If the order was a secret, then their destination must be as well.

Solace posed her questions to Tabetta, who answered them succinctly. "We will travel southeast to reach Andressa Cave, so you will have to backtrack to cross the border at Shulamorn. Further, we will be passing through dangerous territory, patrolled by various gangs with a penchant for robbery or worse. As for your friends, you may not tell them anything, other than you will be conferring with a wise woman who insists on anonymity."

"Does that mean no one else from our party may join us? That we'll be traveling without any security?" asked Solace, who wasn't afraid so much as cautious. She'd encountered highwaymen before and preferred to avoid them.

"Not exactly," said Tabetta. "Brother Alyn knows of our order and may accompany us, along with Brother Evryst and Miss Peka. And three Magians await us in the foothills beyond this farm. While I cannot guarantee your safety, I assure you we know these lands better than anyone."

Solace debated the wisdom of visiting High Magus Rebezza versus leaving immediately for Shulamorn, where she'd say goodbye to Fenwith, Evryst, and the rest of her Toreszan friends. Then she and Arik would cross over the low hills into Yelosha. They'd travel for another week or so before reaching her father's farm. If she didn't deviate from her plan, she could be home in two weeks.

Solace nodded, her mind made up. "Very well. I wish to visit your high magus and hear for myself what she has 'seen.' When do we leave?"

"As soon as you have breakfasted. There is no time to waste." Tabetta bowed. "I must excuse myself now, before anyone rises. I shall be waiting with my Magian sisters on the eastern side of this valley. Head in that direction with Miss Peka, Brother Evryst, and Brother Alyn, and I will find you."

Peka brewed a pot of coffee for Solace, Evryst, and Alyn, and handed them each a hard roll, wedge of cheese, and piece of jerky for the journey. Alyn had filled their water skins the night before, using a hand pump in the yard connected to the old, almost-dry well.

Solace slipped her knife onto her belt, tucked her slings and stones into her pouch, and tossed her leather traveling cloak over her shoulders. She went into the yard, where Jenx waited patiently, already saddled by one of the monks. Evryst, Alyn, and Peka stood with their horses a short distance away.

She was rubbing Jenx's nose when she heard Arik call out softly, "Where are you going? I thought we were all leaving together for Shulamorn in another hour."

"Arik," she turned toward him. "I've been called away for a brief visit with a wise woman...someone who may be able to shed some light on my current situation."

"Your current situation? What could she tell you that you don't already know?"

Solace pressed her lips together in a firm line. "She is considered very wise, and I wish to confer with her."

"And where is this 'very wise' woman located?"

"A day's ride to the southeast, in the Andressa Mountain range."

Arik threw his hands in the air. "And a day's ride back. So we're going to lose two travel days whilst you go off with on a wild goose chase. Meanwhile, our fathers are sowing and planting right now, and they sorely need my help. They're not getting any younger, Solace."

Arik's words tugged at Solace's heartstrings, and she wavered. But she shook her head. "I'm sorry for the delay, but I must do this."

"Fine. Then I'll come with you."

Evryst cleared his throat. "I'm afraid that is not possible, Arik," he said gently. "The wise woman is very shy of men and only trusts a handful of monks who are known to her."

Arik grunted, his face in shadow. "Alright, Solace. If you are determined to go, so be it. I'll await your safe return in two days' time. Please do not be late."

CHAPTER 12

"SEE THAT PEAK STRAIGHT AHEAD, THE ONE THAT LOOKS LIKE AN incisor?" Tabetta pointed at a range of craggy hills, with one pointy mountaintop thrusting above the rest. "That's Andressa Mountain; our cave's entrance is located at the base. We'll arrive by nightfall."

Unfortunately, they first had to cross an uninviting-looking valley dotted with random boulders and rocks that must have tumbled down from a long-ago avalanche, and several stands of sad-looking sumac trees. They'd been riding nearly all day, and Solace's back, bottom, and thigh muscles were sore.

Even though they'd encountered nothing more threatening than the picked-over carcass of a mountain lion, Solace couldn't shake the feeling they were being watched by something other than the goshawks circling overhead. She chalked it up to fatigue and stress, but the uneasiness lingered.

The sun had dipped below the horizon by the time they wended around the large, sand-colored boulders camouflaging the cave entrance. Two of the Magians peeled away from their group and rode ahead to alert the high magus, although Solace figured the old seer was probably aware of their arrival.

Soon a cluster of veiled Magians flocked around Solace and her companions. Some took their horses' reins while others led them to an antechamber. Torches, mounted in iron sconces on the bedrock walls, bathed the interior in yellow light. Elaborate, multi-colored blankets were spread out on the ground, a welcome touch after a long day on horseback. One of the Magians offered them a simple supper of whitefish stew, and another refilled their skins with fresh water, and then the women withdrew from the room.

Solace glanced at Evryst. "I have a feeling you've visited here before and haven't seen anything beyond this small room."

Evryst nodded. "As you've heard, the Magians rarely entertain visitors, and none leave this antechamber unless invited by the high magus. You are the rare exception, as it should be."

"You mean because I'm a water diviner?"

"And a woman," added Brother Alyn.

"And our queen," confirmed Peka.

"And homeless." Tabetta had reentered the chamber and bowed. "The high magus awaits you, my queen."

Homeless. The word sat like a leaden weight on Solace's heart. Whether or not she made the trip back to Yelosha with Arik, she couldn't go home again—not really. She was no longer the quiet, dutiful daughter of a widowed farmer, but a woman who'd survived kidnapping, attempted murder, a rebellion, a short-lived marriage, and now, exile. There was no returning to the girl she had once been.

Solace squared her shoulders and followed Tabetta,

who lifted one of the torches hanging on the wall and led the way. The shaft of light cast by the torch danced against the bare, sandstone walls of the twisting passage. Solace noticed larger chambers opening to their left and right, but they kept walking until the passage abruptly ended in a drafty, tower-like area hewn from the mountain's rocky interior. Sticks and small logs were stacked in a neat row to the right.

A woman, shrouded in wraps and veils, sat before a fire pit in the center of the room. Burning embers and chunks of charred wood were all that remained of what must have been a cheery fire. Solace heard the sound of wind whistling through the circular chamber. Although she couldn't see the source of the breeze, a steady current of air wafted upward toward the top of the cave.

The woman bowed her head. "Well met, Solace, water-gifted Queen of Toresz."

"Well met, High Magus Rebezza," replied Solace, who didn't feel like the queen of anything, despite the Magians' insistence otherwise.

"Forgive an old woman for not rising for a formal bow, but my legs no longer respond to my wishes. Please, come sit beside me." Rebezza extended her age-spotted hand, and Solace skirted around the charred logs to sit on one of the blankets covering the ground.

Tabetta sat cross-legged across from Solace and Rebezza, who pulled back her veil to reveal white, frizzy hair and a web of wrinkles lining her brown face. Her dark, twinkling eyes reminded Solace of Brother Tomyss, and she felt a slight easing in the muscles across her shoulders. Tabetta dropped her veil as well, and Solace tried not to stare at the stunning Magian. Her thick, curly, black hair was pulled back in loose ponytail, and her lustrous complexion reminded Solace of polished teakwood. She gave Solace a shy smile, and Solace realized it was a rare occurrence for either woman to reveal their identities to a stranger. She was being treated as an honored guest.

Tabetta addressed her elder. "Shall I recharge the fire?"

What an odd way to phrase the question, thought Solace. *Tabetta needs to* start *the fire with fresh fuel—not recharge it.*

"Please do." Rebezza chuckled. "My aged bones are never warm enough these days, despite my layers."

"And the currents are especially strong today."

"Aye. Katya tried adjusting the air flow, but she only succeeded in making the wind blow harder," said Rebezza.

Tabetta rose from her blanket and picked up several logs and an armful of sticks from the stash of wood. She expertly arranged them in the fire pit before sitting back down.

Solace tilted her head to the side, trying to make sense of their conversation. *How can someone adjust the air currents inside a cave?* Rebezza must have sensed her confusion because she explained, "Magus Katya is an air-channeler. However, she is only fifteen and not yet in full command of her powers. Another magus is tutoring her; we have high hopes for Katya."

Solace arched her eyebrows, recalling Tabetta's earlier explanation about the order. Every woman possessed a gift, but Solace had never imagined a young girl could manipulate the flow of air. She turned to Tabetta, wondering about her special talent. The magus removed her gloves, and Solace realized why she wore them: ugly white scars crisscrossed the puckered brown skin of her hands, and when she reached her palms toward the fire pit, Solace could see reddened bumps and fresh blisters in the flesh.

Tabetta touched the twigs and sticks, humming as

sparks flew from her fingers. When the kindling started to sizzle, Tabetta grasped the round logs in her hands. The magus's voice vibrated with power as she clicked her tongue and hissed, the susurrations reminding Solace of crackling wood. Solace watched as the logs began to glow, gasping as bright orange flames burst from Tabetta's hands. The magus raised her arms and waved her hands over the fire, concluding her chant in one final, uplifting note that sounded like, "Burn!"

"Your hands!" cried Solace. "You need a salve right away."

Rebezza patted Solace's arm. "This is Tabetta's gift. Even though her palms blister and peel, she feels no pain, nor can a salve help her."

"Ah," said Solace, thankful for her water gift, which required all her strength and energy, often leaving her with a migraine afterward, but at least she wasn't scarred.

Tabetta tapped the backs of her hands. "Although these scars came from a magistrate who caught me starting a fire when I was fourteen. My parents had forbidden me from using my gift, but it was a bone-chilling winter day, and my best friend begged me for help. His firewood was too damp to light properly, and his little brother was ill with fever, shivering terribly in their drafty, old shack.

"I agreed to help him when his mother wasn't home, but she returned earlier than we expected. Even worse, she wasn't alone—she'd gone in search of the healer, a thoroughly nasty man—and they caught me with the fiery logs in my hands. The healer hauled me in front of the magistrate, who decided I needed to be taught a lesson. One of the men held down my arms, while the other seared the backs of my hands with a hot poker. Then the magistrate returned me to my parents, with the admonition that I must never use my 'sorcery' again, or the penalty would be death.

"It wasn't long afterward that Rebezza sought me out, and I decided to join the Magians, with my parents' blessing. I think they were relieved, knowing I'd be far safer than if I remained with them."

"I'm so sorry that happened to you." Solace shook her head, horrified at the cruel punishment visited upon a young girl who'd committed no actual crime. "Whatever happened to your friend and his little brother?"

"Sadly, the boy did not survive. My friend was wretched at the loss of his brother and guilty over what happened to me. He left home shortly after I did to join a group of ruffians. They drank too much ale, stole from the wealthy, and distributed liberally to the poor—until they were caught. Everyone was hanged, except for the youngest. The judge took pity on my friend and handed him over to the head of the Tor Order, a wonderful man by the name of Brother Tomyss, who took in misguided boys and did his best to turn them around."

"I knew Brother Tomyss! He was very special." Solace arched her eyebrows as another bit of information fell into place. "And your friend...was...is Brother Evryst?"

"Aye." Tabetta nodded. "Evryst has never forgiven himself for endangering my life, although I hold him no grudge. My life as a magus has been far richer than it could ever have been in our home village." She hesitated, her brow furrowed. "We were very young, and there was a time when we dreamed of other things." Tabetta pulled her gloves over her damaged hands and stared into the fire, lost in her own thoughts.

"The hurt and pain endured in our youth remains with us all our lives, leaving an indelible mark on our spirits," observed Rebezza. "We can never run fast enough or far enough to outpace our past."

Perhaps Rebezza was trying to remind Solace of something important, something to do with understanding herself and her motivations. She thought of Rhees, who'd suffered ridicule and bullying throughout his youth because everyone believed he'd been born out of wedlock, when in fact his mother had been secretly married—to the king of Toresz! And then in one horrific day, Rhees lost his entire family. He became consumed by despair and loneliness, two emotions Solace knew all too well, having walked a similar road after the loss of her mother.

It was one of many bonds they shared, their mutual understanding of grief. Her chest ached as she thought of Rhees, the husband of her heart, if nothing else. Despite his bitterness and anger over her departure, she knew he was grieving again—for her. She wiped a tear from her cheek.

Tabetta pulled her veil forward and adjusted its folds. She rose from her blanket, bowed from the waist, and left the two women alone.

"May I?" Rebezza nodded at Solace's clasped hands.

Solace extended her right hand, and the seer grasped it between her gnarled fingers. "It has been a long time, too long, since I have greeted a water witch. Your gift is as scarce as water itself, and even rarer since Neuss executed all the diviners in our kingdom. He is a truly wicked man...I am surprised you didn't kill him when you had the chance."

"*What?*" Solace withdrew her hand and stared at the old woman. "I realize you are a seer, but very few saw what truly happened that day."

"You mean when Neuss pretended to surrender and then rushed King Rhees with a knife?"

"Aye."

"And you brought Neuss down with a single stone from your sling, shattering his collarbone?"

"Aye." Solace took a deep breath, and then another. "Did you have a vision of that battle scene?"

Rebezza gazed up at the soaring interior of the mountain for what felt like a long time, but was probably less than a minute. Eventually, she turned her head toward Solace. "On the day of the battle itself, I fell into a deep trance. No one could rouse me. Tabetta thought perhaps I was passing on. Toward evening I came around and told Tabetta and the others attending me everything I'd seen. Later, one of the Magians heard an eyewitness account, which closely matched my revelation." The old magus hesitated. "Please forgive my curiosity, but I must ask. After all he'd done to you and King Rhees—and to all of Toresz— why did you show Neuss mercy?"

Solace hadn't given the tyrant much thought since that last day of battle, when Neuss had fallen to the ground, screaming curses at Rhees and her. She shuddered. "I thought he should face Rhees and answer for his crimes at a public trial."

"Interesting that you trusted Neuss's fate to a Toreszan court, when you've been unfairly treated by the same legal system."

Solace couldn't disagree, but there was another reason she'd aimed for Neuss's collarbone. She whispered, "I didn't want his blood on my hands."

Rebezza picked up a long stick and stabbed at the logs in the fire pit. "No one would have blamed you if you'd aimed higher."

"Why are you asking me about that day, and about a battle I'd much prefer to forget?"

"To gain insight into your motives. You *are* the water-gifted queen of Toresz, royal pronouncements notwithstanding."

Solace shifted around on the blanket to face Rebezza. It was time she heard the seer's most recent vision. "Tabetta asked me to travel here because you 'saw' King Rhees's coronation and the aftermath. I assumed you wanted to share something with me, some detail for my ears only. I assure you, I can handle whatever you wish to tell me."

Rebezza pursed her mouth, tilting her head to the side and gazing intently at Solace like a small, inquisitive bird. Rebezza finally shrugged and gave her a sheepish smile. "I have a confession to make. I asked Tabetta to entice you to visit me here under somewhat false pretenses."

Solace's forehead puckered. "But why…"

"I wanted to meet you," said the old prophet. "And to make you aware of our order."

"Oh," said Solace, profoundly disappointed she'd traveled so far for so little, and miffed at the wizened, old woman. "So you have nothing additional to tell me, no grand vision to share?"

Rebezza waved her hand. "No grand vision, just what I call my 'flash-views.'"

Solace folded her arms across her chest. "Then would you please share your 'flash-views' with me."

"Alright," she said with another shrug, "although I'm not sure you'll find them very helpful."

Rebezza described, with remarkable accuracy, Maude-Lyn's abrupt arrival at the rehearsal and Valyss's declaration of a prior betrothal commitment. Her vision jumped to the next day and the actual coronation, when Evryst placed the crown on Rhees's head, followed by the protestor rushing down the aisle, dagger in hand, until he was tackled by Arik. Rebezza relayed three more scenes in rapid succession: when Chancellor Zeffen nullified Solace and Rhees's marital contract, when Rhees shouted Solace was nothing to him, and when she ran sobbing from the reading room in the Great Library.

Solace felt hollowed out inside by the time Rebezza finished. The old woman's descriptions of each scene were startlingly complete, right down to the way MaudeLyn had sneered at Solace. She clasped her stomach. "Is there anything else?" *Anything I haven't suffered through already? These feel like fresh stab wounds from my own memories.*

Rebezza sighed heavily. "The rest is hazy at best, as it should be."

"Please tell me whatever you can," pleaded Solace.

Rebezza pinched her lips together, as if deciding how much to impart. She eventually nodded, more to herself than Solace. "Soon you will reach a crossroad that will test your mettle, where you will face the most important decision of your life. There will be other crossroads, of course, each with their own choices and complications; such is the pattern of our existence. Each path taken...and not taken... has its own consequences, one leading to the next. However," the seer leaned closer and grasped Solace's forearm. "Your choices from this day forth will determine much more than your own path. They will shape our nation for years to come."

"But how can that be?" whispered Solace, creasing her brow. *I've already made the toughest decision of all—to leave Rhees! What else is left to decide? Besides, how can my crossroad choices shape anyone else's life at this point? It makes no sense.*

Rebezza ignored the interruption. "You will grow weary, my dear queen, with all the demands placed upon you. You will even be tempted at times to give up, but you must not lose hope. Follow your instincts, for your heart and head must always be aligned. And if you recall nothing else from our conversation, recall this: the future of Toresz lies within you!"

Solace's head spun as she tried making sense of the old woman's words, which felt more like platitudes than prophecy. *What does Rebezza mean about the future of Toresz being within? That seems philosophical but hardly revelatory. My thoughts are more jumbled now than when I arrived.*

Rebezza placed her hand on Solace's head and whispered, "And now, Solace, water-gifted Queen of Toresz, may you traverse these hills in safety, may you find rest when you are weary, and may your labors be honored and your water be plenty."

Solace had so many questions, but she didn't get to ask any of them because the old soothsayer pulled her veil over her face and immediately started to snore. Stifling a sigh, Solace rose to her feet. "Thank you, High Magus Rebezza. This is the true path."

Rebezza murmured, "This is the true path," and resumed her snoring.

CHAPTER 13

SOLACE HELPED HERSELF TO ONE OF THE TORCHES AND STOOD NEAR the room's entrance. She didn't trust herself to find her way back to the antechamber and waited for Tabetta, who reappeared within minutes to escort her.

They followed the twisty passageway in companionable silence, Tabetta pausing at some of the rooms so she could explain their purpose. The kitchen contained a massive stone fireplace on the back wall, including an oven for baking, and a teakettle and cauldron suspended on a rail above the hearth. Barrels of water stood along one wall, with a stone ledge cluttered with clay jars on the opposite side. The common sleeping area revealed about thirty or so bedrolls lined up in three neat rows, and soft snores emitting from within.

They lingered outside a spacious chamber with several spinning wheels and hand looms on one side, and on the opposite wall, a wooden plank sat atop several low boulders to form a table. The makeshift work table was littered with bits of candle, twigs, string, rope, stones, and pieces of metal, pottery, and glass. Several stone shelves on the far wall contained a smattering of old books and scrolls, a small lending library for the inhabitants.

A lone woman, unveiled, sat at one of the spinning wheels, working by the light of a tallow candle. She did not glance up when they peered into the room but maintained her focus. Solace's eyebrows rose in surprise when she saw the woman was not spinning thread—but filaments of gold!

Tabetta must have noticed Solace's shock. "Magus Joella is metal-gifted. She can take any sort of metal, in any form—a silver cup, a gold coin, an iron bar—and spin it into metallic fibers endowed with special properties."

"What sort of properties?"

"Oh, many things. Calming properties for healers' instruments. Curative properties for slings and canes, and so forth."

Magus Joella glanced up briefly from her wheel, her amber eyes twinkling in the candlelight. Black hair escaped from her wimple in corkscrew wisps, framing her round, friendly face. "And most popular of all, protective properties for chainmail." She returned her attention to her wheel, her hands moving swiftly as her foot worked the pedal. "I shall greet you properly, my queen, once I am free of this task."

"Well met, Magus Joella. I look forward to seeing you again."

Solace and Tabetta returned to the passageway, the light from their torches dancing along the stone walls. "What other gifts are found here within Andressa Cave?"

"Hmm," said Tabetta, pausing to consider. "In addition to the gifts of soothsaying, fire-starting, air-channeling, and metal-spinning, which you have already encountered, we have one young woman who is an earth-shifter. She is able to move soil, rocks, and even smaller boulders short distances. 'Tis not a gift we call upon often but is quite convenient when needed. About half our women are more commonly gifted as healers, potion-makers, weavers, and needleworkers. And as women of the hills who must fend for ourselves, all of us are skillful with slings and daggers—same as you."

Tabetta guided Solace to a curtained-off area and pulled back a yellow cotton drape. They stepped into a cozy, square-shaped room, where a bedroll and two fluffy pillows were arranged against one wall. A tall pillar candle flickered on top of a wooden crate that served as a night-stand. Two more crates, in the far-right corner, held a water pitcher, washing bowl, and chamber pot. Solace's saddlebags had been unloaded and stowed in the opposite corner.

"I will leave you now. It is late and you must be tired. Your companions are already bedded down for the night, the men in the antechamber, and Miss Peka in the common sleeping room."

"Will I see you again before we leave in the morning?"

Tabetta shook her head. "I must attend to the high magus. She needs extra assistance after a powerful vision." She held her torch high so Solace could look into her face. "Rebezza and I—and all the Magians—wish you to know you are always welcome here. This is a place of refuge for all women whose gifts attract the wrong sort of attention."

Solace swallowed a lump in her throat and murmured, "Thank you. It's difficult to put into words how much that means to me."

"As displaced women who are disparaged for our gifts, we know all too well. 'Tis called gratitude—and make no mistake, it is we who are grateful to you—for your visit today, and for all you have done for the people of Toresz." The magus withdrew from the room with a graceful bow.

Solace slept soundly and opened her eyes with a start, uncertain where she'd laid down for the night. Then she heard rustling in the passageway beyond the drape and came fully awake.

"Queen Solace, 'tis Magus Joella. I've brought you tea and ah...something else...a gift we hope you shan't need but High Magus prays you accept, just in case, as it were. May I enter?"

Solace tried parsing out the meaning behind Joella's words and quickly gave up. "Of course. Please come in."

She pushed herself to a seated position, her stomach churning in protest as she swallowed down a sudden wave of nausea. Solace had never been a finicky eater—as the daughter of a subsistence farmer, her survival had depended on her knack for eating anything and keeping it down—including snake, pigeon, and even insects, although that had been on a dare from Arik when she was nine. She'd not repeated that particular experience. But lately, she'd awoken each morning with bile in her throat and lead in her belly.

Joella entered with a breakfast tray bearing hot tea, fresh bread, and a small pot of honey, which she placed on the wooden crate next to the bedroll. The magus used a flint to light the tallow candle next to the tray. She straightened and proceeded to peel off her gloves—no, actually, they were sleeves or arm protectors—and her outer vest.

Solace raised her eyebrows, wondering why the woman was disrobing, and why her raiment glinted in the dull candlelight. *What sort of fabric glows like that?* Then Solace recalled the gold filaments Joella had been spinning the night before. Had she been up all night, weaving her metallic thread into something wearable?

Joella draped the garments across her forearms and bowed low. "Solace, water-gifted Queen of Toresz, please accept this humble gift of gold-spun armor, woven for your protection by the Order of Righteous Magians."

Joella handed Solace the golden vest and vambraces, which weighed far less than Solace expected. She ran her fingers over the fine pattern, impressed by the artisanal workmanship. This was no ordinary chainmail, but beautifully crafted, lightweight armor suited for her smaller frame.

Solace glanced at the metal-gifted magus and inclined her head. "Thank you for this handsome and practical present. And please thank High Magus Rebezza for her hospitality. I will wear this whenever I'm traveling—for protection, as you suggest—and as a continual reminder of the wonderfully gifted women living here."

"You are most welcome, Queen Solace." Joella bowed solemnly a second time before pulling aside the curtain. "This is the true path," she murmured as she slipped into the passage.

Jenx and the other horses were saddled by the time Solace had dressed and finished her tea. She'd donned the chainmail vest and vambraces out of respect, intending to remove them later when she became too warm, but she soon forgot about the feather-light garments. Peka complimented her on the "golden armor" and wondered aloud whether she could barter for her own set. Solace and the others rode out of the cave, eager to return to Peka's farm by sundown.

Although it was still early, the sun had risen high enough to heat up the wide valley separating Andressa

Mountain from the foothills farther west. Other than the odd boulder formations and gnarly trees punctuating the brown, pebbly basin, there would be little shade until they crossed into the next range of hills.

Solace's companions restrained themselves from peppering her with questions about her visit with Rebezza, which she appreciated. She'd share the highlights when they took a meal break later, but some of what Rebezza had said—about coming to a crossroad soon, and not losing hope no matter what—Solace would keep to herself.

They'd ridden halfway across the valley when Solace noticed Peka yawning and blinking her eyes to stay awake. "Poor night's sleep?" she asked with a grin.

"Short night's sleep, more like," Peka snorted. "I'm an early riser—up when the rooster crows—but the Magians have me beat. They were folding their bedrolls and reciting their matins at least an hour before me. A very industrious group of women."

Solace chuckled. "A very interesting group as well. Such a remarkable array of skills and abilities, and yet, not everyone perceives their value. It's such a shame they feel the need for secrecy."

"But not surprising, given their history."

"The Magians could do so much more—benefit so many others—if they were able to use their gifts openly."

"Can you imagine what would happen to Joella if someone found out about her gift? And she's not the only one who can spin metal, although she has a particular affinity for gold." Peka shook her head.

"I suppose you're right, it's just—" Solace felt a sudden, sharp jab in the middle of her back. She hissed but kept riding, the pain easing into more of a dull ache.

"What's wrong?" asked Peka.

"It's nothing." Solace flapped her hand dismissively. "I think one of the horses kicked up a stone."

Peka glanced over at Solace and shrieked, "There's an arrow protruding from your vest!" Worry lines creased Peka's brow, and she hollered at the two monks riding in front. "Solace has been hit by an arrow!"

"What?" shouted Evryst.

"How?" cried Alyn.

As if to underscore the danger, two more arrows struck the sandy soil near the men, whether a warning or a lucky miss, no one could guess. Solace scanned the hills surrounding them, looking for the archer. Given their isolated location, she had no doubt they were the target—but who was attacking them? And why?

"Quick!" shouted Alyn, pointing to several large, reddish-brown boulders near a sumac tree. "We'll have some protection over there."

They reached the boulders and pulled up their horses, Jenx neighing a warning. Several arrows struck the tree trunk.

Peka yelled, "Where are these thugs? There are too many places to hide out here!" Peka grabbed her bow and quiver from her horse, nocked an arrow, and took up a position behind the largest boulder.

Solace dismounted, grimacing as she straightened, and Evryst took her elbow. "Come, lie down on your side so I can see to your injury."

"But we need to fend off the attack first," argued Solace.

Evryst pulled his black healer's kit and spare water skin from his saddle bag. "Alyn and Peka can handle a couple of highwaymen." He knelt down, patting the sandy soil. "Now, before you damage yourself further. Please."

Solace knew the master healer would continue

haranguing her until she gave in, so she harrumphed and stretched out on her right side.

Evryst grunted, "I'm going to pull up your vest and tunic to examine the wound. I'll do my best not to dislodge the arrow until I'm ready to remove it, but it still might hurt."

"Fine, do it." She heard the whir of arrows flying overhead and wondered what was happening, but she didn't want to distract Evryst with her questions. She figured Peka and Alyn had some idea of their assailants' location, because they'd not waste a good shaft otherwise.

Evryst rolled up her vest and the edge of her tunic and grumbled, "Huh."

"What's that supposed to mean?" muttered Solace, who was itching to grab her sling and stones.

"Who made you this chainmail?"

"Joella, one of the Magians. She presented it to me this morning. Rebezza asked that I wear it whenever I'm traveling."

"Hmm," grunted Evryst.

"Why are you grunting?"

Evryst ignored her questions, his fingers gently probing beneath her chainmail and shirt. Solace hissed a few times but didn't cry out. She heard the monk open his bag, probably to grab rags for cleansing and bandaging her wound, and a tincture to prevent infection that she was sure would sting. "Alright. On the count of three, I'm going to remove this arrowhead...one, two, three!"

"Ow!" howled Solace, sucking in her breath to keep from crying out loud again. She gritted her teeth as Evryst poured water and then his tincture over her wound, the latter burning so much her eyes teared up. Evryst expertly stitched the wound in her back, which he bandaged with a piece of clean cotton, and then he wrapped gauze several times around her torso to secure it. He turned away to rinse the blood from his hands, giving Solace a modicum of privacy to readjust her garments.

"That chainmail is remarkable. The finest I've ever seen," said Evryst as he packed away his kit. "Without a doubt, it saved your life today. You must wear it until your circumstances are more settled."

"Who knows how long that could be?"

"Precisely the reason the Magians gifted you that vest."

Solace started to rise, but Evryst waved her back down. "Oh no, you stay right where you are."

"But I can't see anything from here."

Alyn called over his shoulder. "There's nothing to see, except three men down. Looks like the others have scrambled, but we can't be sure."

"I'd feel better if you two scouted ahead while Solace rests awhile. I'll stay here to keep watch," said Evryst.

"I'm not an invalid," sputtered Solace.

"Nay, you're not, but you'll start bleeding in earnest if you have to break into a gallop with that wound. We're going to have to take our time heading back to the farm. We'll need to camp overnight in the hills."

"Fenwith will start to fret, and so will Arik," pointed out Solace.

Evryst shrugged. "Perhaps, but there's nothing we can do about it. They know the dangers of traveling these hills, same as the rest of us."

Solace didn't realize she'd dozed off until Peka shook her shoulder. "Do you think you can ride? The way is clear for now. We'd best get moving before anyone else comes along."

Solace grimaced as she shifted on the blanket that

someone—probably Evryst—had laid down for her. The wound left behind by the arrow hurt with every movement, and yet she knew it could have been so much worse. She pushed herself to a seated position and drank from the water skin Peka offered her. The sun had shifted its location, sliding toward the western hills. She'd dozed half a day at least. "Who were they?"

Peka hesitated, then withdrew a leaflet from the pocket of her tunic and handed it to Solace. "Thugs, bandits, highwaymen. You know, the usual supporters of old King Neuss."

Solace skimmed the poorly-written tract, which consisted of actual lies and some half-truths, praising the reign of King Neuss, claiming Rhees was not the rightful heir, and urging an uprising to gain Neuss's freedom. She shook her head. "It's an ugly piece of propaganda, and I hate that anyone had the gall to write and produce such drivel."

"Even worse, that anyone believes it."

"Are any of them still out there?"

Peka shrugged. "I assume so. Based on the tracks, I'd say at least two escaped. But it's nothing new; it'll take more than Rhees's coronation to clean up the hills and highways of Toresz."

Solace slowly rose to her feet with only a slight wince. "I'm ready to leave. I know we'd all feel better bunking down on higher ground rather than out here in the open."

Evryst packed the blanket and ensured they left no trace of themselves behind. He even used the heel of his boot to scuff away at a blood stain on the sand. Solace approached Jenx and patted his neck. She'd not be able to use her vaulting mount anytime soon. Alyn wordlessly cupped his hands to give her a foothold.

Solace thanked him for the boost, grunting at the sharp pain in her back when she landed in the saddle. As she followed her friends, she pondered how many people truly believed they were better off under Neuss. It boggled her mind that even one person thought so. She knew Rhees wasn't perfect, but he was a far better man and would be a far better king than his murderous uncle Neuss.

They traversed the boulder-strewn valley without further incident and climbed into the foothills, finding a small, dry cave to serve as a campsite for the night. Alyn, Peka, and Evryst took turns sitting watch, and Solace didn't argue. She was bone-weary, achy, and homesick—not for her father, nor her dog, nor her sheep back in Yelosha—but for the man she thought she'd married. For Rhees, flaws and all.

CHAPTER 14

When Peka's farm finally came into view, Solace had to restrain herself from galloping the rest of the way. Although her wound was healing well enough—even Evryst pronounced himself pleased, praising the Magian vest when he changed her dressing—she was still sore, weary, and looked forward to sleeping under an actual roof for the night.

Bray and the remaining monks surged around their horses as Solace, Evryst, Peka, and Alyn rode into the barnyard. The chickens raised a ruckus, clucking and flapping their wings. Fenwith stepped out of the stone cottage and scolded them for being late. Maysel limped onto the porch with Wilhm, her giant of a husband, grinning broadly in greeting.

"Solace!" called Arik, stepping out of the barn. "We've all been worried—we were readying the horses to go in search of you!" Chelyss followed behind him, wiping his hands on a rag.

Arik sprinted over to Solace, still seated on Jenx. He took one look at Solace's face and cried, "What's wrong? Have you been hurt?"

"'Tis a minor injury, little more than a scratch, and it's healing well." Solace handed Arik her reins and took her time dismounting. He reached out a strong hand to steady her as she slid from Jenx's back.

"You forget I've known you all your life," Arik grunted, "and you've more than a scratch."

Evryst joined them. "As usual, Queen Solace is understating her own discomfort. We were attacked by highwaymen"—there was a general gasp from the group, everyone crowding in closer to listen—"and the queen took an arrow in her back."

"Let's get you inside!" exclaimed Arik, who wrapped an arm around her waist.

Peka shooed them into the cottage, guiding Solace to the sofa. Arik and Fenwith sat on either side of her, the older woman muttering, "I knew it was a bad idea for you to leave with that strange lady."

"Not at all." Solace shook her head. "I'm glad I went, despite the injury. I learned—" She hesitated, knowing she couldn't reveal the secrets of the Magians.

I learned I'm not as alone as I thought. There are others like me, gifted women who've been misunderstood and even abused because of their incomparable talents, who have so much to offer yet live in fear of discovery. I learned about an amazing group of women who can and do fight back...in their own inimitable way.

Solace accepted a cup of tea from Peka and warmed her hands on the chipped mug. "I learned the benefits of a sturdy vest."

"Huh?" said Arik.

Solace glanced at Evryst. "Perhaps you might explain."

The monk arched his eyebrows at the challenge and then smoothly took up the mantle. He wove a short, interesting tale about their visit to an ancient wise woman and her daughter, who gave Solace a golden vest and matching vambraces, admonishing her to wear them whenever she traveled. It was the very same armor that saved her life when they were attacked.

Arik frowned, not quite taken in by Evryst's storytelling. "If Solace hadn't traveled into the southern hills, which are notoriously lawless, she wouldn't have been injured at all."

The monk thrust out his bottom lip. "Who's to say she may not require such armor again?"

"Let's hope not," muttered Arik, rubbing the back of his neck. "The sooner we can cross the border into Yelosha, the better, as far as I'm concerned."

"Your hills aren't all that much safer, lad," pointed out Chelyss.

Arik shrugged. "They're a mite bit safer. We haven't been dealing with a decade of rule by a crazy king, a rebellion, and all the unrest now unfolding in the capital."

Solace placed her mug on the low, wooden table in front of the sofa. "What unrest?"

Fenwith patted Solace's knee. "'Tis nothing for you to be concerned with."

"What's this about unrest in Urhl?" Solace folded her arms. "I want to hear about it—I must know what's happening."

Since Wilhm and Behn, Peka's older son, had remained in Urhl after the coronation, Solace assumed they were the best source of news. Solace noticed they were standing near the kitchen and waved them over. "Tell me. Please."

Evryst addressed the two men. "We're aware of the street protests after the proclamation about 'Queen Maude-Lyn.' Have they continued?"

Wilhm sighed. "Aye. The whole situation's gotten out of hand."

"Way out of hand," agreed Behn, who had the same large, gray eyes and tawny complexion as his brother, although he wore his dark, curly hair in a ponytail. He stroked his beard, which was fuller and thicker than Bray's. "It's almost as if—"

Behn's voice trailed off but Solace prompted him. "Don't stop now. It's almost as if?"

"As if Rhees wants the strife and disorder to continue," said Behn.

Wilhm nodded. "He's not encouraging it, but he's doing nothing to tamp it down either. In fact, he's doing nothing at all."

"What do you mean?" Solace drew her eyebrows together. Rhees was a man of action, sometimes too much action, without sufficient forethought. What was he up to?

"Rhees is sending out MaudeLyn and her brother to represent the crown wherever he's is supposed to show up," grumbled Wilhm.

"Which is sure to stir the pot," added Behn, "as Rhees well knows. He's a cagey one."

"There's also Neuss's trial in a few days' time." Brother Alyn scratched his beard thoughtfully. "The turmoil will continue until he's sentenced and hanged."

"There's nothing we can do about any of that." Fenwith rose from the sofa. "However, we'll need to be extra diligent when traveling through the hills. I'd like to be as prepared as possible, just in case."

"Just in case?" prompted Arik.

"Just in case we run into any more ruffians." Chelyss supplied for his wife. "Fenwith's right. It'll take a good five days to reach Shulamorn, assuming we don't linger on the way. We must be well stocked and armed to the teeth."

One of the toddlers woke from his nap with a wail, his brother joining the chorus. As Maysel and Wilhm headed down the hallway to see to their boys, Peka chuckled. "Whatever's happening outside this cottage makes no difference to those little ones. They must be fed."

"Come to think of it, I'm hungry myself, Mum," said Bray as he took Maysel's chair in front of the window.

Peka put her hands on her hips. "Don't sit down, lad. I need your help in the kitchen."

Bray moaned, "But I've been up since dawn, doing all the chores."

"Hah! The monks did most of your chores this morning, and you know it." Behn kicked his brother's boots good naturedly. "Come on, let's go help Mum."

Bray rose with a grumble, following his brother and Fenwith into the kitchen. Chelyss, Evryst, and Alyn left for the stables, to brush down the horses and sort out the supplies for the next day.

"You're keeping secrets, Solace," said Arik softly.

Solace turned to face him, her back twinging with the movement. "Aye. Secrets that are not mine to tell."

"Oh, I think some are."

Solace shook her head. "You may have represented my father at Rhees's coronation, but I don't answer to you, nor to anyone else, for that matter."

"True enough," he sighed. "I merely wish you would unburden yourself. Allow me to help you."

Solace scowled. Her oldest friend could be annoyingly perceptive at times. "How so?"

"Tell me what really happened these past two days, and tell me your plans."

Solace fiddled with her hands in her lap. "As to the first, I'm truly sworn to secrecy."

"Very well. And your plans?"

Solace flinched as she rose stiffly from the sofa. Arik stood, his eyes softened with concern. She knew he wanted to help, knew he would do whatever he could to ease her burdens—but they were her burdens to carry, her decisions to make.

"Each day brings its own troubles, Arik," she whispered, "and day by day, I'll face them. We have much ground to cover before we reach the Yeloshan-Toreszan border in Shulamorn Province."

Arik frowned as he took in her meaning. He ran a hand through his dark hair. "You might decide to stay here in Toresz after all. That's what you're *not* saying, isn't it?"

Solace heard the pain in his voice and bit her bottom lip. "I can't talk about this right now!" She walked stiffly from the room, her heart aching as much as her back.

CHAPTER 15

CHELYSS AND FENWITH HAD MADE MORE TRIPS ACROSS THE HILLS and plains to Shulamorn than anyone else, so they took the lead when they left Peka's farm. Since Behn and Bray were accompanying their mother, leaving only Wilhm and Maysel to run the farm, Evryst instructed two brethren to remain behind to assist the couple.

Solace finally figured out why some of the monks looked so alike. Danyss and Devlan, the pair who continued on as part of her escort team, were actual twins, with matching dark hair, thick beards, and arched eyebrows that made them look as if they were perpetually asking a question or chuckling over a joke.

Despite painful twinges from her injury, mostly when she mounted and dismounted Jenx, Solace found the ride soothing. The days were pleasantly warm but not too hot, and occasional white clouds scuttled across the brilliant blue sky, promising rain that never came.

Solace spotted a farmer, hoe in hand, his large, floppy-brimmed hat pulled down low over his forehead just like her father. She thought of the snug cottage built by her father's hands, and how warm and safe she'd always felt there. They passed flocks of sheep grazing in the hills, their wooly coats grown thick during the winter. She smiled, remembering her own small flock back home, and her intrepid sheepdog, Barley. Solace's mind wandered freely, not alighting on any topic as serious as her future.

On the afternoon of their third travel day, Fenwith and Chelyss left the hard-packed soil of the main road and turned their horses toward a village. Solace lowered her brow, surprised they were stopping early, since there were still a few hours of daylight left. On the other hand, one of the horses had started to limp, their water skins were running low, and they needed to replenish their supply of jerky. A hand-lettered wooden sign announced they were entering Manyalan.

The town was larger than any they'd bypassed so far and appeared a tad more prosperous-looking, which wasn't difficult. Most of what passed for villages in Toresz were little more than mining settlements or watering holes for livestock, with a few ramshackle buildings lining one side of the road.

Chelyss led them to a large stable yard, where the hostler greeted them with bows and smiles before shouting instructions to his grooms. As Solace dismounted, Jenx snorted and shook his sleek, reddish-brown head. She leaned over to pat his neck. "'Tis only a stopover. I'll not be gone very long."

It panged her to think of leaving Jenx behind on Chelyss and Fenwith's farm when it came time for her to cross the border. But he was Rhees's horse, and while Rhees had given her Jenx, the beautiful stallion would never be content living on a small Yeloshan farm. Solace sniffed; best not to think about that until the time came to say goodbye.

She had two days left before they reached Shulamorn, and she still hadn't decided whether to go home with Arik.

A clean but worn-looking stone inn stood adjacent to the stable. Several shops and a tavern lined the road next to the inn. On the opposite side of the street were a haberdasher, a blacksmith, and an ugly, mud-colored edifice that was neither a house, nor an office, nor a shop. Several young boys, wearing patched, baggy pants and homespun cotton shirts, gathered in front of the building. A pock-marked door and two windows, their peeling shutters sagging open, faced the road.

One of the boys dashed inside and hollered something unintelligible. Soon a dozen boys and girls poured out through the doorway, jumping up and down and flailing their thin arms. Their ages varied, with none of them much older than nine or ten. All the children were similarly dressed in ill-fitting clothes, the girls in raggedy skirts and the boys in mended pants.

They streamed across the road, surrounded Solace, and shouted in high-pitched voices, "All hail, Queen Solace of Toresz! Well met, well met!" Solace stared over their heads at Arik, who ran out of the stable at the commotion. He shook his head, a perplexed look on his face, and threaded his way to her side.

A harried-looking woman, wearing a gray cotton frock and starched white apron, dashed out of the building. She bowed deeply to Solace before turning to her charges. "Children, please line up. Come along, right now, you know the drill. Lonyss and Oraden, that means you! Back in line. Let's make our queen proud."

The two smallest, loudest boys sprang to attention at her voice. The children ordered themselves, shortest to tallest, and then the woman clapped her hands twice. Every child bowed from the waist and then stood straight. The rest of Solace's traveling companions, plus the innkeeper, a tall, skinny, somber man, and his rounder, cheerful wife, gathered to watch. The merchants, the smithy, the tavern owner, and several other curious onlookers stood in clusters on both sides of the road.

The two shortest boys—Lonyss and Oraden?—opened their mouths, and Solace tried not to wince in anticipation of their shrill voices. But instead of shouting at the tops of their lungs, all the boys and girls burst into song.

The children's sweet soprano accents struck a chord deep within Solace's breast. Her eyes welled up unexpectedly. She'd sung the same little melody as a young girl, leading her sheep out to graze each morning. It was a song of the hills, of the dry, brown, rocky land spanning Toresz and Yelosha; a song without borders.

Solace smiled and led the applause when the children finished their performance. She praised them and then went down the line, beginning with the tallest girl and working her way to the smallest boy, asking their names, ages, and where they lived.

Solace learned from Bekkah, age ten, the building across the road "was an orphanage, mum, 'n a right good 'un. Leastways 'ats wot Auntie Emmie says, 'n I cain't disagree. We 'as two meals a day, mor 'er less, plus daily book learnin'."

"Auntie Emmie?" asked Solace.

Bekkah bowed a second time and averted her eyes. "I meant ta say Miss Emmie. Thot's 'er name, Miss Emmie." Solace thanked the flustered young girl and moved on to the next child, Lissah, who spoke so softly Solace had to bend low to hear her say she was almost nine, and "Bekkah's cuzzin."

Oraden, age five, informed Solace, "Thot 'afore 'e wuz king, Mister Rhees use' ta visit 'n bring us goodies." Oraden then peered up at Solace, his solemn brown eyes hopeful. Solace chuckled and assured Oraden she would deliver treats before she left Manyalan.

While she'd been chatting with the children, Arik stood at her left elbow. Evryst and Fenwith, who'd been speaking with the innkeeper's wife, reappeared near her right elbow. Solace wondered why her friends were hovering like body-guards, until she spoke with Mrs. Emmaline Wellsun to thank her for the children's performance.

Mrs. Wellsun bowed from her shoulders. "'Tis our plea-sure to sing for you." The attractive woman appeared to be in her late twenties, with a creamy brown complexion and lustrous, dark hair pinned up in bun. "I'm glad you are trav-eling with a large party, ma'am. With those murders a few days ago, everyone's on edge."

"What murders?"

Mrs. Wellsun leaned closer, her voice a soft whisper. "A young woman matching your description—beautiful, long black hair, on the road to Shulamorn—and her male companion were beaten, robbed, and left for dead. A trav-eling merchant came upon them not long afterward; they were both still breathing. He and his sons brought them to Manyalan and paid for the healer to see to their injuries, but neither survived. We buried them yesterday, the poor dears."

Despite the warmth of the afternoon sun, Solace felt a sudden chill. She shivered and rubbed her arms. "How dreadful! I trust the king will do all he can to subdue such lawlessness and punish those involved."

Mrs. Wellsun compressed her lips. "One can hope."

"Do you doubt King Rhees's sincerity?"

The matron hastily shook her head. "Ach, no, ma'am, nothing like that..." She drew her dark eyebrows together. "'Tis that other woman, the northerner who claims to be our queen. She doesn't care about us; she can't possibly understand hill folk. With a woman like that by his side, I fear our new king will forget about the rest of Toresz."

Solace canted her head. "Since you've heard the news about Queen MaudeLyn, why are the children still hailing me as their queen?"

Mrs. Wellsun looked her straight in the eye. "Because *she* is not queen of Toresz. *You* are, ma'am." The woman bowed and left to round up her charges, reminding them of their chores. The children gave good-humored groans as they trooped behind her into their mud-colored home.

Solace waved as they left, but her mind was elsewhere, the woman's words joining a chorus of others inside her head, echoes of conversations she'd had at every stop along her route to Yelosha. But Solace wasn't about to delude herself. She was not the queen and never had been—not legally, not in any way that really counted. Besides, Rhees had all but evicted her from his life. The only queen in Toresz at the moment was the prickly, pouty MaudeLyn of Censarra.

"I had such high hopes for our rebellion. I'd even convinced myself such horrific crimes were a thing of the past." Fenwith shook her head. "Seems like things are as bad as ever, and now, we can't even blame old Neuss."

"I wouldn't be so sure about that," offered Evryst.

"Do you think he's directing ruffians from his cell in the dungeon?" asked Arik.

Evryst ran a hand over his bald head. "Perhaps not directly, but Neuss has some very powerful friends on the outside who would gladly raise a ruckus if they thought it would help advance their own criminal ambitions."

Arik nodded toward the west. "All the more reason for us to make haste for Shulamorn and the Yeloshan border as soon as possible."

"I'm afraid that's not going to happen, at least, the 'make haste' part," said Chelyss, who'd joined them in front of the inn.

"Why not?" sputtered Arik. The string of travel delays was clearly straining his patience.

"Two of the horses need new shoes, and a third has thrush, which needs treatment. While we can leave one horse behind here with the hostler, we can't leave all three. We'll be able to leave the day after tomorrow, minus the horse with thrush. Brother Alyn and I have made arrangements—the inn can accommodate the ladies and half the men. We'll rotate, some sleeping in the barn tonight and the others inside, then we'll swap tomorrow night."

Arik rolled his eyes. "Fine, there's nothing to be done but stay the extra day and re-shoe the horses." He turned to Solace. "At least you can rest up before we make the final push for home."

Solace didn't mind the delay, but she couldn't very well say that to Arik. "I know you're anxious to get back to help our dads. They rely on you so much."

"True enough. But more to the point," Arik lowered his voice, took her by the elbow, and walked a little distance away from the others, "I'm anxious to get you away from all this craziness."

"You mean the highwaymen? Yelosha has them as well."

"I know, but I don't like hearing that a young woman matching your description was attacked on the road to

Shulamorn. That tells me it may not have been a random crime. And let's not forget you got an arrow in your back while visiting that wise woman. But mainly, I want to get you away from all this crazy talk about you still being the queen. It's as if everyone in these hills has closed their ears to the news."

Arik was right, but Solace could also understand why people were wary of MaudeLyn. Censarrans in general, and the royal family in particular, had a reputation for thinking they were better than their Toreszan neighbors. "I guess it's a bit of wishful thinking on their part."

"Wishing something is true won't make it so."

Solace rubbed her forehead, suddenly exhausted from the constant drama her life had become. She mumbled that her head was starting to hurt, and Arik hurried her into the cool shade of the inn.

CHAPTER 16

WHEN THE INNKEEPER'S WIFE SHOWED HER TO THE MODEST, whitewashed bedroom prepared for the "queen's privacy," Solace had expected to spend half the evening pacing the floorboards. Her mind was awhirl with murdered girls, stray arrows, the Order of Righteous Magians, and Arik's stalwart focus on crossing into Yelosha—and taking her with him.

Solace placed her candlestick on the nightstand next to the double bed, which took up half the room. She edged around the foot of the bed and stood before a small, oak dresser that held a pitcher of water, a washing bowl, and a rough burlap towel. A square window, with a wooden chair beneath it, occupied the far wall, and a chamber pot was tucked into the corner.

She hanged her leather cloak on the iron coat hook next to the dresser, removed her armor and her tunic, and tossed them onto the chair. Gingerly, she unwound the bandage from around her waist and examined it for any telltale spotty brown stains from her wound. She nodded with satisfaction. This was the first evening her dressing had come away clean, and she felt only occasional pangs of discomfort in her back. She'd been lucky, far luckier than the poor young woman and her companion.

Solace washed up, changed into her nightgown, and went to the window. Pulling aside the faded cotton curtain, she stared at the western hills behind the inn, illuminated by the full moon, and thought of home.

Home is where you belong, where you don't need to explain yourself, where you fit in, like hand to glove, horse to bridle, hearth to... Shaking her head, she let the curtain drop, blew out the candle by the bed, and crawled under the covers.

Solace joined Fenwith, Peka, and Arik for breakfast in the inn's cramped lobby. Just inside the front door sat an old pine desk; a set of cubbyholes for storing room keys and any messages for guests hung on the wall behind it. Two fraying, green armchairs were crammed in front of the fire-place, and four rough-hewn, plank tables filled nearly all the remaining floorspace. Depending on the time of day, the room served as a dining area, reading room, and front parlor.

Solace sipped her piping-hot tea and considered the boiled egg, slice of burnt toast, and strip of bacon on her plate. Her stomach roiled so she looked away. Perhaps she'd be able to swallow down the toast in a little while.

Behn and Bray must have risen earlier, because they burst into the inn, slamming the door behind them and earning a hard stare from the innkeeper. "We just heard the herald, passing through on his way to the next town!" Bray was barely able to contain his excitement. "Old Neuss has been tried and convicted of multiple counts of murder, treason, and fraud, plus a long list of other crimes. He was sentenced to death, to be carried out immediately. Neuss must be hanged by now, as the trial happened a few days ago."

"That old fox is dead at last!" exclaimed Fenwith. "Good riddance to a bad man."

Peka nodded with grim satisfaction at the news. Her husband and eldest son had been murdered by Neuss. "Finally! Justice was served the moment he swung at the end of a rope."

Solace felt simply a hollowness inside. She didn't regret Neuss's death, but knowing he'd been executed didn't make her feel any better either. She hoped Toreszans, including Rhees, could begin to heal from the wounds inflicted by their monstrous former king. Thinking of Rhees caused her to rub the spot on her chest above her heart, but she quickly dropped her hand. If Evryst spotted her, he'd assume Solace had strained her heart again and urge her to spend the day in bed.

Fenwith went in search of Chelyss to give him the news, and Peka left the inn with her two sons. Solace nibbled on her toast and pushed the rest of her plate toward Arik, who hesitated. "Are you sure you can't eat this? Perhaps later?"

Solace shook her head. "I won't eat it. Please help yourself."

Arik nodded, quickly consumed the bonus breakfast, and wiped his mouth on a threadbare linen napkin. "You don't seem particularly moved by Neuss's sentence. I'd have expected you to be happier."

Solace shrugged. "I'm glad it's over, that's all."

Arik hesitated, seemed about to say something, and thought better of it. He pushed back his chair. "I hear there's an able leatherworker next to the smithy. I have a harness in need of a new strap. Can I pick up any sundries for you on the way back?"

"No, thank you." Solace tapped the book she'd carried down from her room. "I have all I need right at the moment. I intend to put this day to good use."

Arik leaned over her chair to read the title stamped in gold letters on the worn leather cover. He laughed softly. "You are the only person I know—man or woman—who finds map-reading an enjoyable pastime." Still chuckling, he skirted around the scattered tables and exited through the door.

Solace couldn't possibly explain her love of maps to anyone else, except perhaps to another water diviner, but Neuss had purged them all a decade earlier. She pulled the atlas toward her with a happy sigh. Wherever Solace went, she adjusted the mental map of water sources inside her head. Often, she was only half-aware she was doing it, until the need arose to identify the location of a new well. Then she'd call up her mental map and find new nodes she hadn't realized existed.

She opened her book, turning the pages until she found her current location, the village of Manyalan. Solace traced the path to Shulamorn. Once they left the inn, they'd travel another two days before reaching the border town. Two more days before she'd have to make a decision: say goodbye to her friends and cross the border with Arik, or remain in Toresz, homeless and jobless. Sighing, she used her finger to follow the winding route between Shulamorn and her father's house, deep in the Yeloshan hill country.

Solace had been so preoccupied with leaving Urhl and Rhees behind, she hadn't given much thought to the last leg of the journey—traveling through Yelosha with Arik—or what came afterward, when she arrived home. She clutched her head with a soft groan and leaned her elbows on the table.

Stupid, stupid Solace! What was I thinking? If I return home with Arik as my only companion, then everyone—Dad, Arik, his father, and every single neighbor—will expect us to marry. In their minds, traveling unchaperoned with another man who is neither my father nor my brother could mean only one thing: we are betrothed. And if I refuse, I will be shunned by everyone, even my dad.

Then another thought struck her. *Has this been Arik's plan, or at the very least his assumption, all along?* Her face flushed with anger at Arik and her father, who'd sent Arik in his place, putting her in this untenable position. She wanted to rail against men in general—and the arcane set of laws that put their own interests ahead of women everywhere—and at Neuss, who'd been the root cause of her hasty, non-legal marriage, and all her current troubles.

Solace discovered, with a start, the only man she wasn't angry with at the moment was Rhees. She still felt a stab in her chest whenever she thought of him. And while she held him accountable for his awful, hurtful words when they'd separated, she realized he'd been lashing out in pain. Catching her bottom lip between her teeth, she reached for her book. After ordering a second pot of tea, she carefully flipped through the pages. A calm settled over Solace as she studied her maps.

Nothing broke her concentration, not the scullery maid chatting with the innkeeper's daughter, nor the shuffling of footsteps in the bedrooms overhead, nor the harness bells ringing in the stable yard. Nothing, that is, until she heard raised voices outside, and one man shouting to be heard above the rest. Sighing, she grabbed her book and got up to investigate.

Solace threw open the door and stepped outside, surprised to find the Tor monks and most of the towns-people surrounding a herald astride a horse. A thick layer of dust coated the man's face, hair, beard, and blue tabard with Rhees's coat of arms stitched onto the front. The man's companions—four well-armed knights—waited for him near the hand-painted sign, where the main road to Shulamorn turned off into Manyalan.

Why had the man returned? Heralds normally covered an established circuit, quickly delivering the king's proclamations and then traveling onto the next town. They stopped only briefly, to change horses and grab a hasty meal, and they never back-tracked. Then again, they generally traveled in pairs, with just one guard at their side.

Fenwith, Chelyss, and Peka joined the crowd in the street, everyone speaking at once. Arik emerged from the leatherworker's shop with Bray and Behn. It became apparent this wasn't the same messenger when Brother Evryst called out, "What is being done to recapture the scoundrel?"

"King Rhees and his knights are in pursuit," the herald replied, his deep voice booming over the din. Everyone paused to listen, the promise of news silencing even the children who'd spilled out of the orphanage from across the road.

"Thus proclaims His Royal Highness, King Rhees of Toresz: 'Escaped convict Neuss Axium Orillya is wanted, dead or alive. I hereby order every town and village with ten or more men to immediately form a posse and seek out the fugitive. A bounty shall be paid upon confirmation of his death or capture.' Thus concludes the king's proclamation."

An eruption of voices, mostly shouting questions, followed the terse announcement. The herald, obviously accustomed to such a reaction, nosed his horse forward, forcing his way through the throng. He joined the knights waiting at the village's outskirts, and the five men galloped off toward the next town.

Mrs. Wellsun's young charges surged forward, Oraden claiming he wanted to see "'ole Neuss truss't up an' led off to 'is imm'nent demise." The woman clucked her tongue as she rounded up the boys and girls.

Bekkah lingered near Solace, staring at the heavy tome in her arms. "Pard'n, mum. Is thot a book 'o maps yer carryin'?"

Solace's mind was awhirl. How had Neuss managed to escape? Were his loyalists—little more than criminals and assassins—behind the attack on her near Andressa Mountain and the murder of the young woman and her companion on the Shulamorn road?

Bekkah licked her lips nervously, and Solace forced her attention back to the girl in front of her. She smiled. "Aye. Are you a fan of maps?"

"Oi." Bekkah's eyes lit up, and she nodded her head vigorously. "A big fan, mum. Sum'times I dream 'o maps." Bekkah's face clouded. "Pleez don't say nothin' mum. Miss Emmie says ta keep it secret, like. We don't want folks thinkin' I'm pecul'ar."

Solace nodded, only half listening to the girl. Mrs. Wellsun called out to Bekkah, who bowed toward Solace and ran to catch up with the other children.

A dozen separate conversations had sprung up around Solace, but she paid them little heed. She was dimly aware of Evryst speaking in low tones with his Tor brethren, Bray declaring they should join the Manyalan posse, and Peka reminding her youngest son they had a more pressing obligation—to protect their queen. Arik murmured something about needing to press on toward the border, and Fenwith agreeing, albeit without enthusiasm. The innkeeper, the blacksmith, and several shop owners debated the wisdom of leaving their town undefended, given recent events on the road to Shulamorn.

What Solace heard, as clearly as if she was still seated on a blanket inside Andressa Cave, were the high magus's final words. Solace would have an important choice to make, one that would affect her life and others. She glanced toward the hand-painted sign near the turnoff to the village. She'd reached the crossroad sooner than she'd expected—and it was a physical junction, as well as a figurative one—with Urhl to the east, Shulamorn and Yelosha to the west, Censarra to the north, and Andressa to the south.

She knew, with the same certainty she felt every time she divined for water, what she had to do next. She couldn't possibly foresee all that would ensue following her decision, but wasn't that like the way of water itself? Twisting, turning sinuously beneath the ground, tricksome, even dangerous at times, but also soothing and life-sustaining.

Solace pushed past the gathering of friends and Manyalans. She passed the inn, the stable yard, and the small desert flowers that had sprung up overnight on the side of the village road. She sensed others following behind, her friends for certain, but probably also the curious towns-people. When Solace reached the crossroad, she turned around. Everyone had followed her, even the hostler's mastiff, who barked once as if to call the crowd to order.

Solace took a deep breath and said, loudly and firmly, "I will lead the Manyalan posse. Neuss must be recaptured before he can harm anyone else. Decide amongst yourselves who shall remain behind to defend your town, and who shall join me. But make haste—we ride in an hour!"

CHAPTER 17

Solace's announcement was met with cheers from the townspeople, Peka, and her sons, applause from the Tor monks, Fenwith, and Chelyss, and furrowed brow from Arik, who stalked back to the inn alone.

Solace sighed. She would have to speak with Arik and try to help him understand. But first, she needed to confer with Evryst, who was shouldering his way through the crowd. The rest of her companions hung back, as if in silent agreement the monk could speak for them all.

Evryst brought his hands together in a prayer pose and bowed deeply, greeting her as one would greet their sovereign after a long absence. Solace arched her eyebrows, clasped her hands in front of herself, and returned the bow, careful that her head remained above his. She had made her choice, and he was acknowledging it. From this day forward, she would be the Water Witch Queen of Toresz, and her demesne would be the poor and displaced, the outcast and homeless.

"My queen," said Evryst, "are you certain?"

"Aye."

"Very well." Evryst nodded. "The Brothers of the Tor Order are at your disposal."

Solace tilted her head. "And what if King Rhees directs you otherwise, opposing what I command?"

A half-smile flitted across Evryst's lips, but he quickly schooled his features, the diplomatic head of a monastic order once more. "Allow me to amend my initial statement. Half the Tor brethren shall be at your continual service, and the other half reserved for King Rhees. Should the king's orders align with yours, then you shall have the full complement of warrior-monks at your disposal."

Now it was Solace's turn to smile, but briefly. Then she placed her left hand under her right forearm, and extended her right hand to Evryst to seal the pact. He followed suit and shook her hand, his dark eyes twinkling. "Welcome home, Queen Solace."

"Henceforth I shall be known as Solace, Water Witch Queen of Toresz," she said. "I do not wish to be mistaken for MaudeLyn, Queen of Toresz."

"So mote it be," replied Evryst. "Although MaudeLyn is technically Princess of Toresz. Contrary to earlier reports, the king has not elevated her status to Queen. I spoke with the first herald while he was changing horses this morning. He says the king keeps to his chambers and has made no public appearances, except at Neuss's trial, which lasted less than two hours."

"Ah," said Solace, who tried not to show her relief at the news Rhees and MaudeLyn were not actually together.

"Apparently MaudeLyn and Valyss have been conferring with Chancellor Zeffen. Their advisor was overheard saying there were no legal remedies to the king's enforced singlehood."

"Hmm," said Solace, delighted to learn the Censarrans

had hit a wall they couldn't scale by misapplication of the law. She wanted to cheer but instead replied, "Thank you for the update."

"Indeed." Evryst bowed a second time.

"Please don't leave us in suspense any longer," called out Fenwith, standing some distance away with the rest of Solace's friends. The Manyalans had already dispersed. "Does this mean you're staying?"

When Solace nodded, a whoop rose from Behn and Bray. Peka said, "Alright, boys, enough hoopla. We have much to do and very little time. Hop to it!"

Behn and Bray turned toward the village, but Solace called them back. "Could one of you please see that treats are delivered to the orphanage? I promised Oraden." Behn waved his hand to acknowledge her request.

She glanced down at the book she held in her arms, recalling Bekkah's enthusiasm for maps, which even permeated her dreams. Could the child possibly be water-gifted? If so, Solace would look in on Bekkah from time to time, and when she was old enough, Solace would introduce her to the Righteous Magians.

She handed the book to Bray. "Please deliver this to Miss Emmaline, for Bekkah and Lissah to use when they study geography." Bray took the book and then joined his brother, the two of them jogging back into town.

Solace found Arik in the stable, securing the repaired harness on his horse. He didn't look up. "I met a Yeloshan man and his son at the leatherworker's. They invited me to travel with them back to Yelosha. I've settled my account at the inn and will be leaving shortly."

"Arik," she said quietly.

Her oldest friend turned toward her, his brown eyes gentle. "There's no need for you to explain yourself to me."

"Isn't there?"

"Nay." Arik shook his head. "I've spent the past week trying to deny it, but I can't any longer. You belong here, just as I belong back home, tilling the land with our dads. Let's face it; you've always been just out of reach, always on the cusp of leaving me and Soren."

A tear slid down Solace's cheek, which she swiped with the back of her hand. All her earlier anger at Arik and her father was gone, replaced by a dull ache deep inside her soul—in that place reserved for childhood memories safely tucked away, until some future time when it might not hurt so much to visit them again. "I'm sorry," she replied, her throat thick.

Arik moved closer and brushed back a loose lock of her hair, his calloused fingers rough against her cheek. "Don't be. You can't alter who you are, and I wouldn't want you to change anyway." He stepped back, pointed out the stable door, and said firmly, "Now go capture that knave and save the kingdom!"

Solace nodded silently through her tears, which she didn't bother swiping away this time. She walked back to the inn, head down, and didn't look back.

Two-and-a-half hours later, after the horses needing new shoes had been swapped out temporarily, after saddlebags and water skins had been resupplied, and after tearful goodbyes between family members, Solace and Jenx led the posse out of Manyalan. Fourteen towns-people accompanied them, including Giulia, the innkeeper's raven-haired, ax-wielding daughter, and Hossin, the blacksmith's son, who was at least the height and breadth of Wilhm. They rode northeast, toward the mines and caves dotting the hills between Manyalan and Urhl, where Neuss would be more likely to hide, and where it would be much more difficult to flush him out.

Solace left the main road, following a hard-packed dirt trail that horses' hooves had beaten into a path. Although her stomach still churned, mostly in the mornings, and her heart was still burdened by her separation from Rhees, she hadn't felt so at peace since she and Rhees had defeated Neuss the first time. The fact that Neuss had escaped rankled her. Nothing short of betrayal could account for his clean getaway.

Someone had double-crossed Rhees and aided the ex-king-turned-fugitive. But who? Could it have been one of the Censarrans? Solace slowly turned the idea over, examining the political angles—something she'd learned to do from Brother Tomyss—but she eventually dismissed the notion. MaudeLyn and Valyss sought a closer alliance with Toresz through their association with Rhees. They'd gain nothing by weakening his hold on the kingdom.

No, she decided, it must have been a disgruntled Toreszan—a member of the palace staff, perhaps even a knight—whose palms had been sufficiently greased to look the other way, leave a door unlocked, or serve as a lookout while Neuss fled.

The traitor would need to be discovered and quickly brought to trial. Before the Censarrans had invaded their lives and wrenched them apart, Solace and Rhees would have solved the crime themselves, swiftly uncovering the spy in their midst and recapturing Neuss before he'd fled from Urhl.

Solace drew her eyebrows together. She needed to stop her unhelpful train of thoughts. She was no longer Rhees's closest confidante, no longer "queen of his heart" as he'd once called her. Time to focus on finding Neuss and forgetting the what-if scenarios clogging her brain.

Peka and Fenwith came alongside her on the trail, their horses kicking up clouds of dust. "Well, have you worked out who helped Neuss escape?" asked Peka.

"Not yet. Have you?" said Solace.

Peka tilted her head at Fenwith, who was riding at Solace's right side. "Fen has some suspects in mind."

Fenwith squinted at the hills in the distance and sighed. "It must have been one of Neuss's soldiers whom Rhees pardoned after he defeated the old king. A few of them became guards later."

Solace nodded. "Could have been one of them, or anyone on the staff whom we haven't had time to vet."

"My coin is on one of the guards," said Peka. "They had the best access to Neuss."

Solace nodded. "That's the likeliest scenario. Let's hope whoever betrayed Rhees has fled with Neuss."

Fenwith glanced at her sharply. "Are you thinking Rhees himself could be in jeopardy, if the traitor is still in his employ?"

"Aye," Solace replied grimly. "Although at least Rhees will be on guard, now that Neuss is at large."

"The sooner we capture Neuss, the better for us all," said Peka, her mouth turned down. "And if I come across the scoundrel, I'll finish him myself."

"What's that dark cloud behind us?" yelled Bray from the back of the line of horses.

Solace slowed Jenx and turned sideways for a better look over her shoulder. "It looks like smoke, but that doesn't make any sense. We've had no lightning strikes, and there's nothing to fuel a fire out here, except tumbleweeds and the occasional tree."

"I think that's Manyalan!" cried Giulia.

"That's definitely Manyalan—and it's burning!" shouted Hossin.

CHAPTER 18

THE ENTIRE POSSE TURNED THEIR HORSES AROUND AND SHOT OFF toward the village. As they drew closer, it became readily apparent that Manyalan was indeed burning. Solace pressed Jenx into a gallop, anxious to reach the town before darkness fell.

By the time they were down to the last mile, Solace struggled to see through the thick haze of smoke wafting toward them, coating the back of her throat. She heard horses neighing, men shouting, and children's high-pitched wailing. The acrid smell of charred wood invaded her nostrils, making her cough, and her eyes teared up from the smoke. When her eyes finally cleared, she inhaled sharply at all the damage in front of her, which made her start coughing again.

The stable was a blackened hulk, and three shops, including the leatherworker's, had been reduced to burning embers. The inn and tavern, streaked with soot, appeared mostly intact—for now. Men and women tossed buckets of water on the buildings, while hollow-eyed children milled about in the street. The hostler and his grooms were rounding up frightened horses that had, thankfully, escaped from the stable and run off in different directions.

The Manyalans dashed ahead, their horses skittish and snorting at the smoke and fire, Evryst and the monks fast on their heels. Solace knew they'd be seeing to the injured and comforting the despondent. She followed them, dismounting when she spotted Lonyss and Oraden clinging to each other and crying. She knelt on the ground, and the two small boys hurled themselves into her arms.

"Bad men!" Lonyss hiccupped. "Vewy scawwy."

Oraden sobbed. "They'z grapp't Miz Emmie an' Bekkah an' Lissah!"

"Someone grabbed Miss Emmaline and two of the girls?" Solace felt a chill ripple down her spine. "Who took them?"

"Bad men!" the boys cried in unison. "Yer half'ta find-'em! Pleez, mum."

"Emmaline's gone!" shouted Hossin, sprinting out of the orphanage.

"Who's Emmaline?" asked Fenwith, coming alongside Solace.

"Mrs. Emmaline Wellsun—she runs the orphanage," said Solace.

"My Emmaline." Hossin's voice cracked. He clutched his frizzy, black hair in two meaty fists, as despondent as the two small boys clinging to Solace's legs. Hossin's reaction told Solace two things: pretty Emmaline Wellsun was a widow, and the blacksmith's son was courting her.

"We will go after them—but first, we need informa-tion," said Solace firmly. She glanced around. Evryst and Alyn were kneeling on the ground, attending to the injured wherever they'd fallen. Most of the patients seemed able to speak, with non-life-threatening burns and wounds. But not all; Danyss and Devlan spread a horse blanket over two bodies lying in front of the leatherworker's shop. Chelyss, Peka, and her sons were helping to toss buckets of water on the inn and the tavern, the two buildings closest to the smoldering shops.

"I hate to say it aloud," said Fenwith, "but this has all the hallmarks of..."

"Of Neuss," supplied Solace. "Although he couldn't have gotten quite this far, this fast. But this certainly looks like the work of one of his gangs...but why here, why now?"

"I should think it would be obvious." Hossin sighed wearily.

"Please explain." Solace nodded at the huge man.

"The whole country is in an uproar over you and that northerner claiming to be our queen. We follow only the Water Witch Queen, and every town, village, farm, and ranch between Urhl and the border has been keeping tabs on you. We knew you would be near Manyalan the day before you arrived."

"So if you knew of my whereabouts, it stands to reason so did Neuss's men—the same ones who probably attacked that young woman," said Solace. She felt sick to her stomach. Had she led Neuss's goons to this village?

"Aye," agreed Hossin. "And since you're more of a threat to old Neuss than anyone other than King Rhees himself, you're naturally a target—you, and anyone associated with you—even Manyalans who offered you hospitality."

Solace shook her head. "Me? A threat to Neuss?"

"Of course you're a threat," said Fenwith, "you're the one who brought Neuss down last time. You broke his collarbone and prevented him from killing Rhees. Do you think that old fox has forgotten? Come to think of it, Neuss might even have a bounty on your head."

"Which he could only pay if he escaped the hangman's noose," added Hossin.

Solace pursed her lips as she peered at the mayhem all around her. She was the root cause of all this? "This ends now! We will rescue Emmaline Wellsun and the girls, and we will take down Neuss once and for all!"

"Neuss could be setting a trap for us," said Evryst, his black kit slung over his shoulder. Solace hadn't noticed when he'd joined them, but he knew about the kidnappings and had more details about the attack on the village, which occurred an hour after the posse had left town. The raiders wasted little time setting buildings on fire and terrorizing the residents. While everyone was distracted, several men broke into the orphanage and snatched Emmaline, Bekkah, and Lissah.

Solace nodded. "I think you may be right. But Neuss is also sending a message." Thugs had trafficked in women and girls during the ex-king's reign. Solace had nearly fallen victim herself, but Rhees had stopped the men in time. Gang activity had slowed dramatically after Neuss's capture, but not any longer. "Now that Neuss is free to roam these hills once more, his ruffians are back in business, and they want everyone to know."

"But even if it's a trap—we're still going after Emmaline and the girls—right?" Hossin asked anxiously.

"Of course," said Solace, "but we need a plan."

"And some idea of where to start looking," added Evryst.

Bray had been lingering, an empty water bucket in his hand. "I have an idea."

Evryst nodded at the young man. "All thoughts are welcome."

"The kidnappers need a place to secure Miss Emmaline

and the girls, and they need to move about quickly without being seen." Bray glanced around. "The mines are the perfect hideout, if you're already familiar with them.

"And an absolute rat's nest if you're not," grumbled Hossin.

"Our friend, Wilhm Imyns, knows the mines better than anyone," exclaimed Bray, who'd grown up around his brother Behn's two best friends, Wilhm and Rhees.

Solace knew Bray could be starry-eyed around both older men, but he was also correct. Wilhm had worked in the mines for years to support Maysel and their boys. "I'm sure Wilhm would want to help," Solace said, "but it'll take too long to ride to your farm and bring him back. Besides, we're going to need more than Wilhm if this is a trap."

Evryst waved the towel he was holding at the sky. "I agree we can't wait for Wilhm's arrival—although I'd like to have him as backup, in case we need to thoroughly search the mines. In the meantime, I could raise a general alarm."

"How?" Solace arched an eyebrow at the middle-aged monk, who wasn't making any sense. He was probably in dire need of a hearty meal and pint of ale. They'd ridden hard to return to Manyalan when they spotted the smoke and hadn't eaten since breakfast.

"Peerless Petrie and Daring Dahlia."

Solace's eyes widened. "But are they reliable?"

"Better than a herald, and faster too. I'll need to write a short, identical message for each bird, secure it to their leg, and release them. If our pigeons leave tonight, my Tor brethren will receive the news by morning. I'll ask them to join us in the search for Neuss and to send word to Wilhm at the farm, requesting his aid."

"They'll need to know where to meet up with us," pointed out Fenwith.

"The kidnappers can't afford to be in the open for very long," said Evryst. "What mines are fairly close, about a day's ride from here?"

Solace mentally reviewed the maps she'd been studying; had it been only that morning? "If they're heading east toward Urhl, which is likely, then it's got to be Oressa Cave. Several large mines and a smattering of smaller ones operate inside that cave system."

Hossin agreed. "Aye, Oressa is known for its large deposits of gold ore." He snapped his fingers. "But one of the veins stopped producing last year, and that mine's been abandoned."

Solace glanced at Evryst, who nodded. "Sounds promising as a hideout." He and Hossin worked out the optimal meeting spot for the Tor monks to congregate, and then Evryst left to write out his instructions for Peerless Petrie and Daring Dahlia to deliver.

While the innkeeper's wife organized temporary homes for Emmaline Wellsun's orphans, the women with intact kitchens went to work. Soon, blankets were spread out like a patchwork quilt up and down the street, and everyone— the newly homeless, the bereaved, and Solace and her friends—were invited to eat the hastily prepared meal of hot vegetable-barley soup, crusty bread, and hard cheese. The tavern owner contributed several kegs, serving ale to the thirsty crowd. The only thing missing was a nice cup of tea.

After the meal, Solace, Fenwith, Chelyss, and Peka followed the innkeeper back to the inn. Although the interior smelled smoky, it was undamaged. Evryst, as the master healer of the group, suggested everyone try to get some rest before they set out in the morning to track down Mrs. Wellsun and the children. Hossin had objected, until Evryst reminded him even the kidnappers would have to sleep at some point, and they couldn't mount a rescue without rest and reinforcements.

Solace knew she wouldn't be able to fall asleep right away. She tossed her leather cloak around her shoulders, crept down the stairs, and slipped out of the inn's front door. She needed fresh air, without the acrid smokiness clinging to everything inside the village. Solace walked to the crossroad where she'd stood that morning and announced her decision to remain in Toresz.

Stars twinkled in the dark dome of the sky, and the moon shone down on the pebbly soil. Small desert flowers hugged the road, their tiny blooms shut tightly until morning. Solace turned toward the eastern hills, in the direction of Urhl and the palace—and Rhees. She wanted to see him, yearned with all her heart to hear his voice, to feel the touch of his hand, his lips. *Stop this madness! Rhees is beyond your reach.*

Solace started back toward the inn; she needed to get some sleep before morning. As she walked, she kept her eyes on the moonlit ground, and stooped to retrieve something from the sandy soil. Straightening again, she fingered her prize—a smooth, flat stone, perfect for slinging—before dropping it into her pouch.

CHAPTER 19

"It's deathly quiet—are you sure they're down there?" asked Hossin for the third time in the past hour.

Solace sat between Fenwith and Evryst, tucked into a crevice on a bluff overlooking Oressa Cave. The three of them shared Evryst's spyglass and took turns training it on the opposite hillside. Hossin, too restless to sit, paced behind them. The waxing moon cast just enough light to see shapes and shadows. Chelyss and the Manyalan posse —minus the hostler's daughter and tavern owner's son, who'd stayed behind to help with the cleanup—waited with the horses at the bottom of the crag, ready to pursue anyone fleeing the cave.

They'd ridden the entire day and half the night, arriving after midnight at the steep peak that served as their lookout post. Evryst expected most of the Tor brethren by the next afternoon, but Wilhm wouldn't arrive until later from Peka's farm, far too late for the blacksmith's impatient son. Hossin had wanted to storm the mine immediately upon their arrival, until Evryst reminded him that was the surest way of getting someone killed, probably Emmaline or one of the children.

Evryst nodded patiently, providing the same answer he had twenty minutes earlier. "When Danyss and Devlan crept to the mine entrance the first time, they heard girls' voices coming from inside the cave."

"But they didn't hear Emmaline." Hossin's voice wobbled.

"She may simply be asleep. Don't lose heart." Solace didn't relay what Evryst told her: Danyss and Devlan had heard girls *crying* inside the cave, but no other sounds. And no other voices either.

Alyn, Danyss, and Devlan had returned to the cave, joined by Peka and her sons. They planned to split into two teams and work their way into the abandoned mine using Oressa's vast set of tunnels. Although they wished for Wilhm's expertise, they feared waiting too long to rescue the girls. Hossin wanted to accompany them, but Evryst had convinced the blacksmith's son his skills were better suited to apprehending kidnappers rather than stealth and spying.

Solace raised the spyglass to her eye and scanned the rock-strewn base of the opposite hillside, searching for any movement in or out of the cave. Hossin cleared his throat, but she hissed, "I hear someone coming!"

She aimed the spyglass at the entrance to the abandoned mine. "Look!" Two small figures dashed out of the cave with Peka right on their heels. Raising her arms to the sky, Peka crossed them over her head and waved several times, the all-clear signal. Behn and Bray exited last, carrying a limp body between them.

The blacksmith's son shrieked, "Emmaline!" and scrambled down the pebbly bluff, nearly tumbling over in his haste. Solace, Fenwith, and Evryst followed behind him more slowly, picking their way in the dark.

Peka stepped in front of Hossin and placed her hand on his massive chest. "She's alive but hurt. Brother Evryst needs to examine her injuries. I promise to call you as soon as he's finished. Go with Fenwith and tell the others the kidnappers have fled, and we have the girls and Miss Emmaline."

Hossin whispered, "But will she live?"

"Go now," replied Peka. Hossin nodded, his face a mask of grief as he followed Fenwith and Peka's sons.

Evryst had retrieved his healer's kit earlier, when Danyss and Devlan had told him of the crying girls. He dropped to his knees next to Emmaline Wellsun and lifted her arm to check for a pulse. "Quick—I need a torch. I can barely see."

"On it." Peka dashed back into the cave.

Solace saw why Peka had stopped Hossin from coming any closer. Emmaline's face was battered and swollen, and a long gash on her forehead had crusted over. The top of her dress was ripped, revealing cuts and bruises along her neck and collarbone.

Solace's stomach lurched as she fell to her knees next to Emmaline. "What can I do?"

Evryst glanced up, his eyes in shadow. "Hold her hand for now. She needs to know she is safe." Nodding, Solace gripped Emmaline's hand.

Peka returned with a couple of sticks as thick as her arm. "These were near the entrance, but we need to light them."

Lissah, who'd been softly crying next to Bekkah, hiccupped and stepped forward. "I can light 'em, ma'am. Please stack 'em on th' ground, like so."

"But how—" said Peka.

Bekkah swiped at her eyes and sniffled. "Lissah's fire-gifted. Auntie Emmie won't be mindin' if it's an emergency."

Lissah grasped the wood and began humming, sparks flying from her fingers. The young girl lifted her voice to the sky, warbling and hissing, until the thick sticks caught fire. Peka gasped, her eyes widening. Evryst, who'd seen his fire-gifted friend, Tabetta, wield burning wood in her hands, merely nodded his thanks.

Peka and Bekkah held up the flaming torches as Lissah cradled her hands to her chest. Solace helped Evryst clean the cuts on Emmaline's face and neck before they rolled her onto her side, where they discovered a bump the size of a robin's egg under her matted hair. While Evryst used bronze scissor-blades to trim the hair from Emmaline's scalp, Solace peered through his healer's kit, selecting two jars. She prepared a tincture of honey and vinegar to disinfect the lacerations. As Solace spread the mixture over the lump on the back of Emmaline's head, Evryst withdrew a rolled ball of cobwebs from his kit. He pressed it over the wound and then wrapped Emmaline's head in a clean strip of cotton.

They carefully rolled her onto her back again, and Solace gently applied the same solution to the cuts on Emmaline's face and neck. Evryst examined the rest of the woman's torso, arms, and legs, and he used his long, silver tube to listen to her heartbeat, which was slower than it should be, but he attributed that to her concussion.

When Evryst finished, he insisted on inspecting both girls, who were uninjured other than a few cuts and bruises, and Lissah's burned, puckered hands, which would heal on their own. Solace considered what she knew about both girls; Lissah, who was obviously fire-gifted and claimed to be Bekkah's cousin, and Bekkah, who dreamed about maps and called Emmaline Wellsun her auntie.

She asked Lissah, "Miss Emmaline is your mum, isn't she?" When the young girl nodded, Solace turned to Bekkah. "And your aunt?"

Bekkah said, "Aye, but 'tis a secret."

"Because all three of you are gifted." Solace stated it as a fact, which neither child disputed. "You can divine for water, can't you?"

Bekkah nodded, adding, "And Auntie is like Lissah. No one else, not e'en Mister Hossin, knows."

Lissah whispered, "But Mum was goin' ta tell 'im soon."

"Thank you for trusting us with the truth," said Evryst. "And now go on with Miss Peka. We'll take good care of Miss Emmaline." Peka guided the two girls to the other side of the bluff, where Hossin and the others were eagerly awaiting news.

Evryst waited until the children were out of earshot and then pointed at the tincture in Solace's hand. His curiosity evident, he asked, "Where did you learn to mix honey and vinegar together for an antiseptic? Most people rely on saline water or a tincture of white sage."

"From Brother Tomyss's book on healing."

"Ah," said Evryst, "he would be pleased to know how well you've studied the books he gave you."

"I only wish..." Solace stopped herself from saying it aloud.

"Only wish what?" prodded the monk.

"That Tomyss had written an ironclad marital contract."

Evryst nodded. "It certainly would have saved us all from a lot of upheaval—and you from a great deal of angst and heartache. But Tomyss would never have forged your father's signature, and there's the rub."

"I figured as much. Too bad he couldn't have foreseen this mess and avoided it altogether."

Evryst furrowed his brow. "Oh, I wouldn't be so sure about that. Tomyss was the most astute man I've ever known. I'm sure he grasped the potential complications, and he would have known about Prince Heris and Crown Princess MaudeLyn's betrothal."

That hadn't occurred to Solace. "But then Tomyss must have expected the truth to come out eventually."

"I'm sure he did—and Tomyss would have trusted you and Rhees to figure out how to address it."

"And now it's too late."

"Is it really?" asked Evryst. "I believe that depends on you and Rhees, and in the end, what you decide to do."

Now Evryst was starting to sound like Rebezza, using fuzzy language about the future. Solace refrained from an eye roll. "Which decision, precisely?"

"Whether to forgive Rhees and take him back, when the time comes."

"But... but..." sputtered Solace. "Rhees is legally obligated to MaudeLyn."

"Aye, 'tis true. Although I believe with the right incentives, MaudeLyn would agree to an annulment."

"An annulment! Is that even a possibility?"

"Aye, it's quite possible and entirely legal."

Solace stared at Evryst. "Why didn't you or Ghrier speak up about this earlier, back in the library?"

"Because you and Rhees were so emotional, and MaudeLyn and Valyss so adamant, there was simply no way we could negotiate at the time."

Solace blew out an angry puff of air. The more she

thought about it, however, the more she could see Evryst's point. No one could have mediated a settlement in the aftermath of Rhees's crowning and the revelation their marriage wasn't legal. "Even so, I still can't imagine the crown princess ever giving in."

"Really? I'd think she's probably reached her fill by now."

"Her fill?"

"Aye." Evryst cleared his throat. Twice. "Ah...well, to put it succinctly...the king is not an easy man to live with under the best of circumstances, and I expect the crown princess and her brother have not seen Rhees at his best. I would be very surprised if they are not regretting their trip to Toresz and wishing for a way out."

"'Tis true living with Rhees can be challenging." Solace snorted. *And yet I loved every minute of it, every argument and debate, right up to the moment Rhees shouted I was nothing to him.* "But even if MaudeLyn would agree to an annulment, there's one more intractable obstacle—my father. You heard Arik. Soren will never sign the marital contract."

"Oh, I think he will, when you tell him your news. He will want to help."

"I don't have any news for my dad." Solace frowned at Evryst. Maybe the master healer was trying to tell her she'd overtaxed her heart and didn't have long to live. But then why was he smiling?

"Actually, you have quite momentous news, my queen." Evryst hesitated and then gave her a small bow. "You are increasing."

"Increasing?" Solace inhaled sharply. Quickly handing the tincture to Evryst, she turned and stumbled toward the cave behind them. Cradling her stomach, Solace thought of her nauseous mornings and extra fatigue and odd cravings.

Just that morning, she'd awoken from a dream about the orange trees growing in the palace courtyard. She could have sworn she smelled their blossoms.

All of which she'd attributed to her long flight from Urhl, and her sadness at leaving the man she loved. Solace turned back toward Evryst. "You mean to say, er, you're trying to tell me, um, what exactly?" She stopped speaking and waited; she needed Evryst to spell it out for her.

"My dear queen, you are carrying the heir to the throne of Toresz!"

CHAPTER 20

Solace retreated several steps until she felt the wall of the cave at her back. Feeling unmoored and even a little lightheaded, she leaned against the solid rock to anchor herself. A sharp denial sprang to her lips. *"No, you're wrong! It's impossible!"* she started to shout but stopped herself. Of course it was possible.

She and Rhees had spent five glorious weeks together, first visiting Yelosha to see her father and then crisscrossing Toresz, before duty had forced them apart in Urhl. Solace had departed for her water divining trip, and Rhees had remained in the capital to form a new government.

Solace frowned, trying to recall the last occurrence of her monthly courses, which had never been regular. Could it have been before the final battle with Neuss—almost three months ago? She clutched her head. "Oh sun, moon, and stars! How can this be?"

Evryst cleared his throat again, but Solace flapped her hand at him. "Don't answer that. What...what do I do now?"

"You carry on, just as you're doing."

"First things first, you mean." Solace took a deep breath, and then another, forcing herself to calm down. She needed to stop the swirling inside her head and focus. "First, we continue the hunt for Neuss until he's recaptured. Everything else—our future as a nation—hinges on ridding ourselves of his scourge."

"Aye," agreed Evryst.

"Then I...I'll speak with Rhees...and then we'll see."

"Precisely."

"It's not much of plan," Solace objected.

Evryst shrugged. "But it's enough for now."

Solace heard a scraping noise behind her and reached for the knife tucked into her belt. Evryst scurried over to the other side of the cave entrance, a blade in his hands. They both relaxed when Alyn, Danyss, and Devlan emerged from the cave. The monks were vastly relieved to learn Mrs. Wellsun and the children had been rescued.

Hossin chose that moment to dash into the clearing and fall to his knees beside Emmaline with a whimper. Evryst placed a hand on the man's beefy shoulder. "Miss Emmaline will recover, but she requires bedrest until her head injury is completely healed. We need to move her to the closest town. Any suggestions?"

"Aye." Hossin exhaled shakily. "Axelan is nearby, about seven miles, and I have a cousin there who will take us in."

Evryst nodded. "Alright, she'll need to travel slowly, lying down in a basket. Best to leave while it's still dark, so you can arrive before it's too hot. Take the two girls and half the Manyalans with you for protection." Evryst provided Hossin with additional instructions, clean rags for bandages, and the remainder of the antiseptic tincture.

Danyss and Devlan left to strip the branches from a nearby tree, which they'd use to fashion a litter. Meanwhile

Alyn spoke with the villagers, who quickly reassembled into two smaller teams, one to accompany Hossin, Emmaline, and the girls, and the other to remain with Solace and continue the search for Neuss.

After Hossin left for Axelan with Emmaline and the rest of their party, Evryst insisted Solace and her party get some rest. The Manyalans volunteered to take turns sitting watch, while everyone else spread out their bedrolls under the craggy overhang of the giant bluff.

Solace complied without complaint. Her arms and legs were heavy with fatigue, and she was mentally exhausted. As she drifted off, she brought her hands to her stomach, marveling at the tiny life inside her—unplanned and most definitely inconvenient—but not unwanted. Whatever the future held for her, she would do her best for this little one.

Then another a stray thought wandered into her weary brain. *Why had the kidnappers fled without taking their hostages?*

Too tired to work out an answer, Solace rolled onto her side. "I'll have to ask Evryst and Peka about it tomorrow," she murmured to herself before sleep claimed her completely. But when morning arrived a few short hours later, she'd forgotten all about her question.

THE APPOINTED time to meet up with the Tor contingent came and went with no sign of them. With desert animals dozing in the daytime heat and not even a small breeze stirring the gray tumbleweeds and spiky grasses, the hills and plain were eerily still—as if nature had taken a single, great inhalation of breath and then simply held it. By late afternoon, the Manyalan posse was downright jittery.

Even the normally placid Evryst rubbed his bald head anxiously.

Bray and Behn climbed to the top of the bluff with Evryst's spyglass and took turns sweeping the horizon. The Manyalans debated whether to remain or leave to continue the search for Neuss on their own. Chelyss reminded them there was strength in numbers, and they decided to wait a bit longer.

Bray called out, "Hang on—I think there's something out there, coming from the east!"

Behn took the spyglass from his younger brother and fiddled with the viewfinder, everyone impatient for confirmation. Behn carefully scanned the dry, brown plain spread out before them. Finally, he shouted, "There's a small cloud of dust. Looks like riders heading our way."

Brother Alyn ascended the bluff to see for himself. Huffing, he asked, "But are they Tor riders?"

Alyn removed his belt, swords, and navy habit, turning them over to Bray for safekeeping, and climbed a lone cypress hanging precariously over the edge of the crag. Behn handed him the spyglass. Straddling the *V* formed by two tree limbs, Alyn peered in the direction Behn and Bray were pointing. Solace paced around the bottom of the bluff, wondering whether Petrie and Dahlia had delivered the message—and if so, why the reliable warrior-monks were so delayed.

"There are riders, alright, but not nearly enough!" called down Alyn. Everyone groaned and waited until Alyn could provide more details. Some minutes passed. "I count only five of 'em...all wearing Tor robes, plus a couple of extra horses." Alyn climbed down from the tree, donned his habit, strapped on his belt and swords, and descended the hill.

Evryst peered over at his second-in-command, who merely shrugged. Evryst blew out a puff of air and went to his horse, retightening all the straps and ensuring his saddlebags were securely fastened. Solace had never seen Evryst so edgy.

"That's the third time you've adjusted your saddle," pointed out Solace.

Evryst patted his horse's neck. "Something's off."

"Because only a few monks responded to your message?"

"I issued direct orders. I'm sure they responded, but they've been diverted by something else. And then there's the matter of the kidnappers." His voice trailed off.

Solace suddenly remembered the question she'd been pondering when she'd fallen asleep. "You mean why did they run off without Emmaline Wellsun and the children?"

"It makes no sense to me," grunted Evryst. Alyn, Fenwith, Chelyss, and Peka had wandered over, not even pretending to be looking after their own horses. They gathered around Evryst and Solace.

Fenwith crossed her arms, her dark eyes staring at the expanding cloud of dust containing five riders and three extra horses, now plainly visible. "No one snatches women and children and then leaves them behind for no apparent reason."

"Which means they had something else in mind," agreed Peka.

"I don't like it. Feels too much like another of Neuss's schemes," said Chelyss, scratching his gray beard.

Solace considered all the evidence: the raid on the village, timed to occur shortly after she and the posse had left Manyalan; the fires and kidnapping, which had lured them toward Oressa; and now the tardy and altogether insufficient response by Evryst's monks. "This all adds up to one monstrous distraction," she blurted out. "Neuss's thugs wanted to keep us occupied and out of the way, while the main action is happening elsewhere."

Chelyss slapped his thigh. "I think you're spot on."

"Unfortunately," said Evryst, "I have to agree."

"But why should they bother?" Solace frowned and spread open her hands, palms out. "We are small in number."

Evryst gave her a wry smile. "But big in heart—and impact. Neuss knows when you and Rhees combine forces, you're practically unstoppable. I'm convinced the ambush in the Andressa foothills was an assassination attempt on you. Neuss's men would have tried again, but for whatever reason, they decided against another direct attack. Instead, they did the next best thing. They slowed you down."

Bray stood behind Peka, listening to every word. "Why don't Behn and I ride out to greet the monks. The sooner we know what's happening, the faster we can prepare for what's next."

Solace shook her head. "We need to make a visual identification of those riders before anyone approaches. Just because they appear to be wearing navy habits does not make them Tor monks."

Evryst agreed. "Well said. We wait."

Peka scolded her youngest son for eavesdropping, but Bray just gave her an impish grin. "You'd do the same, Mum, and you know it."

She chuckled but didn't deny it. "I confess I'm anxious to hear any news and won't rest easy until Neuss is found."

They waited until Alyn, still using the spyglass, shouted, "It's alright—they're ours! I see Josaph, Lamkin, and three novices whose names I don't rightly recall."

While Danyss and Devlan saddled up and rode out to greet their Tor brethren, Behn and Giulia, the Manyalan innkeeper's daughter, began preparing the evening meal. It was nearly dusk by the time the monks arrived.

A heavily-stooped, white-bearded monk named Josaph appeared to be the leader. He accepted a swig from Alyn's hip flask with a grateful nod, bowed low to Solace, and then raised his sorrowful brown eyes to her. Pounding his chest with his fist, he cried out, "I'm sorra ta bring ye such sad tidin's. Our dear 'n glorious leader, King Rhees of Toresz, is dead!"

CHAPTER 21

Solace's heart and head both hurt, and sharp little prickles stabbed her back. She had no idea why she was staring up at the dusky sky, or why all her friends were peering down at her from such a great height.

"Step back, please—she needs some air," said Evryst hoarsely.

Solace frowned. She didn't need air; after all, she was still breathing. What she needed was to remember what it was the old monk had said right before she'd passed out.

"Oh!" Solace brought her hand to her trembling mouth as tears leaked from the corners of her eyes. "Oh, no...it can't be." Then she heard Fenwith keening somewhere behind her, Peka crying softly, and Chelyss sniffling, and she knew it must be true.

Evryst crouched down beside Solace. He carefully probed her head and neck before rocking back onto his heels. "You're very lucky. You fainted in a patch of grass that broke your fall." Evryst gently eased her up to a seated position.

Tears continued streaking down Solace's face. She

shook her head. "Not lucky, never lucky again...now that Rhees...is gone." She dropped her face into her palms and wailed. Deep, wracking sobs shook her shoulders and hurt her chest. Her heart exploded in a starburst of agony, and she crossed her arms in a vain attempt to stop the pain.

Solace's sobs eventually turned into harsh, painful hiccups. She heard Fenwith still crying, although more softly, and Peka sniffling into a handkerchief. Evryst, his voice thick with emotion, asked Josaph to tell them what had happened. Solace remained on the ground, her knees tucked up to her chest, her cheeks wet and her nose running.

As she listened to the old monk, Solace's thoughts revolved around the same refrain: *Rhees is dead. Rhees is dead. Rhees is dead.* And then: *I can't go on. I can't do this alone. I can't raise Rhees's child without him.* Solace glanced eastward, toward Tor Mountain and Urhl. *I'll stay right here on this rocky ground until my skin falls off and my bones melt into the earth, until I fade to nothing, until I am nothing but dry, brown, Toreszan dust.*

Solace tried again to concentrate on the ancient monk's account. The old man took another swallow from Alyn's hip flask. "It's been chaotic-like since yer departure, Brother Evryst. Yer already aware of th' coronation and pronouncement about 'Queen MaudeLyn.' Ev'rybody knows she ain't th' real queen!"

Josaph paused to spit on the ground. "Even so, the northern princess an' her kingly brother started poppin' up ev'rywhere all ov'a sudden, givin' speeches filled wi' hot air, handin' out worthless baubles to th' children. But King Rhees remained secluded. Rumors had it he permitted jest th' chancellor an' head o' th' guard into his chambers. The king emerged only for Neuss's trial an' sentencing, which occurred inside th' keep—so no one beyond th' palace walls has seen King Rhees since th' coronation.

"Folks nat'relly became concerned 'n a bit unruly. And ev'rywhere MaudeLyn and Valyss of Censarra went, fist-fights broke out. Th' people started booing th' royal siblings, demandin' to see their rightful king an' queen—that would be King Rhees an' you, Queen Solace." Josaph paused to give Solace another bow. "Then in an instant, ev'rythin' changed." Here the elderly monk had a coughing jag that lasted a full minute. His eyes watering, Josaph waved at Lamkin. With a narrow fringe of silver hair encircling his bald pate, and his extreme near-sightedness, Lamkin appeared every bit as aged as his fellow monk.

Lamkin bowed from his shoulders and picked up the tale from Josaph. "Whilst th' palace guards were transferrin' ole Neuss to the gallows, a scuffle broke out. We later learnt a third o' th' men on duty that day 'ad once worked fer Neuss. They killed er injured th' other guards—'n helped th' scoundrel escape!

"Well, our king Rhees was mighty angry, rightfully so, 'n he decided to go after ole Neuss himself, along with 'is loyal knights 'n soldiers. Th' king demanded 'is brother-in-law, King Valyss, accompany him, prob'ly 'cause he didna trust the Censarran enough to leave 'im unsupervised in th' palace. Apparently th' princess refused ta stay behin', claimin' she feared th' staff would poison 'er if she remained." Lamkin rolled his eyes. "About dis time, th' king sent us word, commandin' all Tor monks ta aid in th' capture of Neuss 'n his followers."

"All the monks?" interrupted Evryst.

"Aye, excep' for th' younges' novices, those under fifteen—'n old timers like me 'n Josaph," said Lamkin.

Josaph piped up, "Plus Arneld 'n Bently. But they cain't

even set in th' saddle no more. So, when th' pigeons arrived with yer message, Brother Evryst, we 'ad a choice ta make—ride out 'ere 'n meet up with you, or ride t' Miss Peka's farm to seek Mister Wilhm. We figured we'd best come to see you."

"Then who's looking after the monastery and all our livestock?" asked Alyn.

"Arneld, Bently, 'n the rest o' th' novices," replied Lamkin.

A pained expression crossed Evryst's face, but he waved his hand. "Alright, please continue."

Josaph had stopped coughing by then, so he described how the warrior-monks of the Tor Order rode out with the king and the rest of the soldiers and knights from the palace. Rhees decided to split up his forces, since he had two promising leads on Neuss's whereabouts. He sent half the knights, soldiers, and monks, who were known for their exceptional skills with the longbow and sword, with Sir Kryss to search for Neuss in the Andressa Mountain range. Meanwhile, the rest of the brethren accompanied Rhees and his army into the foothills west of Tor Mountain, where they encountered Neuss and his makeshift militia.

"Th' fightin' was somethin' fierce, wi' heavy casualties on both sides," said Josaph. "After a two-day battle, our dear king was mort'ly wounded—took an arrow in his heart. Even th' northern princess was heard to be wailin' about th' king's untimely death."

The monks subsided into silence, and Solace forced herself to stand on shaking legs. Her voice sounded harsh and distant, as if someone else were speaking. "Everything, up until the last part, makes a cruel kind of sense. But there's no conceivable way Crown Princess MaudeLyn would have been mourning over Rhees."

Evryst glanced up at the sun setting over the western hills, pursed his lips, and sighed. "I agree, which begs the question: who actually witnessed the battle, so we may question them?"

One of the novices stepped forward and dropped his cowl, which had been obscuring his face. Solace stifled a gasp when she saw a long, angry, pink scar zigzag from the right side of his forehead near his hairline, cut across the bridge of his nose and down his cheek, and end somewhere behind his left ear. The young man, who appeared to be about Solace's age, was fortunate to have retained both his eyes.

He bowed to Evryst and Solace. "I was there, in the foothills west of Tor Mountain."

"Brother Maximyss, I believe?" asked Evryst.

"Aye, sir, though even my mum used to shorten it to Max."

"Very well, Brother Max," said Evryst. "Since you were in the foothills with the king's troops, how did you come to be here?"

"I'm the fastest rider, sir, so Brother Calvryss sent me back to the monastery with the news that King Rhees had fallen. He sent a second messenger to Sir Kryss to inform him and request his assistance."

"Max intra'cpted us as we were leavin' 'n offer't ta come along. We gave 'im a fresh 'orse 'n 'ere we are," explained Josaph.

"Did you see the king actually fall?" Solace addressed her question to the scarred novice, her eyes watering again.

"No, ma'am," replied Brother Max "I was too far away. I'm a bowman and spent most of the battle firing arrows from my perch in the hills. But I saw the fighting, and our side taking the worst of it."

"How did you come to hear King Rhees had been struck by an arrow?" While Solace didn't want to give herself any false hope, she needed to confirm the accuracy of Max's account.

"Some of the injured knights told Brother Calvryss we'd suffered heavy casualties, and the king had fallen along with the rest. Plus, there was a lot of wailing that even I could hear. Everyone said it must be the princess, who'd been helping the healers inside the field tents." Max folded his hands and waited, as if ready to offer up a prayer for the dead.

Solace's heart sank even further. She knew Rhees would have been right up front, trying to hold the line where the fighting was fiercest. Unfortunately, Max's account had the ring of truth, except for the part about the princess. Solace couldn't quite imagine MaudeLyn helping the healers or weeping over Rhees, unless it somehow would make her look better.

Solace took a shaky breath and swiped her eyes with the back of her hand. "All of this occurred near Tor Mountain?"

"Aye, ma'am." Max nodded.

"And that is the last known sighting of Neuss as well?" she asked.

"Aye," he replied.

Solace looked down at the ground and winced at the fresh pain radiating through her chest, the ache drilling deeper than her physical injuries ever could, piercing to her very core. She'd encountered the gnawing ache of grief once before, when her mother had died. But this was even worse. This time, she couldn't imagine going on, raising Rhees's child without him. For despite Rhees's bitterness at her departure, Solace had no doubt he had loved her until the end, and he would have cherished their baby.

Everyone appeared to be waiting. The old monks shuffled their feet. Max pulled his cowl back up. Fenwith snuffled. Solace thought they might be waiting for her to say something more, something profound that would rally them, but Solace had no words left. She had nothing left to give. Toresz had taken and taken and taken from her.

Finally, Evryst cleared his throat. "My queen," he said gently, "is it your wish that we search for Neuss in the Tor foothills? That we aid in his recapture?"

"Or his prompt execution," spat out Peka.

"The Tor foothills you say?" Solace closed her eyes against the pain and another onslaught of tears. She had trouble concentrating.

"Aye," said Evryst.

Solace blinked her eyes open; she had to make an effort. She recalled the peculiar salute of her adopted homeland and decided to start there. Pounding her achy chest with her fist, Solace flung her five fingers out into the air like a bird in flight. Everyone else responded by pounding their chests and then flicking their fingers.

Solace hiccupped. "Then that is where we shall go next," she whispered, "to ensure Neuss pays for this latest, and most egregious, shedding of innocent blood. And to bury my husband and my king."

Her voice choked when she got to the last part, when she said "to bury my husband" aloud.

CHAPTER 22

Solace sensed a shroud of sadness, tinged with an undercurrent of fear, settle over the group. Even normally rambunctious Bray had subsided into morose silence. She wasn't the only one mourning Rhees that night. But her grief was dark and deep and raw, and she couldn't cope with anyone else's. She turned toward the horses, thinking to pull down her tent.

"My queen," said Evryst, attempting to draw her back to the present. "Shall we establish a watch in short, two-hour shifts and then rotate?"

Solace waved her hand dismissively. "Might as well."

"And then shall we leave for the foothills of Tor Mountain at first light?" Evryst persisted.

Solace exhaled in a long, wobbly huff. "Sounds about right."

She stumbled toward the horses again, but Behn intercepted her. "I've set your tent up, over here." He took her arm to guide her.

Solace mumbled her thanks, and Behn dipped his head in acknowledgment. "'Tis nothing. I only wish…"

Solace paused, her hand on the flap, her legs ready to give out from under her. She didn't want any more conversations or condolences. She wanted to close her eyes and blot out everything. But one of Rhees's boyhood friends was standing before her, grief-stricken as well. "I'm listening."

"I wish we'd killed Neuss when we had the chance."

Solace blinked slowly. Behn's words echoed those of High Magus Rebezza. What Behn really meant was he wished Solace had killed Neuss with her sling when she had the perfect shot.

"Aye," she said softly. "But that alone might not have been enough to stop this uprising and save Rhees. Look at how many followers Neuss has garnered through his years of graft and greed. Someone else would have stepped in, sooner or later, to disrupt everything Rhees and you and I have fought so hard for."

"You're saying there will always be another Neuss, always another villain who opposes us," said Behn.

Solace shrugged. "I suppose there might be short periods of peace and prosperity, but then someone will get greedy again. In the end, I think good people must always be on guard and prepared."

"That's a rather dismal view."

Lifting the flap, she said, "Goodnight, Behn," and crawled into her lonely, narrow, canvas shelter. She pulled off her boots, rolled up her cloak, and curled onto her side. She didn't have long to wait for the tears to start flowing again.

Solace was awake before the birds started twittering to each other, while it was still dark and chilly. For the first few moments, she forgot Rhees was gone. When her head cleared, the heavy weight of remembrance threatened to crush her.

She decided to roll over rather than rise. She would stay in her tent that day. And maybe the next day as well. *Let someone else take over and find Neuss*, she thought. *Let someone else lead the poor, downtrodden people of Toresz. Let someone else try to do the right thing, and keep doing it, day after day, only to lose everything. I have nothing left but my own heartache.*

It wasn't Evryst this time, but Fenwith, who forced Solace back to the present and intruded on her grief. Crouching low, Fenwith pulled back the tent flap and handed Solace a battered tin mug filled with hot coffee. Solace noted the stoop of the older woman's shoulders, her gray hair pulled back in a less-than-tidy bun. They'd not yet spoken of Rhees—the two women who'd loved him most.

Fenwith squeezed herself into the tent and pulled a second tin mug through the tent's opening. Fenwith sat cross-legged on the ground, raised the mug to her lips, and sipped her coffee. Then she inhaled shakily and sniffed. "You need to get up and lead us out of here," she said matter-of-factly. "No one else can do it, lass, er, my queen. You're all we have left."

Solace pushed herself up, gripped the hot mug by the handle, and took a long swallow. "I can't do it."

"Of course you can. One foot in front of the other. You're a girl of the hills; you know how it's done. Must keep moving. Must keep busy." Fenwith stifled a sob.

Solace grasped Fenwith's arm and whispered, "I can't believe he's truly gone."

Fenwith shook her head. "I won't believe Rhees is dead until I see him laid out before me," she said, her voice quaking. "I must touch his wounds myself. Nothing else will do."

"Aye." Based on Brother Max's account of the battle, Solace had no reason to think anything other than the absolute worst. But she wouldn't say that to Fenwith.

"It's nearly first light. I'll step out so you can get ready," said Fenwith, taking both tin mugs with her.

Solace rubbed her bleary, puffy eyes and gave in to Fenwith's need, and the needs of everyone else. *Fine,* she thought, *I can't bring Rhees back, but I* can *stop Neuss. Everything else, even my grief, can wait.*

Solace dressed, her fingers sweeping over the finely-woven, gold mesh fabric of her Magian vest. She silently rolled up her bedding, broke down her tent, and loaded her gear onto one of the pack horses. She wandered over to Jenx, patted his neck, and told him they both needed to be brave. "We're facing our toughest battle yet," she murmured. "And this time, we're doing it alone, without Rhees riding Zirott alongside us."

Jenx turned his head and nuzzled her hair, a comforting gesture. She rubbed his nose and then offered him a dried apple ring. For a massive war horse, Jenx was quite dainty as he accepted the treat from her hand. Solace heard the shuffle of footsteps behind her and turned.

Max, the scarred novitiate, bowed. "Pardon me, Queen Solace, but I couldn't help overhearing. And I wanted to provide assurances you're not alone. In fact, I'd wager more Toreszans are willing to take up arms now against Neuss than before the rebellion."

"Oh? Why do you say that?" Solace fingered her slings. She secured one around her waist, just above the leather belt holding her dagger and scabbard, her pouch of stones, and a small healing kit. She tied her second sling around her forehead.

"Because of our sorely lamented king Rhees," replied

Max, "and because of you. For the first time in a decade, our people have tasted freedom from fear, false imprisonment, and hanging for 'crimes' as innocuous as searching for fresh water."

He pointed to his damaged face. "Which is how I gained this memento. I'd been helping my sister, who was divining for a new well location, when Neuss's thugs came upon us. We didn't know digging a new well had been declared illegal. And because I attempted to fight back, they scored my face so I'd never forget them, and then beat us both to death, or nearly so in my case.

"I prayed that my sister, who'd just weaned her first-born, would escape. But they killed her and left me, an eight-year-old boy, on the side of the road for the vultures to pick over. By the time I'd managed to drag myself home, our other sister had fled. She must have heard about the attack, assumed the worst, and left with the baby. I never saw either of them again."

Max held up his hand at the dismayed look on Solace's face. "I am not seeking sympathy. My story is no different from hundreds of others. I can't think of a single family of my acquaintance—or any of my Tor brethren—who haven't suffered under Neuss's regime, and who didn't rejoice at his sentencing. And now we are angry yet again, and saddened by renewed losses, and ready to fight back, even unto death."

Solace slipped her arms into her vambraces as she considered Max's story. Was he right? Were more Toreszans ready to take up arms? Last time, Rhees's friends and followers, many of them desperate for change and impoverished by Neuss's skullduggery, had joined them. But most Toreszans had remained on the sidelines, probably rooting for their success, but unwilling to make any sacrifices themselves. Although they'd managed to defeat Neuss, neither Solace nor Rhees had had any doubts they'd been remarkably lucky, and their victory was fragile at best.

"I'm sorry, Max, for what you've already suffered and for what's yet to come. And while I'm heartened to hear more Toreszans are willing to help us, I'm not sure how we can mobilize them in time. If we're going to stop Neuss, we must go after him now, before he has a chance to solidify his power base and rise up, even stronger than before." Solace patted Jenx's rump and flexed her shoulders.

Despite the heaviness inside her chest, her back injury was mostly healed, and her nausea was at bay. She scrambled backward half a dozen paces, ran toward the bay stallion, and vaulted onto his back.

"Dam—ah, I mean darn!" exclaimed Max. "I've heard about your mount but couldn't quite imagine it."

Max jumped when Brother Evryst clapped a hand on his shoulder. "It's time to move out, son."

"Aye, sir. I was just explaining to Queen Solace that we're at a crossroad."

Solace peered down at Max. There was that word again. "A crossroad?"

He nodded. "With a bit of coordination, I'll bet, um..." Max looked at Evryst, whose black eyebrows had shot up when he mentioned "betting." The young monk took a deep breath and tried again. "I believe we can muster a small army of wily, willing Toreszans—and quickly too."

"But Rhees had a trained army and look what happened," said Solace hoarsely, her eyes tearing up.

"That's just it—they were good knights and soldiers in the traditional sense—but they didn't know how to fight dirty!" exclaimed Max.

"Fight dirty? I don't like the sound of that, Brother

Maximyss." Evryst folded his arms across his chest, a stern expression on his face. "Please explain."

Max waved his hands in the air. "It's just what I call it, because Neuss's men are tricksome. Unlike our knights, who lined up in proper formation and fought out in the open, Neuss's army was more cunning. They lulled our side into thinking victory was assured because of their smaller numbers on the battlefield—but that was all a ruse. Half of Neuss's men hid in the hills and caves, attacking us from the sides, from behind, from everywhere all at once. And they used slingers too, like our queen did during the revolt. Neuss beat us because he kept surprising us."

Solace listened intently to Max's explanation. When he finished, she swiped at the tears on her face and said, "These are some of the tactics my father used during the Yeloshan campaigns—he called it monkey warfare—it's a way to even the odds by surprising your enemy." She glanced at Evryst. "We did some of the same things during the rebellion, if you recall."

"Aye. I'm not opposed." Evryst rubbed his bald head and addressed Max. "You mentioned an idea for mustering more support for our cause?"

Max bounced on the balls of his feet excitedly. "Aye, sir. I propose splitting off from you and the queen. I figure I can take the other novices with me, and we'll serve as heralds—the queen's heralds—riding into every town and village between here and Tor Mountain, with a call for volunteers. Sort of like the king's heralds did before, only we'll ask for anyone with a knife or sling or bow or pitchfork to come help us. And we'll tell them we're going to be fighting like... um...like monkeys!"

Jenx snorted, as if in agreement with the plan, and Solace leaned over to pat his neck. "It's going to take too long if you plan to stop in every town between here and Tor Mountain," she said, slowly warming to Max's idea. "I suppose we could send out two groups of 'queen's heralds.' You could take the towns on the northern side of the Urhl-Shulamorn turnpike, and another team could visit the towns to the south."

Evryst scratched his beard thoughtfully and finally shrugged. "It's as good a plan as any. I'll go tell the others, and we'll ask for volunteers to serve as these heralds."

Solace watched as Evryst explained the plan, as Behn and Bray argued with Peka and Fenwith, the Tor monks conferred with the other novitiates, and the Manyalans whispered among themselves. It wasn't long before Giulia stepped forward and bowed to Solace. "Due to Neuss's machinations—the fire and attack on our village, and the kidnapping of Miss Emmaline and the children—we're down to five Manyalans from our original posse of fourteen. My friends wish to serve as your heralds, ma'am, but they have appointed me to remain with you. I shall represent Manyalan when we are victorious against Neuss!"

The Manyalans applauded, and so did the young monks, and Behn and Bray, until Evryst shouted, "Thank you for your service and sacrifice—your bravery shall be recorded in our annals. And now, please reassemble into two teams and then listen to Queen Solace, who will dictate her message to you."

Solace dismounted to personally thank each volunteer, and then she relayed aloud what she'd been composing inside her head. This was her first official proclamation without Rhees by her side, and she wanted to get it right. She debated what to call herself, finally settling on her proper, legal name—if her marital contract had been valid.

"Thus proclaims Her Royal Highness, Solace Blu Orillya,

Water Witch Queen of Toresz: 'Fugitive Neuss Axium Orillya is killing our families, friends, and neighbors. Neuss is bent on destroying our kingdom, and I will not rest until he is defeated. If you are willing to help, gather your weapons, your courage, and your wits—and inform my heralds, who shall provide further instructions."

Once she confirmed her new heralds could repeat back her message, Solace explained what she wanted them to do when they arrived in the Tor foothills with their new recruits. Her voice shaking, she recited the old hill blessing, with everyone else joining in. "May you traverse these hills in safety, may you find rest when you are weary, and may your labors be honored and your water be plenty."

Fenwith and Chelyss came alongside her to watch as the Manyalans and novices rode away. "We'd best leave now too. The sooner we reach Tor Valley, the sooner we can bring Rhees home," said Chelyss, his voice gruff with emotion. His brow was a mass of furrows, and his shoulders sloped downward. Solace was aghast at how much older he seemed, as if losing his nephew had aged him overnight.

"Home to the palace?" asked Solace, her voice cracking. She'd kept it together while instructing the heralds, but all she really wanted to do was collapse into a heap.

Chelyss shook his head. "Rhees may have been King of Toresz, but he had two great loves—the hills of his boyhood home in Shulamorn—and you, his dear queen."

"Besides, Rhees would balk at a fancy sendoff, especially after the debacle of his coronation, when he gained the crown and lost you," said Fenwith, dabbing her eyes with her handkerchief.

Solace's mouth quivered as she fought for composure.

"Then let's go bring Rhees home," she whispered. Turning and running toward Jenx, she leapt onto her stallion's back for the second time that morning. And not a moment too soon; once she landed, Solace's eyes brimmed with fresh tears, blurring her vision.

CHAPTER 23

HIGH CIRRUS CLOUDS OCCASIONALLY SCUTTLED ACROSS THE SUN, granting horse and rider alike some welcome relief throughout the day, and the stars shone brightly on them as they traveled at night. Solace maintained a good pace without overtaxing the animals or elderly monks, stopping for short meal breaks and to rest their horses. They lit no fires and took care to remain as unobtrusive as possible.

The group was sharing a cold meal of jerky, dried fruit, and crackers, when Giulia asked how much longer before they reached the low hills that formed the starting point of the Tor Mountain range.

Evryst said, "I'm figuring about eight hours."

"Aye," agreed Chelyss. "Give or take."

"Any thoughts on how we can get into the Tor foothills unseen?" asked Solace.

Devlan and Danyss scratched their thick beards in unison and glanced at each other. Danyss nodded at Devlan, who said, "Aye, there's a twisty little mountain pass we can take that'll keep us mostly out of sight."

Josaph thrust out his bottom lip. "Yer not contemplatin' climbin' Daemon's Doorstep, are ye?"

Devlan and Danyss shrugged at their monastic elder. "It's the best means of avoiding detection."

"And tumblin' off a cliff, whilst we're at it!" harrumphed Josaph. "Ye young'uns er always seekin' thrills, ain't ye?"

Evryst raised his hands to ward off any further debate. "Alright, one option is Daemon's Doorstep. Any other thoughts?"

Lamkin tapped his forefinger on the side of his nose and nodded thoughtfully. "Mebbe one other thet's not quite so...perilous-like."

"Please continue, Brother Lamkin," encouraged Evryst.

"Anvil Pass."

Evryst nodded reluctantly. "A second option, certainly, although some would argue it's uncomfortably warm and somewhat unpredictable."

Lamkin shook his head. "But ole Anvil ain't truly erupted in decades."

"Erupted?" said Solace.

"Anvil Pass is a long, narrow strip of hardened lava that forms a sort of conduit through the lower elevations of the Tor foothills," explained Alyn. "It's arguably the fastest means of accessing them. It's also the hottest. Although the last recorded volcanic eruption was eighty years ago, it's still hotter than any other part of the mountain range, hence the name."

Alyn must have noticed Solace's confusion, because he supplied the missing clue. "What do you find in every blacksmith's forge, near the furnace?"

"Ah," she replied. "An anvil. Of course."

Giulia summarized, "So our choices are to cut across

through Daemon's Doorstep, which is so treacherous every traveling merchant who's stayed at the inn has told me they've taken the long way around, or we use Anvil Pass, which will be fiendishly hot, but hopefully not as dangerous."

She glanced around at the group and then looked at Solace, who shrugged and said, "Seems like Anvil Pass is safer and faster, so let's try it."

If she hadn't been heartsick and weepy every time she thought of Rhees, Solace might have enjoyed the ride toward Anvil Pass. The evening was pleasantly cool and the air sweet with the promise of spring. They startled a small pack of wild dogs halfway through the night, and spotted the occasional owl scouring the desert floor for its next meal, but otherwise encountered nothing else. A bright canopy of stars twinkled above their heads, and the crescent moon shone on the rocks and boulders, creating odd shapes on the desert floor.

The first bands of gold were stretching across the eastern horizon when Lamkin announced, "Jest beyond them two acacia trees, thar's an openin' in th' side o' th' hill —that's th' startin' point o' Anvil Pass."

Josaph agreed, adding, "Best get yer torches lit. 'Tis dark as death inside th' Anvil!"

Solace gave the order to dismount so they could tighten straps and harnesses on their horses, remove outer garments or armor that would prove too warm inside, and ready the torches. She took off her cloak, chainmail vest, and vambraces, stowing them in her saddlebag. Everyone else did the same, peeling off armor, tabards, and habits.

Solace offered Jenx an apple ring from her dwindling supply and ran her fingers through his mane. "That's a good boy," she whispered. The stallion gave a soft whicker in reply.

Evryst joined her and patted Jenx's neck. "If it's alright with you," he said to Solace, "I'd like to take point. I've traversed Anvil Pass half a dozen times, and it can be tricky."

"Of course. I was hoping for someone with knowledge of the pass to lead us through." She leaned forward to whisper, "I'd feared one of the elderly brethren might step forward if I asked for volunteers. I'm not so confident they're up to the task."

Evryst smiled. "They have good hearts and willing spirits, but I'd prefer not to leave the guiding to them."

"Aye," Solace agreed. "Do you have any advice for the rest of us?"

"A few words of instruction, which I may as well give to everyone now."

When Solace nodded, Evryst turned back to the rest of the group and shouted, "Alright, we're about to enter Anvil Pass. As Brother Josaph has said, it's black as pitch inside, and we only have a few torches to light the way. We need to be extra vigilant. We'll be traveling single file—no exceptions, even when the pass widens—because it narrows again very quickly. Remain on your horses the entire time. If you are guiding a pack horse, ensure you've tightened the leads.

"You'll know when we've reached the center of the pass, because the heat is intense. You're going to feel as if you can't breathe, but you can. Remain calm and continue moving forward. Whatever you do, don't stop, because you'll hold up everyone behind you, and you may cause someone else to pass out. Any questions before we line up?"

"Jest a suggest'n. Young'uns should ride ahead of

old'uns, like me 'n Lamkin, cuz we'll slow ev'ryone else down," said Josaph.

Evryst looked ready to argue the point, but Josaph put his hands on his hips and jutted out his long, white beard. Evryst sighed. "Fine, you and Brother Lamkin will take up the rear. I'll take point, followed by Brother Alyn, who will carry on if I should encounter anything untoward. Queen Solace will follow behind us. I'll ask the rest of you to sort yourselves out now, before we light the torches."

It took another five minutes of jostling and shuffling, plus several trips behind the acacia trees for anyone needing to take care of personal business, before the group was lined up and ready to enter the pass. They had three torches, which Behn dipped in olive oil and then used a flint to light. Evryst, Peka, and Josaph each carried one. Peka rode in the middle, behind Bray, Behn, and Giulia. The ascending age-order pattern continued, with Danyss, Devlan, Fenwith, and Chelyss riding behind Peka and in front of Josaph and Lamkin.

Evryst raised his torch to indicate they were moving forward. Entering the rocky mountainside through a narrow crevice, Solace rode into a wall of uncomfortably warm air that left her feeling slightly breathless. She knew Evryst and Alyn were directly in front of her, but the torch barely pierced the darkness inside the massive cavern. And although she heard Jenx's hooves striking the rocky surface, she felt a momentary surge of panic, because she couldn't see the ground beneath them. She saw nothing but a faint flicker of light above Evryst's head.

Solace gripped Jenx's reins harder and reminded herself to breath normally. She knew how to follow instructions, and Evryst's had been simple—deceptively so. She found it far too easy to allow her mind to wander in the vast, black, void surrounding them, so she focused instead on the sound of their horses' hooves clopping along and the faint wisps of light from their torches.

No one spoke, not even Bray, who was plodding on the igneous rock-bridge behind her. Perspiration trickled down the sides of Solace's face, and her tunic stuck to her chest and back. Hers eyes gradually adjusted to the near-total darkness, the torches providing the only glimmer of light inside the pass.

Solace began to wonder whether she'd passed the center yet, when what felt like a massive oven door swung open, searing her lungs with hot air. Coughing, she trying to catch her breath as sweat stung her eyes. She blinked a few times and swiped her brow, wishing they'd decided to take Daemon's Doorstep; at least they'd have been outside, inhaling fresh air. Suddenly, Solace heard a muffled thump, followed by a horse's indignant neigh somewhere in the blackness.

Behn cried out, "Bray! What are you doing?"

Peka hollered, "What's wrong with Bray?"

Solace glanced over her shoulder and gasped. Bray's saddle was empty.

"Stop moving, everyone," shouted Solace. She pulled on Jenx's reins, slid down to the ground, and leaned against his sweaty flank.

They were standing on a narrow slip of rock, and Solace feared the worst as she groped her way over to Bray's horse. She slid her hands down the mare's neck and then dropped to her knees in relief. Bray was dangling upside down, unconscious, his left boot heel tangled up in his stirrup.

Solace reached him at the same time as his brother. Behn lifted Bray's head and shoulders, while Solace released Bray's boot from his stirrup.

Peka yelled, "Is Bray alright?"

"Aye, Mum, he's just fainted is all," grunted Behn, who gripped Bray underneath his armpits.

"Whatever you do, do it fast!" called out Evryst. "Otherwise, we're going to have more fainting spells before we're through."

"He's not going to be able to ride on his own," pointed out Solace.

"I'm going to hoist him into his saddle and climb up behind him," said Behn. "Can you keep him from slipping until I'm in place?"

Solace gripped Bray's belt in one hand, and his tunic in the other. Gritting her teeth as Behn lifted him, she strained to keep Bray from careening off the horse. She felt her heart shudder inside her chest with the effort and knew she had to get out of the stifling heat soon, or she'd be fainting next.

When Behn was seated behind his brother, Solace released her hold and handed Behn the reins to his own horse and Bray's. She gingerly made her way back to Jenx. Mindful of the sharp drop off on either side of them, she took great care not throw Jenx off balance when she mounted him. Swiping her perspiring face with the back of her arm, Solace told Evryst they could start moving forward again.

The intense heat gradually lessened, until Solace felt she was riding on the perimeter of a blacksmith's furnace, rather than smack dab in the center of one. As her breathing became less labored, she started worrying about Fenwith, Chelyss, and the elderly monks. If the heat had been too much for poor Bray, how were they faring? Since she couldn't peer that far back in the gloom to see for herself, she had no choice but to wait until they were off the pass.

"Almost there!" shouted Evryst. "Keep a straight line until you feel cool air. And take your time; the surface is very uneven at this end of the Anvil."

Solace slowed her pace to match Evryst's and Alyn's, who'd reined in their mounts. She could feel Jenx straining at his leads a bit, probably because he could sense they were nearing the exit. She was equally impatient but didn't want to risk a stumble, not when they'd nearly cleared Anvil Pass, which she vowed to never take again. Solace recalled Evryst's initial reluctance to use the lava-formed pathway and now understood why.

Finally, Solace felt a cool rush of air wash over her perspiring face. She inhaled deeply as she guided Jenx toward the cave's egress, which widened into a soaring space, almost like a great hall hewn from the heart of the mountain. As they exited, they stepped onto a broad mound of dirt and stone that was strewn with boulders and a few more acacia trees.

Taller mountains ranged all around them, with many suitable hiding places tucked into crannies and crevices. Solace knew her small team would be easy to observe from nearly any vantage point. They needed to climb to a higher elevation as soon as possible to avoid detection.

She turned to watch her friends and their horses scramble out of the cavern, beginning with Behn and Bray, who groaned as he wiped his brow. Solace was relieved to see Chelyss and Fenwith finally emerge, although with their gray hair plastered to their skulls and their chests heaving, they looked as if they'd been racing. Josaph fared no better, wheezing as he joined them.

Everyone waited for the last horse and rider, Brother Lamkin, to trot outside...and they waited some more, until Evryst dismounted and dashed back into the cave. Josaph climbed off his steed and shambled after him, mumbling about Lamkin "al'ays runnin' behin' ev'ryun else."

Solace glanced at Alyn, who'd dismounted and was peering anxiously at the dark opening. She heard Evryst shouting for extra torches. Peka handed hers to Alyn, who jogged back inside. Everyone else had climbed off their horses by then and were staring at Anvil Cave. They heard Josaph's gravelly voice calling, "Lamkin, ole man, where 'r ye?" Peka looked at Solace and shook her head.

Evryst and Alyn eventually emerged, supporting Josaph between them. The old monk made no sound, but his eyes were brimming with tears. Alyn said, "There's no sign of Brother Lamkin or his horse. Since none of us heard a sound, we think they both passed out from the extreme heat and tumbled off the bridge together."

Evryst suggested they take a moment to remember Brother Lamkin before they pushed on, since Anvil Cave was now his final resting place. Solace nodded uneasily as she glanced at the lightening sky. The sun would be rising over the mountains very soon.

Each of the monks shared a little story or memory of the man they'd known. Brother Josaph went last. Sniffling, he rasped, "Lamkin 'n I were novices togeth'r. Tho he was al'ays th' smartes', fastes', 'n witties' of us all, Lamkin wanted ta serve oth'rs, nev'r ta lead. An' tho 'e was young'r th'n me by two weeks, Lamkin insisted on goin' last. He..." Josaph's voice broke. "He must'av known he'd not make it across't th'Anvil agin, him 'n his b'loved mare."

Josaph turned toward the mouth of the cavern and called out, "Rest up, ole fren, 'cuz when I join ye, we'll be kickin' up ar heels wunze agin!"

Josaph's image of two white-haired monks "kickin' up thar heels" again reminded Solace of her own near-death experience. She had passed through the veil separating the living and the dead after a knife attack by one of Neuss's guards. Her mother had greeted her and given her a choice: Solace could join her mother in the bright, sparkling light, which she'd sorely wanted to do—or she could pass back through the veil to be with Rhees—who'd desperately needed her.

Solace had chosen to return to Rhees. And though the raging fever that had nearly killed her had also weakened her heart, she'd never regretted her decision. She brought both her hands to her mouth and choked back a sob.

Where is Rhees right now? Is his spirit hovering at the veil's border? Or like Mother and Lamkin, has he already passed far beyond it?

CHAPTER 24

By the time they'd finished reminiscing about Brother Lamkin and toasting his long life, the sun had crested the tallest of the eastern peaks. Solace glanced up at the ring of hills surrounding them, her brow creasing with worry. They were clustered on a low mound of pebbly soil in front of Anvil Cave—far too exposed to anyone wishing them harm.

Solace wondered whether they should wait for reinforcements that might never come, or break into smaller teams now to search for Neuss. She was about to pose the question to the group but never got the chance. Peka yelped as an arrow struck the ground in front of her, and everyone dived for cover.

Neuss's thugs had found them.

Solace slapped Jenx's backside and pointed at the cave they'd just exited. "Go wait for me!" The bay stallion dashed into the Anvil's great hall, the other horses following in his wake.

She dropped to her hands and knees as more arrows whizzed past her head, and crawled between two boulders. Peka and Behn were already there, and Bray was nearby, tucked into a narrow fissure in the rockface. Everyone else scattered, some retreating to the cave with the horses, the others hiding behind boulders.

As another barrage of arrows fell from the sky, someone yelped. Solace started rising to see if anyone needed help, but Behn pushed her down as several stones struck the ground next to them. "Neuss has archers and slingers tucked into these hills," he grunted.

Solace groaned in frustration. "Any ideas where they're firing from?"

Peka waved her hand in the direction of Tor Mountain. "They're tucked up in those foothills to the east, which makes sense. They can fire down into Tor Valley, on the other side of the ridge, where our army is bogged down. And they can pivot and attack anyone trying to outflank them."

"Like us," sighed Behn.

"We're sitting ducks 'til nightfall," grumbled Bray, hiding in the narrow crevice nearby.

"If we last that long," replied Behn, "which is doubtful."

"I don't intend to sit here all day being fired upon," hissed Solace. "We're going to find whoever is hiding in those hills and stop them."

"We're going to need a distraction," said Peka.

"What sort of distraction?" asked Behn.

Peka and Behn traded a few ideas with Solace, who kept shaking her head. Their options were either foolhardy or just plain impossible. She hadn't led her friends halfway across Toresz and endured Anvil Pass to quit now, but they were pinned down, in broad daylight, without any backup.

"Will that do?" Bray was pointing at the mountain directly opposite them.

Solace squinted. She didn't see anything at first, but

then she noticed vaporous, purple tendrils rising from the summit. *Purple smoke?*

Peka gripped her elder son's shoulder. "Behn, do you think it could be—"

"Aye!" he said excitedly. "Smoke signals!"

"What are you two talking about?" Bray sounded annoyed. Solace recalled her grandparents had used smoke to send out alerts to other hill families back home, but that was ages ago.

Peka stared at the rising purple wisps and scratched her chin. "It's been a long time. Do you recall what purple means?"

"Enemy subdued," replied Behn.

Peka squinted at her son. "How?"

"And who?" asked Solace. "If those are smoke signals you recognize, who's sending them?"

"Smoke signals?" said Bray. "But we've never used them before."

Behn nodded. "You're right—we never got the chance. King Meade had become interested in the idea of using smoke to send messages. A couple of months before Neuss murdered his way onto the throne, Rhees, Wilhm, and I learned how to..." Behn's voice trailed off.

"Then who's sending that signal now?" Solace repeated her question.

Behn said, "Wilhm! It's got to be him! But what's he doing here?"

"Wilhm! Where?" Bray peeked out.

Solace cautiously peered over the boulder they'd been hiding behind. "Whoever it is, they appear to be helping us. All's quiet across the way."

"Stay down while I get a better look." Behn crept to the acacia tree and swung up into the branches. He climbed partway up and pulled out a spyglass. Everyone else waited quietly for confirmation they could come out of hiding. Everyone except for old Josaph, snoring in rhythmic puffs beneath the tree, oblivious to the fact they'd been under attack.

Behn jumped down from the lowest branch and called out, "It's alright—they're friendlies! I spotted a monk in a navy habit, a few folks just milling about, and a very tall man who's got to be Wilhm."

Peka stood up, her hands on her hips. "Which begs more questions. Who retrieved him? And is everyone else safe at the farm?"

Bray put a hand on his mother's shoulder. "Wilhm wouldn't leave the farm undefended, Mum. I'm sure all's well back home."

As the group slowly reassembled, Solace did a quick scan for injuries. Chelyss held a blood-soaked rag to his upper arm. "'Tis only a flesh wound—an arrow grazed me," he grunted.

While Evryst cleaned Chelyss's arm and applied a fresh bandage, Solace explained about the significance of the purple smoke. "I have little doubt Neuss is still hiding somewhere in these hills." Her voice shaking, she added, "While Rhees is lying somewhere in the next valley."

Tears leaked from Solace's eyes at the thought of Rhees, her often rash but always brave warrior-king, lying still. She wiped her damp cheeks with the back of her hand, and when she spoke again, her voice was steady. "It's time for us to split up and go our separate ways."

After a chorus of protests about the need to "protect our queen," squashed by a stern frown from Solace, the group eventually agreed to split into three teams—two to search for Neuss, and one to search for Rhees. Solace was torn between what her heart demanded, which was to find Rhees and cradle him in her arms one last time, and what her head urged, which was to finish off Neuss. She thought of Rhees's baby and her head won.

Fenwith, Chelyss, and Peka would leave immediately for Tor Valley to locate Rhees. Since Fenwith nursed the faint hope Rhees was alive, Solace asked Evryst to accompany them. If Rhees needed the skills of a master healer, Evryst would know what to do. He reluctantly agreed. Solace sensed the monk was torn between duty to his queen and her unborn child, and duty to his king, if Rhees still lived.

Solace would lead Giulia, Behn, and Bray to inspect the source of the purple smoke and continue the search for Neuss in the eastern ridge of hills. The rest of the monks volunteered to look for Neuss near Daemon's Doorstep, located on the other side of Anvil Cave, where a second chain of foothills ran farther to the west.

The Neuss search teams would be working more or less in parallel, since the foothills meandered in two squiggly lines around Tor Valley. Alyn estimated it would take each team roughly a week to hike through their section of the hills—longer if they ran into trouble.

"If we do find Neuss, how will we notify the rest of you?" asked Devlan. "We don't have pigeons, trumpets, or heralds."

"Why not use smoke?" suggested Giulia.

"Good thought, but we don't have any means of sending colored smoke," Alyn pointed out.

"Let's keep it simple," said Solace. "Smoke sent from a hilltop means Neuss has been found. The other search team will suspend operations and help the team that signaled.

Smoke sent from anywhere else—from midway up the hill or from the valley—means something is wrong. The other team won't suspend their search, but they will send in reinforcements as soon they arrive." Solace added silently, *if they arrive.*

She waited until everyone nodded. "Alright, let's see to our horses and then get moving."

Evryst said, "May I have a word, my queen?"

"Of course." After everyone else had dispersed, Solace added in a low voice, "I know you're going to remind me to be careful and not strain my heart further. And to be mindful of the child—our future king or queen."

Evryst sighed. "I don't expect you'll forget the child, but I do fear you will take unnecessary risks, since it's in your nature to do so. All I ask is that you remember who you are —the Water Witch Queen of Toresz—the only woman who can lead this kingdom until your child comes of age. We need you now more than ever. And we need you hale and hearty."

"Fine." Solace folded her arms across her chest. "I'll do my best to stay alive."

"And not take unnecessary risks or stress your heart."

"Aye, that too."

"Thank you, my queen. That is all I can ask." Evryst gave her a low bow and turned to leave. He paused, as if he wanted to add one more admonishment but then reconsidered and walked away.

THEY WERE LESS than halfway up the mountain where they'd observed the purple smoke when Solace called out, "We need to leave our horses here and climb the rest of the way by foot." The slope leveled off into a mostly flat bluff before rising again sharply above them.

Solace dismounted and rubbed Jenx's nose. Tufts of grass grew amid the rocks, providing an ideal grazing spot for the horses while they waited. She led Jenx to a rivulet trickling down the hillside. As she bent down to refill her water skin, Jenx raised his head and neighed a warning. Solace's hand went to the dagger in her belt. "Quick," she whispered to the others. "We have company."

Behn and Bray withdrew their swords, while Giulia clutched her ax. There was nowhere to hide. Not even the grasses were tall enough to offer any cover. Solace brought her finger to her lips, and they crouched against the rugged mountain wall, Solace's heart pounding in her chest. She heard a man speaking quietly as he descended the path above them, and a woman's low reply.

Jenx gave a soft, friendly whicker. Solace glanced at the smartest horse she'd ever known. *Could it be true?*

Bray dashed onto the narrow ribbon of a trail and rounded the corner.

"Bray!" hissed Behn. "Get back here."

Bray shouted, "But it's Wilhm and Maysel...and Brother Max too!"

Behn resheathed his sword and sprinted after his brother. Solace straightened and exhaled slowly. She glanced at Giulia, who'd slipped her ax back into the holster on her belt.

The innkeeper's daughter shook her head. "Bray is too rash. It's obvious Behn worries about him as much as their mother does."

"Aye," agreed Solace. She suspected they were thinking the same thing: *Bray may get himself killed someday, if he's not more careful.*

Behn and Bray returned with Wilhm, Maysel, Max, and several men carrying machetes. Between the newcomers, Solace's small team, and the horses, their bluff was becoming rather cramped.

"Well met, Queen Solace." Wilhm boomed in a deep voice as he bowed. "The mountain is secured, and the thugs who were attacking you will cause no further trouble."

When Wilhm hesitated, Maysel stepped forward and bowed. "We wish we were meeting under happier circumstances. We are devasted about King Rhees."

"There's no need for bowing among friends," said Solace, her voice catching. *Focus,* she thought. *Don't fall apart.* "We saw the smoke and came to investigate. I had high hopes we might encounter you, Wilhm, but I'll confess I'm surprised to see Maysel with you. And Brother Max."

"When we heard about our army's losses, and about our king, Wilhm and I both had to come." Maysel glanced at Behn and Bray. "But don't worry—the farm is in good hands—the two monks are still there, and my sister and her husband are there with our boys. They'll look after things until we're all home again."

"No doubt." Behn nodded. "But how did you hear about the army and Rhees?"

"My sister and her husband live near Tor Valley and fled during the battle," said Maysel. "They told us our army suffered heavy casualties, including our dear king Rhees."

"We left as soon as we could," added Wilhm, "and encountered Brother Max on the road."

"Queen Solace." Brother Max pushed back his cowl and dipped from the waist. "We have delivered your message from Manyalan to the turnoff for Jaryss, the village just south of Miss Peka's farm, which is where we ran into

Wilhm and Maysel. I'm happy to report we've secured a good number of volunteers."

Solace sincerely hoped the three machete-wielding men had brought along their friends. Max must have read her thoughts, because he added, "These are Wilhm's friends from the mines, whom we met on our way here. The volunteers we recruited are hiding in the hills, awaiting your signal."

Solace thought she may have underestimated Max's persuasive skills, which went well beyond heralding. "Well done, Brother Max," she said. "How many do we have?"

Max beamed at her words of praise. "About three score, with more trickling in.

"Excellent work," exclaimed Solace. "Do they know what to do next?"

Max started to pucker his lips but Solace shook her head. "Not yet. We need to explain to Wilhm, Maysel, and their friends first."

Max gave her a wide grin. "Already done!"

The tallest of the machete-wielding miners, a man named Jerwyn, bowed low. "Aye, Queen Solace. We stand ready ta assist ye."

Solace inclined her head to indicate her thanks. "Then it's time to let everyone know we're here, and we're ready to take on Neuss. Max, if you would do the honors?"

Max climbed onto a boulder, cupped his hands around his mouth, and called out, "Chip-chir! Chip-chir! Chip-chir!" Wilhm and the miners climbed up next to Max and added their voices, repeating the quail call, which started to echo across the hills rimming the valley.

After a full two minutes of "chip-chirring," Max, Wilhm, and the miners changed their quail call and tempo. They shouted, "Tuck-too! Tuck-too! Tuck-too!"

The hills fell silent, which meant Solace's "army" was following instructions, replying to the first call and not the second. She expelled a puff of air. "Alright, let's move into position."

"Where to?" asked Wilhm, once he'd hopped down from the boulder.

Behn explained, "Solace's plan is to move methodically through the foothills overlooking this side of Tor Valley. We'll rid one hill at a time of Neuss's ruffians—which is why we need so many volunteers—and then move on to the next hill to the north."

"So once we've cleared a hill, how do we let our friends coming up behind us know to move on to the next one?" said Wilhm. "There's no point in duplicating efforts."

"Great question," replied Solace. "We're using quail's calls to communicate position, and rocks to indicate a 'safe hill.'"

"Rocks?" repeated Wilhm.

Solace arched an eyebrow at Max, who waved his hands at the hills in the distance. "Don't worry, ma'am, everyone else knows, but I didn't get a chance to explain it to Wilhm and the others yet."

Solace pointed down at the pebbles and stones dotting the hard-packed ground. "We'll be using rocks to form cairns along the way."

Maysel snorted. "Using rocks is brilliant. They're about the only thing we have in abundance around here."

Bray quickly demonstrated by building a cairn out of five stones, and they descended the mountain, leading their horses by foot until they reached level ground again. While Bray built a second cairn at the base of the hill, Wilhm, Maysel, and the three miners retrieved their horses, who were waiting under the widespread limbs of an ancient cypress.

Wilhm offered to take point, with Solace and Maysel following directly behind him. They plodded along, single file, through a narrow trail between the first hill and the next. Solace expected another round of arrows and stones to rain down on their heads, but none came. Other than the sound of their horses' hooves striking dry ground, and small creatures rustling through the tumbleweeds and grasses, the hills were silent. She heard distant shouting from Tor Valley on the other side of the foothills and prayed that Rhees's beleaguered army could hang on a bit longer.

By dusk, Solace and her team had climbed and inspected two more hills. Both had been lower and easier to scale than the mountain where they'd met up with Wilhm and Maysel. Even so, Solace's heart shuddered painfully from the constant climbing, Maysel was limping more than usual, and Max was trying but failing to hide his yawns.

Solace and her team stood in a narrow canyon with their horses, the lower knolls behind them and the next set of hills straight ahead. She knew they needed to stop and rest. Besides, they couldn't very well be sneaking up mountain trails at night without using torches—a dead give-away. "Let's find a cave or some other protected area to bunk down for the night. We can resume the search at daybreak."

"Aye," agreed Wilhm, who craned his neck to get a better look at the craggy peak in front of them. He pointed at a crevice near the base of the mountain and turned to Jerwyn. "I think you used to mine in these parts, didn't you?"

Jerwyn scratched his long, soot-colored beard. "As a boy, wif me dad."

"Will that cave work for the night?"

Jerwyn nodded slowly. "We cin all fit inside, includin' ar animals. That partic'lar mine was abandoned a while back. Th' tricky thing is—"

Solace heard the swoosh of an arrow as it sliced through flesh, but she was too late to shout a warning. Jerwyn fell dead at their feet, a shaft protruding from the center of his chest.

CHAPTER 25

"Run!" yelled Solace as she mounted Jenx, arrows striking the soil on either side of her. Everyone scattered, some to the hills behind them and others, like Solace, forging toward the crevice ahead. With enemy archers firing on them from above, she prayed the opening in the mountain's base would offer refuge. It didn't occur to her until she slipped into the fissure's rocky embrace that she could be heading right into one of Neuss's dens.

Fortunately, the opening in the mountainside appeared deserted, except for the burnt ends of several spent torches and charred remains of a fire—evidence of recent use that no one had bothered to hide. As a rule, hill people respected the land and were a cautious bunch, even more so after a decade of abuse by Neuss. They knew how to cover their tracks. Whoever had camped there last was neither cautious nor respectful.

Solace dismounted as the others thundered into the cavern behind her: Behn, Giulia, Bray... and no one else. *Oh no! Where are the others? Max and the miners? Maysel and*

Wilhm? Were any of them hit? She thought of Maysel's little boys and dashed back to the opening for a look.

"Maysel took an arrow. I saw Wilhm carrying her into the low hills behind us," said Behn softly.

"How bad?" whispered Solace.

Behn shook his head. "I couldn't tell—everything was happening too fast."

Solace glanced back outside at Jerwyn's still form and murmured, "Looks like the others made it to the hills with them."

"Why are we whispering?" asked Bray in his normal tone of voice.

"Hush!" hissed Behn and Giulia simultaneously.

Solace pointed down at the blackened, ashy logs behind Bray. She could practically hear Bray's wheels turning. He murmured excitedly, "Neuss must be here somewhere."

Solace put up her hand, palm outward. "Hold on," she whispered, "we can't be certain of that. All we know is we're being attacked from above, likely by some of Neuss's sympathizers, but I still believe the man himself is holed up elsewhere, ready to escape if his uprising fails."

"Either way, we need to stop those goons," mumbled Bray. "What's our plan?"

Solace blew out a puff of air. "I'm working on it."

"Jerwyn was trying to tell us something about this mountain before he was killed," said Giulia softly.

Behn agreed. "I think a quick reconnaissance of our surroundings is in order."

"Good idea," said Solace. "Why don't you and Giulia scout ahead. We'll wait here with the horses."

Solace and Bray worked in companionable silence, brushing down the horses' dusty coats and checking hooves for stones. Solace kept her ears primed for any sounds coming from the cave's interior or exit. She returned the brush to her bag and arched her back. She'd just begun to worry about Behn and Giulia, when she heard footsteps coming from inside the cavern.

"Quick," she hissed, withdrawing her dagger from her belt. "We have company."

Bray stood at her side, his hand on his hilt, his shoulders tensed. She felt him relax ever so slightly next to her as he whispered, "It's Behn and Giulia."

"How can you be sure?"

"I'd know my brother's footfall anywhere, and Giulia shuffles a bit when she's tired."

Solace resheathed her dagger just as Behn and Giulia came into view. She noticed Giulia had fresh blood splatter on her vambraces, and Behn had a new gash on his forehead. "What happened?"

"Neuss's men got the jump on us," grumbled Behn as he wiped a trickle of blood out of his eye. "This cave is like a giant echo chamber. They must have heard us arriving with our horses and figured we'd be checking things out. If it wasn't for Giulia, I'd be a goner."

Giulia waved away the praise. "They were on us so fast; all I did was react. I got two of 'em, but the third one slipped away. I'm sure he's alerting the others even now."

Solace's eyebrows pointed downward. "Then we need to make our move very soon. What can you tell us about this cave?"

While Bray quickly cleaned and bandaged Behn's cut, Giulia explained, "A few things. We're at the entrance to a very twisty passage. Around the bend, there's a mine shaft on the left that's silent as a graveyard, which we passed by. We jogged ahead a bit and then wound around three more bends—two right-hand turns and then a left—before coming to a fork. We were attacked from both sides at the fork, and I think I know why. When the last thug got away from me, I saw him make a flying leap straight up, onto a stone ledge. From there, he disappeared into another passage. But I heard his footsteps for a while after he'd run away, and they were leading further upward."

"There's a way to ascend this mountain from the inside," added Behn.

"Aye," said Giulia, "and that's probably what poor Jerwyn was trying to tell us."

"Hmm," Solace sighed. "If we go up that way, they'll be expecting us. But if we try climbing the trail outside, they'll be able to pick us off, one by one. We need a third option."

"It's getting pretty dark outside," said Bray. "If we split up, we can try to surprise them. Solace and I can sneak up the trail outside, and you two can wait for them partway up the inner passage. When you hear a commotion above you, that'll be your signal to rush in and give us a hand."

Behn grunted. "That's a terrible idea. You'll get picked off before we can get there in time."

"In daylight, aye, but we'll have a decent shot at escaping their notice at night," said Solace, who wasn't thrilled about a nighttime climb, but she saw the merit in Bray's idea. "If you have a better idea, let's hear it."

She waited until Behn and Giulia reluctantly shook their heads. "Alright then, let's do this."

Solace grabbed a water skin, and some nuts, dried berries, and jerky from her saddle bag and tucked them into the pockets of her cloak. She re-tied the slings at her waist and around her forehead and fingered the stones in her pouch. She counted nine and hoped that would be enough. "I'll be back soon...I promise," she whispered to Jenx, wondering whether it was right to make promises she might not be able to keep. The stallion blew warm air in Solace's face and then lowered his head. "Love you too."

Behn lingered near the cave opening, hissing instructions to his younger brother until Bray finally threw his arms around Behn's neck and murmured, "I'll be careful, and you do the same."

Solace and Bray sidled along the wall of the mountain as they slipped outside. They waited a few beats to be sure no one spotted them before they crept up the trail to begin their ascent in the dark.

Bray insisted on taking point. "I'd never forgive myself if you stumble off this path into thin air. Not only would I feel terrible, but I'd become the most hated man in Toresz —the fool who allowed the Water Witch Queen to fall off the mountain."

"Fine," Solace huffed. "Take the lead. I wouldn't want to inconvenience you with my premature death."

"Aw, come on. You know what I mean."

"You'd better not tumble over the side either. Your mother and brother would never forgive me," hissed Solace.

"Then let's make a pact: none of us dies tonight."

"It's a deal," she said softly.

The moon cast the mountain above them in shadowy relief, making their nighttime hike feel even more surreal and creepy. They trudged along, sticking close to the hillside on their left as they ascended the path. Solace's shoulders were taut with tension, and her thigh and calf muscles burned with the strain of climbing so much in a day. She and Bray had no choice but to keep going; fear-laced adrenaline motivated her now. They had to surprise the goons hidden in this hill, or all four of them would be dead before dawn.

More than halfway up the hill, they approached an

opening in the rock wall on their left and slowed down, their hands going to their daggers. Solace peered down into the pitch-black hole that smelled strongly of bat dung and wrinkled her nose. "This must be where the twisty passage lets out. Very convenient as a hideout."

"And we've confirmed how that one thug got away from Behn and Giulia," muttered Bray.

They continued their climb, and Solace wondered how everyone else was faring: Wilhm and Maysel, who'd been injured; Alyn and the monks traveling toward Daemon's Doorstep; Fenwith, Chelyss, Peka, and Evryst, entering Tor Valley to search for Rhees, or in reality, for his remains. She bit her bottom lip and shook her head. The time to dwell on her heartache would come later, after she'd rid the kingdom of Neuss.

As they neared the summit, Bray stopped abruptly, causing Solace to bump into his back. "What's up?" she whispered.

"I thought I heard something."

Solace peeked around Bray's shoulder. "I don't see anything." Nonetheless, she uncoiled one of her slings and reached into her pouch for three stones. She raised her head to peer at the craggy outcropping that extended over the trail ahead and stilled.

"Duck!" she hissed, shoving Bray to the ground. Dropping a stone into the leather cradle of her sling, Solace slipped her middle finger through the looped end of the braided cord, then gripped the knot at the other end. The sling whirred in the still evening air as she rotated it above her head. When she reached the velocity needed to propel the stone, she released the knotted end of the cord. The projectile flew with deadly accuracy toward her target: the dark shape of an archer perched on the overhang above them, his arrow aimed at Bray.

The bowman tumbled from the crag to the sharp rocks below, but Solace didn't pause in her task, swiftly seating another stone in her cradle. As Bray started to rise, she said, "Keep your head down!" Solace gripped her sling's knotted end, rotated the cord, and released—striking a second archer in the head—and then she quickly reloaded for a third shot. She waited, panting slightly, for any movement above them.

After a few minutes of silence, Bray asked, "Can I get up now?"

"Aye," whispered Solace, "but someone else could be tucked up there, out of sight for the moment."

"Agreed," said Bray. "We know four are definitely down—two in the cave below and two just now—and that could be all of them. But we have to check the ledge above us to be sure."

They cautiously rounded the curve of the path as it wound beneath the drape of rocky overhang, creeping onto the bluff from the other side. The slice of moon had slipped behind a cloud, plunging the mountain into utter darkness. Solace could barely make out Bray three feet in front of her. But then the hairs on the back of her neck bristled, and she sensed someone nearby, someone with a score to settle.

With a flick of his wrist, Bray's dagger whipped past Solace, who jumped to the side when she heard a garbled yelp behind her. Bray jogged in the direction of the sound, stumbling into a body sprawled on the ground.

"Let's see if they can tell us anything useful," suggested Solace.

Bray seized his sword, ready to defend himself in case

the assailant suddenly jumped up. He knelt down for a closer look. "Too late, I'm afraid."

Solace peered across the top of the bluff as the moon emerged from its cloud cover. No one else was crouching in the shadows ready to pounce on them. She blew out a puff of air. "I think we can declare this a 'safe hill.'"

"Finally," replied Bray. "I'm ready to call it a day." He dragged the body toward the edge of the summit, and a dagger clattered to the ground. Solace realized she'd been seconds away from having her throat slit. Bray gave the dead thug a firm push, and then he tossed the dagger over the side as well.

"What are you doing?"

"I'm tidying up for future hikers. This is a nice hill. I don't want some mum and her kids to climb up here and find that."

"I don't think anyone will be doing recreational climbing while there's a battle raging down in the valley," she pointed out.

"It's still good to clean up one's messes," he mumbled defensively.

Solace could just make out Bray's outline as he lifted his shoulders in a half-shrug. She knew something about that last kill bothered Bray, which she struggled to understand. Bray had fought by her side during the rebellion. He'd felled dozens of men and women with his slinging skills, which were on a par with hers. However, he'd brought only his sword and dagger when they'd left the farm. Solace suspected he was trying to emulate his father, who'd been a knight before becoming a farmer. Knights were definitely not slingers.

"What's wrong, Bray?"

He shrugged a second time. "Nothing."

"There's definitely something. Tell me."

Bray sighed. "She was softer and smaller than I expected."

"Oh. Well, she was about to attack me, so you saved my life. Thank you." When Bray didn't reply, Solace added more gently, "She chose the wrong side in this fight."

"I know. It's just...I hate all this fighting over such over a crap king like Neuss. He's not worth anyone losing their lives over."

"You'll get no argument from me there." Solace grimaced as her heart stuttered suddenly and then beat on, but not before a jolting wave of pain shot across her chest and down her right arm. She'd overstrained herself again, which was difficult to avoid when pursuing a fugitive ex-king. Hissing through her teeth, she took a steadying breath, and then another. Fortunately, it was too dark for Bray to notice.

"Bray? Solace?" Behn whispered hoarsely from some-where below them. "Are you alright?"

Bray shouted, "Aye, we just cleared the summit. We're coming down."

"We never heard a commotion so decided we'd better come investigate," said Giulia.

"There were three of them," called out Solace. "They'll bother us no more." Although she realized, as the words left her mouth, that wasn't entirely true. The girl's death would linger in Bray's head for some time to come.

CHAPTER 26

WHEN SOLACE RETURNED TO THE CAVE, SHE LEANED HER HEAD gratefully against Jenx's neck. He gave her a low whicker in reply. Behn hung back while she greeted her horse, but she sensed he had something on his mind. Bray and Giulia had left in search of a few more logs and sticks to build a fire, which they wouldn't light until dawn. No sense drawing unwanted attention to themselves.

"What really happened up there?" said Behn under his breath.

"Why do you ask?"

"Bray isn't talking, which isn't like him. He's not eating either. He told me he'd lost his appetite, but I know he's got to be half starved."

Solace gazed at Behn in the flickering glow of the single, nearly spent torch they'd dared to light inside the cave. "Do you remember your first hand-to-hand, up-close fight, when the other person died right in front of you?"

Behn dropped his eyes. "Aye."

"Well Bray experienced his first tonight. Give him some time."

"But he fought in the war."

"Aye, as a slinger; most of our targets were hundreds of feet away. Tonight, it was close range."

"How bad was it?" asked Behn.

"It was a girl, who was about to attack me. A knife-throw from Bray stopped her."

"Ah," muttered Behn. "My sentimental little brother."

"Who would like to be treated as an equal."

Behn frowned as he considered her words. Eventually, he nodded. "Fair enough. I'll do better."

Hot, chicory-laced coffee and steaming porridge seasoned with cinnamon greeted Solace the following morning, compliments of the innkeeper's daughter. As Giulia handed Solace a tin mug and bowl, both filled to the brim, she said, "We decided to let you sleep in. Behn and Bray left to look for Maysel, Wilhm and the others. I've seen to the horses."

Solace and Giulia resorted supplies and then began cleaning up all evidence of their campsite. They dug a hole to bury the ashes from their fire, carted the larger pieces of charred wood into the brush, and covered bloodstains with sand. Most gruesome of all, they had to deal with the two dead thugs lying in the twisty passage. They prodded, pushed, and dragged their bodies to the abandoned mine shaft, where they deposited them in the deep, dark hole that Giulia declared a fitting burial site for the criminals who'd almost killed Behn.

They were taking a much-needed break when Bray dashed into the cave, followed closely by Behn. Solace and Giulia jumped up in surprise.

"Don't just charge ahead like that," admonished Behn. "Always stop and check your surroundings first."

"But Jenx was standing in the entrance. He wouldn't be

hanging out there if something was wrong," huffed Bray, vibrating with excitement.

Solace thought he must have found their friends. Why else would Bray be so bouncy? "Where are Maysel and Wilhm? Are they waiting for us outside?" she asked.

"They were already gone by the time we got there," said Bray, with a shake of his head. "But we did find a second cairn, this one with six stones. And the top stone was long, pointy, and angled toward the valley."

Solace drew her brows together and glanced at Behn, who explained the significance. "I'm certain Wilhm left us a message, letting us know he was heading to Tor Valley with Maysel. Max and the others must have gone with them."

"Then Maysel must need the skills of a master healer," said Solace slowly. "Which means she's well enough to travel. Wilhm wouldn't move her otherwise. That's some good news, anyway."

"Speaking of good news," said Bray, impatiently rocking on the balls of his feet. "There's more."

"Well don't keep us in suspense any longer," grumbled Giulia. "You're practically bursting at the seams."

"We saw smoke rising near Daemon's Doorstep," exclaimed Bray. "From the top of the hill. The monks have found Neuss!"

An icy chill coursed through Solace's veins, which the warm afternoon sun shining into the cave's entrance did nothing to dispel. She would be facing Neuss again—and for the last time. Only one of them would walk away from this battle, and she earnestly hoped it wouldn't be the convicted killer.

"How long will it take us to ride to Daemon's Doorstep?" asked Giulia. "Assuming we can avoid any further attacks along the way, that is."

Behn canted his head, considering. "If we leave shortly and travel through the night, we should be there by morning."

"I like the idea of traveling mostly by night," said Solace. "Let's head out as soon as you're ready." She led Jenx outside and then vaulted onto his back. His slender ears pricked forward at a low roar emanating from Tor Valley. "What's that noise?" she wondered aloud, patting the horse's neck.

"That's Sir Kryss and his troops," said Behn. "They've finally arrived in the valley and are engaging Neuss's forces."

"We climbed the hill to have a look," added Bray. "I think our side might be winning."

"It looked to be a mighty fierce battle to me," grunted Behn. "I think it's too early to tell."

"No matter how you slice it, Sir Kryss's arrival is good news for our side," said Giulia. "I like to think we've helped the cause in a small way, by eliminating some of the archers in these mountains."

Solace nodded. "And if the rest of the volunteers are anything like Jerwyn, then they will be helping too, as best they can." She added, "Behn, could you take point? You have a better sense of where we're going than I do."

The shallow valley separating the hills near Anvil Pass from those closer to Daemon's Doorstep was all lumps and bumps, low ridges, and little shade—as if some giant had balled up brown tissue paper and then tried smoothing it again without success. Behn rode ahead and before long, Giulia joined him. Bray eventually came alongside Solace. They rode in silence as they guided their horses across the uneven, rock-strewn landscape.

After Bray sighed for the third time, Solace asked, "Are you upset that Behn and Giulia are getting along so well?"

"What?" Bray glanced at the innkeeper's daughter laughing at something Behn had said. "'Course not. Giulia's cool, and her skills with that ax are topnotch. Mum likes her too."

Solace nodded and waited for Bray to speak his mind. She wasn't surprised when he said, "It's just...it's the girl I killed yesterday. I know I had no choice, everything happened so fast, but she was so young, not more than seventeen or eighteen."

"My age."

"Huh?" he mumbled.

"That girl was about my age," pointed out Solace. "Old enough to make her own choices, and unfortunately, old enough to pay the price for them too."

"Funny, but I always think you're older," said Bray, "probably because you're so in control of yourself. I guess it goes with being a queen." Bray looked apologetic and coughed into his hand. "Sorry, I'm sure that whole thing with fake 'Queen MaudeLyn' must still rankle."

Solace shook her head. "She's not the fake queen. I am. But I don't care about MaudeLyn anymore. I only wish I'd been there with Rhees, in the end." Her voice caught in her throat. "I could have held him when...when he passed. I could have comforted him." She looked away with a sniffle.

"Fenwith told me he's still alive."

"She said the same thing to me," said Solace, "but that's just false hope."

Behn's timetable held true. They arrived just as the sun peeked over the foothills behind them. Solace craned her neck as she peered at Daemon's Doorstep, a narrow, high, stone-and-wood bridge connecting two soaring peaks. She decided the reality of the "doorstep" was far more daunting than any of the descriptions.

"Can you identify where the smoke signal originated from?" she asked.

"Aye." Behn pointed to the slope at the northern end of Daemon's Doorstep. "The monks sent the signal from that hill."

"How can you be so certain?" asked Giulia.

"The summit looks like a boar's head."

"No way," said Bray, shaking his head. "It looks like a goat."

"It's a boar, clear as day," insisted Behn. "But you agree this is the right one?"

"This is definitely it," replied Bray. "The goat-head hill."

"Fine, goat or boar makes no difference to me," said Solace with a small sigh. "The question is: where are they now?"

"If yer seeking Brother Alyn, he's awaiting ye at th' top o' the mount," Josaph wheezed as he shuffled toward them. "Good t' see ye, Queen Solace." The ancient monk bowed low, wobbled slightly, and then straightened. He nodded at the rest of Solace's companions. "Well met, all. Took ye long enuf."

"We ran into some trouble," said Behn wryly. "Slowed us down some."

"What can you tell us about Neuss's whereabouts?" asked Solace.

"Jes come wi'me." Josaph hobbled off without further explanation. Solace and her friends dismounted and trailed him. He shambled across the pebbly ground, occasionally glancing over his shoulder at the opposite peak. The old man led them around the mountain's skirt, where they found the monks' horses and a single bedroll tucked into a wedge-shaped cavern.

Solace's horse neighed and nosed his way into the cave. Jenx was probably as tired as she was of riding through the seemingly endless brown hills of Toresz. Even though she'd been raised in the Yeloshan hill country to the west, Solace was equally weary of hiking up one mountain pass after another hunting for Neuss. Her low back constantly ached, she had intermittent heart palpitations, and if she closed her eyes, she feared she'd sleep right through to the next day. Solace itched to find the former king and finish what he'd begun.

After a hasty meal of nuts, berries, and water—Josaph's fire had gone out, and Solace didn't want to wait for the old monk to build a new one—she followed the trail up the slope with Behn and Giulia. Bray remained behind to help Josaph with the horses and to gather more wood.

The three of them chatted occasionally as they mounted the boar-slash-goat-head hill, reserving most of their energy for the climb itself. Solace had neither seen nor heard anything to indicate the summit was inhabited, and they'd ascended more than half the slope. If she hadn't observed Josaph and the monks' horses at the base, she'd think the mountain was deserted. The opposite hill was equally silent. She wondered whether this whole expedition would end without ever discovering Neuss's whereabouts. Perhaps he'd already fled west into Yelosha.

"My legs are killing me," muttered Behn, who unlike his brother, rarely complained.

"Aye, mine too," agreed Giulia. "I haven't done this much steady climbing since I spent the summer at my uncle's ranch. I was eight."

Solace smiled. "I'm glad I'm not the only one who's sore

and achy from all this hiking. I figured I was just out of practice."

Behn chuckled. "Probably just getting 'old' like the rest of us."

"Say, did you see that?" asked Giulia.

"Wha—?" Behn never finished his question but slumped onto the trail, an arrow stuck fast in his stomach.

"Behn!" cried Giulia, who knelt down beside him.

Solace turned around and dropped to the ground next to them as arrows flew overhead, from the peak across the way, and from the summit above them. She glanced around for any place they could drag Behn. "Quick, let's get him behind those bushes." Giulia started to rise, but Solace said, "Keep your head down! I can't drag the two of you."

They managed to pull a groaning, bleeding Behn behind a cluster of scraggly bushes that offered little real protection but at least shielded them from sight. While Giulia examined Behn's injury, Solace dug into the small kit attached to her belt. She withdrew a roll of spider webbing. She didn't bother with her packet of salt; there was no point in cleansing and disinfecting the wound with the arrow still in place. Behn groaned as they gently removed his chainmail.

"There's so much blood," whispered Giulia as she rolled up Behn's tunic.

Solace grimaced as she packed the soft, sticky gossamer webbing around Behn's wound. They could only slow the bleeding for now. Behn would need a healer's skilled hand to remove the arrow and stitch the hole in his gut. Arrows continued whizzing overhead, and they had no choice but to sit tight and wait it out. Meanwhile Giulia held Behn's hand, her face grim.

Some time passed, perhaps fifty minutes, when the

silhouette of a man suddenly loomed over the bushes, blocking the sun. Solace's hand went to the knife in her belt but stilled when Danyss dropped down beside them. "How bad is it?" asked the monk.

"Bad enough," murmured Giulia.

"We can't move him like this," whispered Solace.

Danyss removed the leather bag he'd slung over his shoulder and propped it open on the ground. Although not a master healer like Evryst, he seemed adept at field medicine. Using fabric shears to cut away Behn's tunic, he frowned at the spider silk, soaked dark red, that was packed around the wound.

Danyss fixed his eyes on Solace. "Is this your doing?" When she nodded, he said, "Good thinking." Danyss removed his habit, rolled up the sleeves of his tunic, and asked Solace and Giulia to each grip one of Behn's arms while he removed the arrow. Behn reared up with a loud scream, which dissolved into soft whimpers as he thrashed around, Giulia and Solace holding him down.

Danyss made quick work of threading silk through a bronze needle, and then he doused the needle and Behn's abdomen with whatever alcoholic concoction he carried in his hip flask. Poor Behn screeched again as Danyss stitched up the ragged edges of his wound. When Danyss finished, he covered Behn's sutures with fresh spider webbing, followed by several layers of cotton gauze.

As he wiped his hands on a rag, Danyss asked Giulia to start stripping the branches from the nearby bush, so they could craft a litter for Behn. He glanced at Solace. "Brother Alyn is up top, waiting for you. If you stick close to the mountain's wall, you'll be safe enough. The arrows have stopped for now."

"Are you sure you don't need my help getting Behn back down the hill?"

"We'll manage," replied Danyss softly.

Behn's gray eyes fluttered open. "Go stop Neuss."

As Solace ascended the steep trail, she hugged the shadows cast by outcroppings and crags, hoping Alyn had enough arrows to provide her sufficient cover until she reached the peak. She felt strangely alone for the first time since the coronation debacle, without friends, guards, or even servants at her heels. Solace had already accepted she might not survive this encounter with Neuss. She wasn't fearful of dying so much as determined to take Neuss down with her. She had no intention of expiring prematurely.

Solace's chest felt tight by the time she reached Alyn, kneeling between two boulders, an arrow nocked in his bow. He didn't turn his head, but kept his eyes trained on the opposite hill. "Well met, my queen. Have a seat behind this boulder. Since you're alone, I'm assuming someone in your party was injured, and Danyss is seeing to them."

Solace dropped down beside the monk, but not before she saw Daemon's Doorstep stretched out before her, a daunting, impossibly high, narrow bridge that was part stone outcropping, part wooden slats held together with hemp and a prayer. And beneath the bridge was nothing but a dark abyss. *It makes perfect sense*, thought Solace, *for Neuss to be hiding on the other side of that.*

"Aye," she said, and then she filled him in on Behn's injury, their encounter with Wilhm and Maysel, who was also wounded, as well as the battle in Tor Valley, with Sir Kryss's troops now engaging the enemy. "And Max did manage to recruit a small army of volunteers who are progressing through the foothills, methodically removing Neuss's thugs."

"I'm sorry to hear about Behn and Maysel. I shall pray they both recover to full strength. At least we have some reason to hope, with Sir Kryss's arrival and Max's recruitment efforts. And we've found Neuss," said Alyn, although he did not shift his gaze from the opposite peak.

It dawned on Solace she'd not seen Danyss's brother since her arrival at the mountain. "And how fares Brother Devlan?"

Alyn nodded at the mountain on the other side of Daemon's Doorstep. "Devlan and Danyss have been scoping out Neuss's hideaway and slowly, quietly eliminating any of his men they're finding in the lower elevations. We don't think Neuss is onto them yet; they are terribly efficient. Sometimes I believe their rightful calling was as mercenaries rather than monks, but I'm glad to have them on our side.

"Danyss had just climbed the hill to provide me with his latest report when all hel—ah, heck—broke loose and arrows starting flying everywhere. We figured you'd arrived and were ascending the trail."

Solace had been toying with the idea of serving as a decoy to entice Neuss out of hiding, which she shared with Alyn. "I'd imagined luring Neuss out of some cave or small hut, where I'd have some place to duck and hide—but this setup is impossible. If I so much as put my foot on the stone ledge, Neuss or one of his men can pick me off."

"Aye," replied Alyn. "So then we need another plan, don't we?"

"I'm tired, and I'm hungry, and I'm sad. I don't have any more ideas," grumbled Solace, pulling her knees to her chest. *And I miss Rhees more with each passing day.*

"There's food in the bag next to my extra quiver, though

keep your head down. First you eat, then we cook up another plan."

Solace pulled the bag closer and withdrew some crackers, moldy cheese, and dried fruit, which she offered first to Alyn, who declined, explaining he'd had his fill. Although Solace felt marginally better after she'd eaten, she still had no fresh plan for defeating Neuss. "We're going to need something that'll send Neuss fleeing from that mountain. Something dramatic."

"Like what?" asked Alyn.

"I don't know. Like a rockslide or cave-in, which I suppose is too much to hope for." Solace shrugged. "Isn't there anything Neuss finds more frightening than being shot by an arrow?"

"Anything he finds more frightening...hmm, let me think." Alyn hummed to himself, which Solace found distracting but apparently it helped, because he suddenly blurted, "I know this will sound strange, but Evryst told me this long ago. Neuss is terrified of the dark."

"That's not so unusual," pointed out Solace. "A lot of people fear the dark."

"True, but Neuss becomes irrational if he's alone in the dark. He requires the constant glow of firelight, oil lamps, or candles, preferably in abundance."

"You've got to be kidding me," said Solace. "Neuss is arrogant, self-centered, and brutal. If he has this phobia, wouldn't more people have known and used it against him?"

"He once ordered his valet beheaded because the poor man forgot to light all the candelabras in the king's bedchamber."

"Now that does sound more like old King Neuss. But I'm not sure how it's going to help us now."

Alyn turned from his position between the twin boulders and slid down to the ground next to her. "All's quiet across the way, and by now Danyss and the others are well out of sight from Neuss's archers." He took a swig from his water skin. "I suppose we must find a way to plunge Neuss into total darkness, and then lure him toward a bright fire of our creation."

"Up here, on a rocky summit, with nothing but your bow and quiver of arrows for fuel?"

"We'll not be touching my weaponry," grumbled Alyn. He leaned his head against the boulder. "'Tis truly a long shot, I know. I shall pray for a miracle."

Solace realized the monk had been on watch without a break for many hours. "Why don't you rest and pray while I keep a lookout?" Solace stood up and braced herself between the twin boulders, her sling in hand.

Alyn folded his head over his chest and began to snore.

CHAPTER 27

BROTHER ALYN RELIEVED SOLACE AFTER A COUPLE OF HOURS. SHE tucked herself against one of the boulders and immediately dozed off. When she woke up, Alyn handed her some more moldy cheese and the last of the crackers. "Here, take some nourishment. It's almost time."

She glanced up at the dusky sky. The sun had already dipped below the ridge line. "Time for what?"

"Time to begin executing your new plan."

"*My* new plan?"

"Aye. It was your idea to target Neuss's deepest fear. But first, we need to eliminate any remaining enemy archers hiding in that hillside with Neuss. Bray has joined Danyss and Devlan to do just that. They'll also prevent anyone, either soldier or servant, from resupplying Neuss's snug little mountain hideout. No more food, water, or firewood for the old fox. After that, the rest is easy." Alyn pointed to the neat stack of firewood someone—presumably the ancient but able-bodied Josaph—had lugged up the trail while she'd slept.

"How so?" Solace knew better than to believe anything would be "easy" with Neuss.

"We wait until Neuss's fire burns so low we can no longer see its glow, at which point, he should go into full panic mode. That's when we'll light up the night sky with our blaze."

"And you expect him to...what? Cross Daemon's Doorstep in the dead of night? He may be panicking, but I don't think he'll be suicidal."

"True enough. But at the very least, he'll be shaken and not thinking straight."

"I hope you're not underestimating Neuss and his remarkable instinct for self-preservation," said Solace.

"We shall see," replied Alyn, rubbing his hands together with all the confidence of a major general. Solace stifled a sigh and hoped he was right.

They waited for hours, taking turns watching the opposite hill as the sky continued to darken into inky blackness. The orange glow from Neuss's campfire flickered, as fire does, but remained lit. Solace wondered how much wood Neuss's men had carted up the hill. Neuss could have a ready supply that would keep him panic-free for many nights yet. Then she considered the steepness of the trail and dearth of wood in the area and decided he couldn't be any better off than she and Alyn.

Well past midnight, Alyn pointed through the opening between the boulders. "The fire glow grows faint. Take a look." Alyn handed Solace his spyglass and stepped back to stoke their small campfire, which they'd been carefully tending so it wouldn't go out, all the while hoarding their dwindling supply of wood and kindling.

Solace raised the spyglass to her eyes, her vambraces

flashing golden in the sudden burst of firelight behind her. She heard a whoosh and felt an arrow sail past her cheek. She opened her mouth to cry out a warning to Alyn, but it was too late. The shaft pierced his neck. Alyn swooned slightly, a surprised look on his face, and then he fell at Solace's feet.

"Alyn!" she screamed, dropping to her knees.

She choked back a sob when she realized he was already gone. Even Evryst couldn't have saved the smart, faithful monk. Solace closed Alyn's eyes and pulled a blanket over him, her tears falling onto her hands. She knew Evryst would take Alyn's loss especially hard and dreaded delivering the news—if she survived long enough herself. Solace rose slowly, careful to avoid appearing in the gap between the boulders, fear squeezing the air from her lungs as she turned to face the opposite hill.

Solace heard the raspy voice of the former king, calling her name, and shivered. Neuss hollered, "I have a friend of yours here. Goes by the name of Bray. He has something to say."

Bray's voice shook. "Don't listen to—"

There was a scuffle and a yelp from the other side, and then Neuss shouted, "Bring me a nice, long, flaming torch, girl, and a full water skin, or your friend goes over the mountainside."

Solace's heart thundered in her chest. *Oh sun, moon, and stars! Now what? I have no cover, no backup...and that monster has Bray!* She wondered what that meant for Devlan and Danyss. Were they lying injured somewhere, or worse? She took a shaky breath. "What assurances can you give me you'll not harm him?"

Neuss yelled, "Assurances? Bring what I asked for or he dies now!"

Solace heard Bray scream out in pain, but she couldn't

see what Neuss had done. "Don't hurt him!" she cried. "I'll bring what you asked."

"Hurry up, girl. He hasn't much time."

Despite her knotted stomach and skittering pulse, Solace forced herself to slow down and think. She'd not have any time to consider options once she stepped onto the ledge. Neuss was a dishonest, greedy, homicidal man who was feeling cornered and more than a little panicked—and who wouldn't hesitate to kill her and Bray as soon as he got what he wanted.

It was up to her to make sure Neuss never got the chance.

Solace took Alyn's water skin, which was two-thirds full, and slipped it over her left shoulder. Next, she sorted through the remaining stack of wood, selecting a long, slender log to use as a torch, but she worried the flame might not last all the way across the wind-swept passage. Frowning, she rummaged through Alyn's healer's kit, withdrawing vial after vial, giving each a good sniff and wrinkling her nose until the scent of fresh olives wafted up to her nostrils. She poured the olive oil over one end of the log and then set it aside. She had one, final preparation before she lit the torch and climbed onto Daemon's Doorstep—a weapons check.

First, Solace inspected her dagger, adjusting her scabbard slightly on her belt. Next, she unwound the sling from her forehead, reached into her belt pouch, and withdrew one smooth, flat stone, which she dropped into the leather cradle. She looped one end of the coil over her right middle finger, held the knotted end between her thumb and forefinger, and allowed the cradle to hang loosely at her side. Solace reasoned the stone should stay in place, provided she didn't trip or manage to dislodge it before she needed it.

Now she was ready, or as ready as she'd ever be, to face Neuss. She dipped the oiled-end of the makeshift torch in the campfire and watched as it flared to life. Taking a deep breath, Solace held the torch high in her left hand and stepped between the twin boulders onto the stone outcropping. She kept her right hand low and out of sight, her sling dangling next to her leg.

"I was starting to think you didn't care all that much about Mister Bray." Neuss's smarmy voice cackled into the night.

"I had to find a suitable torch," shouted Solace.

Neuss snorted. "No tricks now, girl. I'm watching you like a night hawk inspecting his dinner."

Bile rose in Solace's throat at Neuss's words. She swallowed hard and held the torch higher to illuminate the slender, rocky ledge before her, placing one boot in front of the next, each movement taking her one step closer to the vile former king. Her burning log illuminated the deep chasm on either side of her, and once, she made the mistake of glancing down. She shuddered and refused to look down again, her eyes focused straight ahead.

She plodded onward, careful to step around piles of rocks that partially blocked the path, until she reached the hemp-and-wood portion of Daemon's Doorstep that connected her gravelly ledge with the long finger of stone stretching down from the opposite mountain. Solace trembled as she stepped onto the man-made bridge, which rocked in the wind. She wasn't sure which would be worse, crossing the wooden slats and hoping they held, or reaching the other side, where she'd be that much closer to

Neuss. She had no choice but to keep moving and pray he didn't spy the loaded sling hanging down by her right leg.

Solace had passed the halfway mark—of the swaying wooden bridge and Daemon's Doorstep itself—when a rotted slat gave way beneath her boot. Her heart thundering in her ears, she tried to steady herself and accidentally dropped the torch. *At least I didn't send it tumbling into the dark gorge below!* But to her horror, the dry wooden slat in front of her caught fire.

Solace quickly snatched up the torch from where it had rolled and leapt across the flames, hoping the rickety bridge wouldn't give way with her still on it. She increased her speed across the remaining slats, panting heavily when her boots touched down on the solid rock of the other hill.

She inhaled sharply as excruciating pain burst from the center of her chest and radiated down her arms. *Have I been struck by an arrow or a dagger?* She froze, terrified until she realized nothing had pierced her body. It was her weakened heart, objecting to the constant activity, strain, and stress. Was her most vital organ giving out now, or was this one more warning to slow down and adhere to Evryst's advice? Either way, she had no choice but to carry on and hope her heart didn't succumb before Neuss did.

Solace had another moment of panic. She was close to confronting Neuss, and while she had the still-burning torch and Alyn's water skin, her sling's cradle felt too light. Beads of sweat broke out on her brow and trickled down the sides of her face. She must have dropped the stone when she'd stumbled on the bridge. There was no way she could reach into her belt pouch and fish for another stone now. Neuss would see her and that would be that.

The royal convict chose that moment to chortle. "Well

done, girlie. You've cut off your own escape route. Ah, this evening gets better and better."

Solace glared in the direction of Neuss's voice. She didn't see him, which meant he was still being cautious, keeping himself and Bray hidden in the dark interior of the cavern. Did that mean Neuss was expecting some trickery —either from her or from Danyss or Devlan? That idea gave her a tiny measure of encouragement, just enough to glance around and wonder how to unobtrusively reload her sling.

That's when she saw her stone, which had fallen and was lodged between the top of her leather boot and her leg. Solace pretended to stumble, dropping her torch on the rocky ground. She used her left hand to sweep over her boot, pick out the stone, and drop it back inside the sling's cradle. As she straightened, she retrieved the torch, which was still lit, thanks to Alyn's olive oil.

Neuss screamed at her, "You'd better make sure that torch doesn't go out! If you want to see your friend alive, that is."

"Speaking of my friend, I'll not take one more step until I see him."

"You're in no position to barter, girl. You have an abyss at your back."

Solace clenched her teeth. She loathed the way he called her "girl," as if she was lower than his lowliest servant. "True enough. But then again, you're not much better off, are you? Oh, granted, you're in a snug little cave—but you're running low on water and firewood. We need each other right now."

"There's nothing I need less than you."

"Well in that case." Solace extended her left arm over the edge of the pass, ready to release the torch.

"Stop!" shrieked Neuss.

"Then let me see my friend."

Solace heard footsteps shuffling, and then two dark heads emerged from the shadows at the end of the passage. "Bray?" she called tentatively. "Are you alright?"

"In a manner of speaking." Bray's voice wavered. At least she knew which of the two heads belonged to Peka's youngest son.

"Now bring me the torch and water skin," urged Neuss.

"Send me Bray first," said Solace.

"Why, so you can plot your joint attack against me? I think not. Besides, where will you go? You have to get past me if you want to descend, and you burned the bridge, you little fool."

Solace winced. She hated that Neuss was right. And she also knew the likelihood of her or Bray surviving once Neuss had what he wanted was extremely low. She inched forward, torch high, sling down low, when Neuss must have realized she was up to something. "Show me both your hands, girl. Now!"

"You want to see my hands?" She rotated her sling, faster and faster, finally shouting, "See this!" as she released the knotted end of the cord.

As the stone left its leather cradle, Bray ducked down. Solace spotted Neuss's blade glinting in the torchlight, his hand upraised to stab Bray, and she screamed. Then the old king screeched suddenly and toppled over. Neuss's shadow merged with Bray's, and the two of them wrestled on the ground. Solace grimaced, realizing her stone had grazed Neuss—but she hadn't stopped him.

As Bray and Neuss fought, all she could see was a single, dark blur of motion. Solace heard fists thumping against flesh, and tunics tearing, and yelps of pain, but she had no idea who might be winning.

"Bray," she yelled. "Hang on! I'm coming." Solace dodged around boulders and scrambled over rocks, her fingers clamped around the hilt of her dagger as she raced toward them.

Then she heard a horrible *thwack*, like a rock smashing into bone, and one of the shadows stopped struggling. "What were you saying, dearie?" Neuss's voice dripped with sarcasm.

Oh my stars, Neuss has killed Bray!

Solace reached deep inside herself, where she'd buried her grief over Rhees, and her bitterness at MaudeLyn, and her fear of Neuss, and she grew deathly calm. She heard Rebezza's voice in her head, telling her not to lose hope, and to press on, no matter what.

Somehow, the torch in her left hand was still lit, although the flame had burned low. Solace held the light up to her face and growled. "I said, I'm coming, you fiend!" Then she tossed the torch aside and dived for the ground, as the whir of Neuss's blade passed over her head.

Neuss must have realized he'd missed, because he dropped to the ground too. Solace crept toward him, her knife grasped firmly in her right hand. When Neuss stopped crawling, she stopped. When he inched forward, Solace moved as well.

Neuss's shadow loomed up suddenly, and Solace jumped to her feet, ready to pounce. But Neuss held something in front of him like a shield. Solace squinted. She could just barely make out the limp form of Bray.

Neuss shook the boy and hollered, "Drop your weapon, girl, or I'll break his neck."

"He's already dead," she replied grimly. Solace hoped she was wrong, but she wasn't about to let go of her dagger.

Neuss gripped the boy by the hair with one hand and

used the crook of his other arm to squeeze Bray's windpipe. Solace thought she heard a small gagging noise from Bray, which both encouraged her and made her wonder whether she should drop her blade.

Then Bray's hand shot out from his side. He jabbed something sharp and small—an arrowhead perhaps—into Neuss's hip. Neuss howled, flinging Bray to the ground, and then he lunged for Solace.

But the old king underestimated the young queen of Toresz, the girl from the dusty, brown hills of Yelosha. She knew how to protect her sheep and her dog. And that girl was ready.

As Neuss raced toward her, Solace ducked under his arm, slashing his upper thigh with her dagger. Neuss stopped, turned around half in shock, and staggered toward her again. Then he spat at her, reminding Solace of the rabid jackal she'd once killed, just as the beast sprang toward Barley.

Solace screamed and leapt onto Neuss's lumbering form. As she landed, she jammed the point of her blade into Neuss's neck, striking an artery. He tumbled backward, striking his head against a boulder. Neuss growled a single "oof" and fell silent.

Solace jumped up, ready to stab him again, but even in the dim moonlight she could see Neuss's head lolling at an odd angle. The convicted king was, without a doubt, dead.

As Solace leaned over to wipe her blade on the sleeve of his tunic, a fresh jolt of pain shot through her chest. She fell to her knees with a loud cry. Sucking in air through her teeth and exhaling through her nose, Solace took short, shallow breaths until the aching subsided. Eventually, she resheathed her dagger and rose, her relief at Neuss's death mingling with a bone-crushing exhaustion. *My child will never have to face Neuss. And now, perhaps, I can finally adhere to Evryst's advice.*

Solace heard a small movement behind her and spun toward Bray, lying on the ground. "Bray!" She dropped beside him. "Say something."

"Ouch," he muttered, rubbing his head. "Neuss hit me with a rock when we were fighting. I literally saw stars."

Solace exhaled in relief and helped Bray roll onto his side. His neck was bleeding from a cut, probably from Neuss's blade, his left eye was swollen shut, and his nose appeared broken. He slowly sat up, spat out a tooth, and mumbled. "It's over, isn't it?"

"For Neuss, aye, it's over." Solace squeezed her eyes shut, unwilling to think about what came next, about all her future days without Rhees at her side. She let out a shaky breath. "What about Danyss and Devlan, are they—?"

Bray said, "They were both struck by arrows, one in the shoulder, the other in the leg, but Danyss said they'd be alright. We'd been taking out Neuss's men as they came down the mountain for supplies. There were five thugs originally, and we'd gotten four of them. I was tracking number five when he got the drop on me."

Solace's head snapped up. "Where's he now?"

"Danyss got him first. Neuss truly was the last man standing."

CHAPTER 28

Solace and Giulia took turns riding point on their way
back through the Tor foothills. Everyone else, except for
Josaph, had been injured, and so they traveled at a slower
pace, stopping more frequently for rest breaks and to
change bandages. They'd debated whether to take Alyn's
body back to the monastery for proper funeral rites, but in
the end, Josaph made the call, claiming Brother Alyn "was a
pract'cul man, who'd be best remb'red fer 'is brav'ry 'n
battle." And so they buried Alyn in a small cave before
departing.

Bray was the first to notice five-stone cairns popping up
at nearly every hill east of Daemon's Doorstep. As they jour-
neyed, they began to encounter some of the volunteers
recruited by Max and the other heralds—farmers, ranchers,
and villagers who'd left their homes and families to join the
fight—and these same men and women fell in behind
Solace as she rode toward Tor Valley. By the third day of
travel, their ranks had swelled to over two dozen, and by
the time Solace reached the valley, more than fifty of the
"queen's militia" accompanied her.

Unlike the last time Solace had been near the valley, she heard none of the sounds of battle, no clanging swords or shouting men. She wanted to see the battlefield for herself before leaving the relative safety of the foothills. She had injured friends as well as scores of volunteers to look after. She and Bray, who complained of headaches but was mostly healed, climbed a knoll to survey the plain as the late afternoon sun cast shadows across the flatland.

Solace gasped at the dismal scene stretched out below. Countless bodies littered the ground, as far as she could see —some wearing the uniform of Rhees's army, but most in civilian garb—and of these, it was impossible to tell friend from foe. Solace wondered whether that distinction even mattered any more, since Neuss was dead, his brief uprising squashed, although not before destroying so many lives, including Rhees's.

Bray found his voice first. "There are so many of them. They can't all be dead, can they?"

Solace shook her head. "The healers must be overwhelmed with so many injured."

"How awful, to be lying there without anyone to offer you even a cup of water."

"Aye," said Solace softly. "It seems we have one more task to do before we can search for your mum, and Fenwith, and Rhees."

Bray nodded. "But first, we need to raise a white banner so everyone knows we come in peace."

When Solace explained to her volunteers the dire situation on the field, nearly everyone agreed to aid the injured, regardless of affiliation. An old farmer, who'd lost his daughters to one of the gangs operating freely under Neuss's reign, objected. "I promise my girls every night afore I go to bed that I'll avenge 'em. I'll not be aidin' and abettin' my enemy."

Josaph placed his brown, wrinkled hand on the farmer's shoulder. "How long, m'frend?"

"They're gone nearly ten years."

"I'm sorra fer yer losses," said Josaph. "I cin only offer this: ye'll not be healin' yer own hurt 'til ye take th' firs' step —wif forgivin' th' misguided folks lyin' out thar, dyin' in this heat."

The farmer heaved a deep sigh and shook his head. "I'll aid those in uniform only. 'Tis th' best I cin do."

"Verra well, son," replied Josaph. "Peace go wif ye." He embraced the other man, who broke down and wept in Josaph's arms.

Bray carried their "banner"—a white shirt tied to a stick—and rode between Solace and Giulia as they entered the valley. A small unit of royal guards approached them, and Solace called out to the men and women behind her. "Wait here until we've announced ourselves."

Solace, Bray, and Giulia galloped ahead, and when they were thirty feet away, a burly man shouted, "It's the queen! Show her your fealty!" The mounted guards all bowed from their shoulders, pounded their chests with their fists, and flung out their fingers toward her.

Solace recognized the man's voice and dismounted. Bray and Giulia climbed down from their horses and stood on either side of her. "Sir Kryss," said Solace. "We bring tidings: Neuss Axium Orillya is dead at last."

Sir Kryss, a barrel-chested man with salt-and-pepper hair and beard, jumped down from his steed. He removed his battered helm and propped it on his saddle. His blue tabard, newly tailored for Rhees's coronation, was now battle-stained and tattered along the hem. Drawing his eyebrows together, Kryss asked, "Have you seen Neuss's corpse with your own eyes, my queen?"

"Aye," replied Solace.

"How?" asked Kryss. Solace knew he wasn't questioning her claim but wanted to understand the circumstances.

"Neuss was killed by my blade."

Bray spoke up. "I was there and can confirm Neuss is dead, and by the queen's hand."

"Then it's truly finished," Kryss murmured. "Thank you, my queen." He bowed again.

Solace gave a deep sigh. "MaudeLyn of Censarra is your queen, not me."

"Nay," Kryss shook his head. "Perhaps you've not heard? MaudeLyn intends to return to Censarra. I'm in the midst of arranging an armed escort for her, but when I heard murmurs about Queen Solace returning, I hastened here."

"MaudeLyn is leaving Toresz?" Solace canted her head in surprise.

"Aye," replied Kryss. Then he nodded in the direction of the camp. "And I believe that's her right now. Oh joy, she's heading our way." He muttered under his breath, "Probably to complain about my lack of attention to her royal needs."

Solace glanced in the direction of Kryss's head nod. "Is that really MaudeLyn?"

"That's her Royal Haughtiness—er, Highness, alright."

"But she looks so..." Solace couldn't find the right words.

"Furious," said Bray.

"Definitely out of sorts," agreed Kryss.

"And quite plain...and ordinary," added Bray.

"Certainly understated," offered Kryss.

"I'd have expected her to be adorned in queenly robes, given all I've heard about her," whispered Giulia.

She was right. MaudeLyn was wearing a dreary, patched cotton dress beneath a dowdy-looking brown cape. Solace couldn't understand what had happened to MaudeLyn's wardrobe, but whatever it was must have been catastrophic.

MaudeLyn had clearly spotted Kryss and Solace standing together. She dismounted from her gray mare, tossed her reins to a startled young soldier, and stalked toward them. Her long hair was limp and untidy. "You!" she screamed, pointing her finger at Solace. "I should have known my departure would be delayed because of you... you witch!"

Solace arched her eyebrows, wondering if perhaps MaudeLyn had gone mad. She didn't think anything else could account for such a transformation in her appearance. "I have no idea how I've delayed you, madam, or why you're leaving in the first place." *Or who will be sitting on the throne in your absence, as welcome as that will be.*

"Why?" MaudeLyn screeched, her hazel eyes bulging in anger. "Why am I leaving?" Little bits of spittle flew from her pouty mouth. "I'm through! Through with his sour temper and his mood swings and his moaning over 'Solace this' and 'Solace that.' You can have him, and his palace, and his horrid kingdom. Good riddance to all of you!"

Solace flinched, bringing her hand to her chest, which ached with everything she'd lost, with all that MaudeLyn had taken from her. *You crazy, selfish woman, how dare you demean what you so arrogantly snatched away! Did you think there would be no consequences? I wanted what you destroyed. I wanted him, all of him, his good days and his bad.*

MaudeLyn stomped away, muttering about wayward

kings and water witches. She turned back once more and yelled, "And I want my dowry returned to me, with interest!" She yanked the reins from the soldier's hands, swung into her saddle, and trotted away.

As MaudeLyn's words reverberated in her head, the tiniest ray of hope bloomed in Solace's soul. But she was afraid to put any stock in hope. Solace turned to Kryss. "So MaudeLyn has relinquished her claim to the Toreszan throne?"

"Aye," replied Kryss, "as well as her betrothal to King Rhees."

"But—" Solace's wounded, battered heart fluttered wildly as her brain struggled to put the pieces together. Her breathing became shallow and raspy. *Both MaudeLyn and Kryss are talking about Rhees as if he's still here. It's too much to hope for.* Solace straightened her spine until she felt it might snap in half. She sputtered, "We'd heard, that is to say—"

Giulia said it for her. "But we'd heard King Rhees was dead. Killed on the battlefield."

"Rhees isn't dead!" Kryss cried. "He's injured, and grumpy, and depressed about his eye—but he is very much alive."

Solace's mouth formed an *O* as she stared at Kryss. "Rhees is alive? Truly?"

"Of course, my queen. Rhees is far too cantankerous, ah, I mean to say courageous, to die from a single knife wound."

Solace brought a hand to her mouth, too overcome to say anything more as tears—of joy, and gratitude, and hope —streamed down her cheeks. Her knees felt weak, and she reached a hand toward Bray, who grasped her arm.

Giulia whispered, "Take heart, my queen. King Rhees lives!"

Solace knew she had to get a grip; after all, she was the queen, sort of. She had no idea what the legalities were, now that MaudeLyn had renounced everything. She'd ask Chancellor Ghrier about that later.

Solace took a shaky breath and sniffled several times. She wiped her cheeks with the back of her hand and pulled up her shoulders. "Sir Kryss." Solace's voice was thick with emotion. "Take me to King Rhees."

"Right away, my queen." Kryss grinned.

Solace turned to Bray and Giulia. "See to the injured—ours and everyone else's—and come find me later."

She mounted Jenx and came alongside Kryss's horse, the two of them riding ahead of the guard unit. "You mentioned something about Rhees's eye and a knife wound?"

"One of Neuss's men threw a knife that punctured Rhees's left eye," said Kryss grimly, "and then he fell from his horse and shattered his leg. Evryst says his left eye couldn't be saved. However, Rhees will able to walk again, with a cane, but only if he follows instructions now. Which as you know isn't Rhees's strong suit."

Solace nodded, still processing the news that Rhees was alive and very close by. What were a leg and an eye compared to his life? "We'd heard MaudeLyn had been wailing about King Rhees's demise, which I'll confess I found hard to square up with what I knew of her."

"MaudeLyn was loudly lamenting her late brother, King Valyss," said Kryss, "who was struck with an arrow in his back as he fled from battle. Although, to be perfectly honest, when the healer reached him, she discovered Valyss's throat had been slashed as well. She couldn't say with certainty which injury had killed him, and so she reported the brave king had died on the battlefield."

Although Solace knew deserters were often killed by their own comrades, she still winced. "A wise choice on the part of the healer. I only wish we'd heard it had been the king of Censarra who'd died, and not our king."

"I am sorry," replied Kryss. "I'm sure you were much aggrieved by the false report."

"Aye. We were all heartsick," said Solace, "but Fenwith refused to believe Rhees was gone." She glanced at Kryss. "And now, before we are interrupted, tell me the truth about MaudeLyn. Why is she leaving?"

Kryss snorted. "'Tis a short tale. Once MaudeLyn comprehended her brother had died—without heirs, or at least, without any legitimate ones—she decided it was her 'duty to the Censarran people' to return home and ascend to the throne. Of course, that was only after she tried once more to cajole Rhees into wedding her. MaudeLyn thought the king would be more amenable following his injury. But Rhees was, shall we say, even more *courageous* than usual."

"I believe you mean Rhees was more *cantankerous*," said Solace, with a knowing smile.

Kryss's eyes twinkled. "As you wish, my queen."

"And so 'Queen MaudeLyn' she is—of her own kingdom," concluded Solace. "And what of her wardrobe? What happened?"

"As I understand it, the trunks MaudeLyn brought with her to the battlefield mysteriously caught fire one evening, after she had a particularly nasty fit of temper."

"I see," said Solace, chuckling softly. "Censarra is more than welcome to Her Maleficence—er, Majesty—may she reign long and leave us alone!"

Kryss grinned. "'Tis good to have you back, my plain-speaking queen."

He guided her through the vast, bloodied plain, where

men and women lay where they'd fallen, one disorderly row after another, so many that Solace averted her eyes so she'd not become inured to the sight. She would not harden her heart to the suffering and anguish of war, unlike so many other queens and kings before her.

They rode past uniformed soldiers and more royal guards, all of whom saluted Sir Kryss and then stared, open-mouthed, at Solace, until they remembered their manners and bowed low, pounding their chests and flicking their fingers in salute. Kryss finally pulled up at a plain canvas tent and dismounted. "If you'll wait here, I'll announce you."

"Nay, Kryss, I'll announce myself," replied Solace, as her feet touched the ground.

She hurried over to the tent flap and then paused when she heard Rhees's deep baritone. She dashed away a stray tear, took a deep breath, and hesitated again. Someone else was in the tent with him.

"Don't coddle me!" hissed Rhees. "She's been gone far too long—you never should have left her side. I hold you accountable, partly anyway, for losing my wife."

Evryst replied, "I obeyed a direct command from my queen, sire. And I still have good reason to hope—"

"Stop!" bellowed Rhees. "I'll not have any more of your false hope and platitudes."

"See what I mean?" whispered Kryss. "Are you sure you don't want me to announce you?"

Solace shook her head and pulled back the tent flap. "Don't berate Evryst, who did exactly what I asked."

"Solace!" cried Rhees, who was propped up in a field cot, pillows piled behind his back. His wavy, black hair was as wild as ever, and his beard long and unruly. "Are you truly here, or am I still ill with fever?" He raised his hand to his forehead, which was wrapped all around with white gauze. A large patch covered his left eye.

"My queen!" Evryst bowed, straightened, and said, "It is so good to see you. I shall be just outside."

Now that Solace was here, standing in front of Rhees, she was suddenly unsure of herself. He'd been so angry when she'd left. But then she saw the uncertainty in his one good eye, and she took another step closer. Rhees held out his free hand, the one not covering his bandaged eye, and whispered, "Come closer, please, my dearest Lace."

She closed the distance between them, dropped to her knees beside his cot, and gripped his hand in both of hers. Biting back a sob, she murmured, "When we heard you were dead, I was in no hurry to return. All I had to look forward to was your funeral."

Rhees dropped his other hand from his eyepatch and cupped her cheek. "I've heard such strange stories of your exploits that I dared to hope you hadn't left me for good— not that I wouldn't have deserved it if you had. What a fool I've been!"

"Aye, true enough," agreed Solace.

Rhees dropped his hand from her cheek and grunted, "And now I have one blind eye and one gimp leg. I'm half the man I was. You should have gone back home with Arik. He's got two good eyes and two good legs, darn him."

Solace nodded. "'Tis true what you say about Arik."

Rhees withdrew his other hand from her grasp, crossed his arms over his broad chest, and scowled at her. "Well then, why didn't you?"

"Why didn't I what?"

"Why didn't you go back home to your dad and your dog and your sheep—and your precious Arik?"

"While I have missed them all very much, I found that I missed you more."

"You missed me?"

When Solace nodded, Rhees grumped, "I missed you too—terribly. I wanted to ride out after you immediately, but Ghrier told me I dared not leave the kingdom in Maude-Lyn's hands, not even for a day."

"Your chancellor is a savvy man. Speaking of Maude-Lyn, I hear she is gone for good."

"Aye, and none too soon." Rhees's lower lip quivered, and he took a steadying breath. He peered at her through his one good eye. "I am sorry, for all I said and did—or didn't say and didn't do—and although I don't merit your forgiveness, I'll ask for it anyway."

"You cut me to the quick, Rhees." Solace frowned. "You hurt me deeply."

"You're right," Rhees cried. "Just leave me, the forlorn man that I am. You're the only woman I've ever loved and look how I treated you! I pushed you away, let you ride off with a Yeloshan farmer. I deserve to die alone."

Solace rocked back on her heels. She did not believe in wallowing in one's misery, and she'd not permit it from the king of Toresz. "Perhaps you're right, after all." She rose slowly to her feet. "I suppose I'll simply have to raise the crown princess or prince by myself. I'm sure Fenwith and Chelyss will want to help. I might stay with them in Shulamorn during my confinement."

Rhees grew quiet and so still, he didn't bother to fidget. Finally, he found his voice and whispered, "What are you trying to tell me?"

"I am with child—with *your* child—Evryst can confirm it. And while I want our baby to know their father, I'm beginning to doubt whether you're up to the task."

"You are increasing? Truly?"

When Solace nodded, Rhees broke into a wide grin. "I'm going to be a father?" Solace nodded again, and Rhees continued grinning until he remembered the rest of what she'd said. "And Evryst knew? That trickster of a monk didn't tell me." Then Rhees arched his good eyebrow. "What do you mean, I may not be up to the task? Surely you're not biased against a man with infirmities?"

"This has nothing to do with your infirmities." Solace rolled her eyes. "But with your attitude toward them. I detest self-pity. And if you start whining about every ache and pain like an old man, I'll not stand for it."

"Then you're staying?"

Solace sat down on the cot, and taking Rhees's face in her hands, planted a kiss firmly on his lips. Rhees gave a quick intake of breath and ran his fingers through her hair with a soft groan. "I love you," he sighed.

"Then make sure you show it," she whispered, kissed him again, and stood up. "And now, I must fill you in—and Evryst too." She stepped to the tent opening and invited the monk back inside.

"Firstly," she said, "We sustained injuries, some of them serious. Devlan, Danyss, and Behn all need your services, Evryst. Look in on Bray too, although he's mostly healed. We patched them up as best we could, but it was a long ride."

Evryst stared at her and then asked quietly, "What are you not telling me, my queen?"

Solace met the monk's steady gaze and shook her head sadly. "We lost Alyn. An arrow intended for me struck him in the neck. He was gone in an instant, Evryst. I'm so sorry."

Evryst's face crumpled. He stared up at the tent's low

canvas ceiling and didn't reply for a minute. When he looked back at her, his eyes were damp. "I shall miss Alyn."

"As will I," murmured Rhees. "Alyn was a good man—and a good friend to us all."

The two men reminisced about Brother Alyn, each sharing a favorite memory. When they grew quiet again, Solace told them the rest. "I have more news." At their look of alarm, Solace hastily added, "This is about Neuss. He is dead, by my hand."

As she described how it came about, Rhees became increasingly agitated at the danger she'd been in, until Solace finally leaned over and put a finger to his lips. "It is done. If I swear to never set foot on Daemon's Doorstep again, will you be satisfied?"

"I suppose that will have to do," Rhees grumbled.

"I promise to avoid Daemon's Doorstep for the rest of my days—I'd take Anvil Pass anytime over that awful passage."

"Anvil Pass!" shouted Rhees. "When were you there?"

Solace frowned at Evryst, realizing he'd not told Rhees some of the more salient details from their trip. The master healer bowed low and said, "Some stories are best told over the dinner table, preferably with a tall mug of ale. Leastways, that would have been Alyn's preference. Now if you would please excuse me, I must see to the new arrivals." He vanished through the doorway without waiting for a reply.

"It's just as well he's occupied," said Rhees, "it'll help take his mind off Alyn."

"Aye." Solace sat back down on the cot beside Rhees and then pursed her lips. She felt suddenly strange, as if eggshells had settled in the pit of her stomach and were shifting about. A faint fluttering in her abdomen brought her up short. "Oh!" she exclaimed.

Rhees leaned forward and brushed a lock of hair from her face. "What's wrong? Shall we call Evryst back?"

"Nay," Solace shook her head slowly. "We don't need Evryst for this." Then she took Rhees's hand and placed it firmly over her abdomen.

Rhees's good eye widened as he glanced at Solace. "I feel...movement!"

"Meet our child." Solace smiled. "The future queen or king of Toresz."

Rhees cocked his head and stared into Solace's eyes. He must have found what he was seeking there—acceptance certainly, forgiveness too, and a yearning to never be parted again—for he whispered hoarsely, "Welcome home, my love."

Then he gave her stomach a gentle pat. "You too, little one."

CHAPTER 29

THE DAYS FOLLOWING SOLACE'S RETURN WERE THE BUSIEST OF HER life. Since Rhees wasn't mobile, and he wouldn't be for months to come, anything requiring physical activity, such as troop inspections, the placement of additional tents for the volunteer militia, or visiting the injured, fell to the queen instead. Solace quickly recruited Fenwith and Chelyss to help her. She would have asked Peka as well, but she was busy fussing over her sons and getting to know Giulia, whom Solace had no doubt would one day become Behn's wife.

Solace was overjoyed to discover Maysel, Wilhm at her side, in one of the healers' tents. When she tried to thank them for their service, they wouldn't hear of it. "'Tis you we'll be thanking, all our days, for ridding us of Neuss!" cried Maysel.

"Aye." Wilhm, that giant of a man, gave her a sweeping bow. "We are forever in your debt."

Solace found herself swiping a stray tear when she left them and then frowned at herself. *Why am I tearing up so much these days? It makes no sense—after all, Rhees is alive— and we're closer than ever.* Solace had moved an extra cot into Rhees's tent, and the two of them would talk late into the night. They left nothing unspoken, neither their dreams, nor their hopes, nor their hurts.

Solace mentioned her overactive tear ducts to Fenwith one day, and the older woman had chuckled. "Tears go with motherhood, lass." Solace was glad Fenwith had started calling her "lass" again, rather than "my queen." And while Solace still missed her own mother very much, Fenwith helped to fill some of the old void.

After several weeks, Solace and Evryst decided it was safe to move Rhees. He couldn't sit atop a horse yet, so the royal guards transported their king in a wagon, transferring him to Evryst's private wing in the Tor Monastery, rather than directly to the palace. It was easier for Evryst to perform his duties as abbot as well as the king's healer if they lived in the monastery. Besides, Solace wasn't ready to return to Urhl just yet.

Since Rhees had removed himself from the public eye and neglected many of his royal duties after MaudeLyn's arrival, Solace urged him to refocus on the business of rebuilding Toresz. Although he suffered headaches after losing his eye, and his leg needed a great deal of rehabilitation, Solace believed Rhees would heal more quickly if he could make progress as a leader. She helped him with his correspondence, advised him on matters involving the poor and powerless, and urged him to do more to empower women.

The first time Chancellor Ghrier came to the monastery for a visit, he gave Solace a spontaneous bear hug and then immediately murmured an apology for his "lack of decorum." Solace rolled her eyes and hugged him back. The old judge grinned. "It's good to see you, my queen."

Solace invited Ghrier to have a seat in Evryst's private study, which they were using for official business until Rhees was well enough to return to the palace. Max had built a contraption for Rhees, a two-wheeled chair with a plush velvet seat, which Solace or one of the servants could push. Ghrier sat down at the oval table next to Rhees's special chair and opened his leather pouch. He handed Rhees a sheaf of papers to read and sign. As Rhees scanned each page, he handed it to Solace for her review. After she'd finished reading the last page, Rhees asked, "Well, what do you think?"

Solace jumped up from her chair, scooted around the table, and wrapped her arms around Rhees's neck. "I think you're amazing." She nuzzled his beard and kissed his cheek before returning to her seat.

Rhees beamed at her. "It's about time we changed the laws of our kingdom. Women are not property, and they should not require their father's or brother's permission to marry. And they should be able to hold land in their own right." Rhees signed the changes to Toreszan law with a flourish and handed the documents back to Ghrier.

The old chancellor nodded. "Most people—women and men—will welcome this change. And while some will grumble, none can argue this is the right thing to do." He turned to Solace, his white eyebrows arched. "I believe you had another matter to discuss with me?"

"Aye," said Solace. "We wish to shore up our marital paperwork. MaudeLyn and her advisor may have returned to Censarra, but they've left Rhees and me in a legal muddle."

"And while I've just altered the law to prevent this from happening to anyone else," added Rhees. "It's not retroactive, as you well know."

"True enough." Ghrier nodded thoughtfully. "Firstly, I took the liberty of writing to Chancellor Zeffen in Censarra, requesting Queen MaudeLyn's signature on this." Ghrier withdrew a scroll from the folds of his cloak.

"What is it?" asked Solace, taking the parchment from his outstretched hands.

"An agreement annulling the betrothal between Rhees, King of Toresz, and MaudeLyn, Queen of Censarra. Given the speed with which that document was returned, we'll hear no more from the Censarrans on that score."

"Well done, Ghrier," said Rhees, reviewing the agreement.

"Thank you. This does provide us with a measure of relief." Solace tilted her head. "But you said 'firstly,' which means there's more to be done, from a legal standpoint, isn't there?"

"Aye," said Ghrier. "I've long believed—and still do—that your father holds the key."

"I was afraid you were going to say that," sighed Rhees. "Soren hates me. I don't see how he'll be willing to help. You heard Arik's response when you asked him to sign the marital contract in Soren's place."

"But the circumstances are quite different now," pointed out Ghrier. "Solace is carrying the heir to the Toreszan throne. Surely this would soften Soren's heart toward you?"

Solace drew a blank piece of parchment toward her and dipped a fresh quill into the inkwell. "I will write to my father, tell him all that has happened, and invite him to live with us after the baby is born."

Rhees gave a small grunt when she mentioned having Soren move into the palace, but Solace couldn't see any other way to secure peace between the two men she loved most in the world. Ghrier promised to send royal guards to deliver her letter to Soren and wait for his reply, and hopefully, his signature on the now infamous marriage license.

Solace knew her father. Soren would want to save her from further embarrassment and secure her baby from any claims of illegitimacy. She also knew he would, eventually, turn the farm over to Arik and come join her in Toresz. Soren loved children. He wouldn't be able to resist the invitation to watch his grandchild grow up.

One morning while they were awaiting the royal guards' return, Solace and Rhees received a surprise visitor at the monastery. Magus Tabetta had traveled from Andressa Cave to meet the king and personally thank him for the new legal protections now offered to women. Solace knew this was a major act of trust on the part of the Magian community; Rhees would be the first sovereign to know of their existence. She asked Evryst and Tabetta to share their story with him.

Rhees listened intently and when they'd finished, Solace told him of her visit to High Magus Rebezza. She shared the seer's visions and described Rebezza's prediction that Solace "carried the future of Toresz" within her.

Rhees, who seemed dumbfounded at first, thanked Tabetta for looking after Solace when he could not. The magus nodded, her veils swaying with the movement. "We were greatly honored to offer our water-gifted queen sanctuary—the same hospitality and protections we've given to all such gifted girls and women since our founding."

"Now that Rhees is king, I hope you feel safer inside

Toresz," said Solace. "Perhaps, one day, you will be able to emerge from hiding."

"Maybe one day, as you say, we may feel it is safe enough to reveal ourselves. For now, it is a comfort to have the support of the king and queen." Tabetta bowed again as she bade them farewell.

When a month passed, and then another, without any word from Soren or the royal guards, Chancellor Ghrier urged Rhees and Solace to return to the palace in Urhl. Rhees's leg was healing, and he'd been able to take several painful, lurching steps using crutches.

With Fenwith's help, Solace began to turn the overly-gilded palace into a place she could call home. Since their treasury was even more depleted following the brief but costly war with Neuss, and the return of MaudeLyn's dowry, Solace limited her refurbishments. She sold off the most ridiculously opulent furniture, draperies, and wall hangings to merchants, and then used the proceeds to repaint some of the rooms and purchase simpler pieces and fabrics.

By the end of summer, as Solace's midsection became rounder and her feet swelled at the end of each day, Rhees found her weeping one afternoon in their blue-and-white parlor. "What's wrong, my love?" he asked, hobbling as quickly as he dared to her side. "Should I send for Evryst?"

Solace shook her head and dashed away her tears. "It's just...I'd hoped you were being overly pessimistic about my father. But it seems Dad is still undecided, or even worse, perhaps he's chosen not to respond to my letter at all."

"I'm so sorry—I'd hoped I was wrong, for your sake. I know you adore your father."

Solace caught her bottom lip between her teeth. "Do

you think the royal guards became lost somehow? Or attacked?"

Rhees bent his visible eyebrow. His injured orb was shielded beneath a blue eyepatch, one of a dozen Solace had commissioned from her seamstress. She thought it lent an appealing, though slightly rakish, air to her husband. "I sent two dozen highly trained knights," said Rhees, "and we are at peace with Yelosha. Nay, I think they are delayed for a very good reason—certainly something to do with your father—and so we must wait and not lose hope."

One of the footmen burst into the parlor, bowed low, and cried, "Beg pardon, Your Highnesses, but there's a flock of sheep, and a big, shaggy dog, and a pair of enormous draft horses just arrived in the stable area. There's an old farmer out there, too, chatting with the hostler—"

"Oh," exclaimed Solace. "How wonderful!"

She jogged out of the parlor and through the back door, ran down the stone steps, and dashed into the stable yard. "Barley!" she cried, as a dusty sheepdog nearly bowled her over, yipping happily and licking her face. She burst into tears as she knelt down and wrapped her arms around her beloved dog.

The old farmer turned from the hostler and swept his floppy hat off his head. He nervously crushed the wide brim in his brown, work-roughened hands. "Solace, my dear lass!" he said, his voice cracking. "By the stars, you look just like your mama when she was expecting you."

Solace rose from petting Barley, who started barking again and running in circles around the sheep milling in the yard. "Oh, Dad," she snuffled, her tears flowing as freely as water in a new well. "I'm so happy you're here—I'd nearly given up all hope of seeing you again. What took so long?"

Soren's eyes welled up and overflowed, his tears leaking

down his heavily lined face. Solace threw her arms around her father's neck, surprised to see his tear ducts were as overactive as hers. Soren had only cried twice before, when her mother had died, and when Rhees had brought Solace back to their Yeloshan farm after her six-month absence.

As Soren gently patted her back, both father and daughter weeping, the heavy rear door of the palace was thrown open by the footman. Rhees carefully maneuvered himself down the stairs and into the stable yard.

Soren straightened, one arm still around his daughter, and nodded at his son-in-law. "I can see Solace did not exaggerate your injuries, sir."

Rhees leaned heavily on his carved oaken cane as he hobbled over to Solace and Soren. "As a retired soldier yourself, I'm certain you've seen worse, sir."

"True enough," said Soren. "But it's generally the infantry that bears the brunt of the damage, not the royals."

"Perhaps that's the case in Yelosha, sir, but not here in Toresz." Rhees's tone was respectful, and Solace reached out her hand toward her beloved husband. Rhees limped closer, and taking her hand, turned it over to plant a kiss in her palm.

"Apparently so," answered Soren amiably.

Solace was glad to see her husband and father agreeing on something, but she was more interested in the answer to her question. "Dad, what took you so long?"

Soren's face softened as he peered at Solace. "'Tis no small feat, lass, for a man to settle his affairs, move to another country, and arrange a dowry for his daughter— particularly when she is a royal herself."

"A dowry?" Solace tilted her head.

"Aye. A flock of sheep, two draft horses, one sheepdog, and this," said Soren, handing Solace a pouch that jangled.

She peeked inside and gasped. "Dad, where did you get all this silver?"

Soren's gray eyebrows rose. "From Arik, who insisted on paying me for the farm. He said you needed a proper dowry, and I couldn't argue with the lad."

Rhees squinted at Soren with his good eye. "Arik said that?"

"Aye," replied Soren gruffly. He ambled over to one of the tall, black draft horses, reached into his saddlebag, and withdrew a scroll, which he handed to Rhees. "Arik also said I needed to stop being a pigheaded fool. So here you go."

Rhees unrolled the document, scanned it quickly, and showed it to Solace. Soren had inserted, in his own hand, the missing clause indicating his consent to the marriage, and then he'd signed the clause and initialed every page of the contract, just for good measure.

Solace kissed her father's grizzled cheek, which was every bit as damp as hers. His familiar scent of pipe smoke and fresh hay reminded her of their old farm in Yelosha. Then she threw her arms around Rhees, who smelled of well-worn leather and rich, dark coffee...and something else...something she couldn't quite identify.

But as Rhees laughed out loud and kissed her on the lips, Solace recognized the outdoorsy scent of the tall, spiky grasses, and dry, gray tumbleweeds and arid, brown hills of Toresz. It permeated her husband's clothes and hair and beard. It was the aroma of home—a home that was strong and real and true. And hers.

Fans of Toni Cabell's Water Witch series and the kingdom of Toresz won't want to miss *An Unfortunate Reputation*, the story of King Meade and Ellanora, Rhees's parents. This bonus novella is available for *free* to Toni's newsletter subscribers.

BOOKS BY TONI CABELL

A fast-paced adventure full of magic, romance, humor, sword fighting, dangerous creatures, and the power of light versus darkness, **Serving Magic** is a YA Epic Fantasy series with Steampunk and Regency vibes. Winner of The Wishing Shelf Book Awards and recognized by Indies Today as a Top 5 YA Fantasy series by an indie author:

- *Lady Apprentice, Book 1*
- *Lady Mage, Book 2*
- *Lady Liege, Book 3*
- *Lady Spy, Book 4*
- *Lady Reaper, Book 5*

In the arid hills of Toresz, there's one thing more dangerous than divining for water... falling in love with the enemy. **Water Witch** is YA Romantasy duology packed with action, danger, intrigue, royal politics, and romance. Winner of The Wishing Shelf Book Awards:

- *The Lightness of Water, Book 1*
- *The Way of Water, Book 2*

If you're looking for sweet, slow-burn romance with swoony kisses, second chances, and funny, heartwarming characters, don't miss the complete **Faeries of Door County** series. Winner of Best Paranormal Romance, each novel is a standalone story set in the same cozy small town:

- *Rhyme, Riddle, and Romance*
- *Half a Faerie*
- *Return to Mooncrest Inn*

Find all Toni's available books and upcoming new releases on tonicabell.com and Amazon. All her novels are also available in audiobook format on Audible and Apple Books.

About the Author

When Toni told her fifth-grade teacher that she wanted to be a writer, neither of them expected Toni's journey to include stints as a nurse's aid, personal banker, instructional designer, real estate broker, systems analyst, and youth director. Toni is thrilled to be an indie author and does at least half her writing in the middle of the night, which may explain her wild plot twists and unforgettable characters.

Today, Toni writes award-winning fantasy stories filled with spunky gals, protective guys, imaginative magic, and romance that sizzles without the spice. Whether you're a fan of fast-paced, YA fantasy adventures with a dash of swoon or cozy paranormal romance packed with heart-stealing kisses and small town charm, you're sure to find something to love.

Toni's novels have earned Silver and Bronze Medals in The Wishing Shelf Book Awards, two Gold Medals in the Global Book Awards, and Best Paranormal Romance from Indies Today.

She makes her home in a small village along the shores of Lake Michigan with her handsome husband, where she enjoys generous supplies of strong coffee, too many pastries, and more books than she can ever read.

Want a free novella and to stay current on Toni's upcoming releases, sales, and giveaways? Then visit tonicabell.com and sign up for her newsletter.

Toni posts regularly about her indie author journey, life lessons, what inspires her, and her books on Instagram and Facebook. Also consider joining her Reader Group on Facebook, @onceuponaswoon, where she hangs out with some of her closed-door author friends and readers like you.

Soli Deo Gloria.